XAN BROOKS is an award-winning writer, editor and broadcaster. He began his journalism career as an editor at the *Big Issue* magazine in London and spent fifteen years as a writer and associate editor at the *Guardian* newspaper. His debut novel, *The Clocks in This House All Tell Different Times*, was listed for the Costa First Novel Award, the Author's Club Award, the Desmond Elliott Prize and the Walter Scott Prize for Historical Fiction.

THE CATCHERS
XAN BROOKS

SALT

CROMER

PUBLISHED BY SALT PUBLISHING 2024

2 4 6 8 10 9 7 5 3 1

First published in Great Britain in 2024 by
Salt Publishing Ltd
12 Norwich Road, Cromer, NR27 0AX United Kingdom

www.saltpublishing.com

Salt Publishing Limited Reg. No. 5293401

A CIP catalogue record for this book is available from the British Library

ISBN 978 1 78463 320 2 (Paperback edition)
ISBN 978 1 78463 321 9 (Electronic edition)

Typeset in Neacademia by Salt Publishing

Printed and bound in Great Britain by Clays Ltd, Elcograf S.p.A

THE CATCHERS

1

H ONEST JIM WAS a catcher, the first and the finest, in the mid-1920s, right before the big flood. He drove out from New York to criss-cross Appalachia with a recording lathe packed in the bed of his van. If you had a good song then you had his attention. He'd pull up a chair and give you three minutes of time.

"Three minutes?" men said. "Why, three minutes is nothing." Not knowing that this was all the time the apparatus allowed: three minutes before the pulley system unwound and the lead weight hit the floor. Not realizing, also, that outside of the mountains the pace of life had sped up and that this was the age of motorcars and Bell telephones, airplanes and film cameras. The world races on and only dawdlers drag their heels. If you can't play a good song in the space of three minutes, most likely it's not worth recording at all.

"Three minutes," he'd tell them. "But then the song lasts forever."

In those days it was said the land was mostly made up of music, as though it was stirred up with the water and the soil, as though the very breath of the wind was God's orchestra tuning up. The people played banjos and fiddles, washboards and dulcimers. They played sacred songs and chicken songs; shanties, reels and laments. Songs poured through the hills like migrating salmon. Songs fell out of the trees like round russet apples. Catching one was so easy, you only had to stick out your hand. But catching the good ones, the sellers, that required real skill.

"Who makes the best songs?" Honest Jim liked to ask, a cigar in one hand, a cup of produce in the other. "Who did it, I mean. Who's responsible for a song?"

"Picture it as a crime scene," said Rinaldi, tapping the table.

"You weigh up the evidence and identify the main culprit."

"So fine, a crime scene if you like. Who did it? Your chief suspect."

"The musician," replied the rookie catcher, John Coughlin, who was on his first trip to the mountains and hopelessly out of his depth. "The performer. The singer. Whoever wrote and played the piece."

They were boarding at the Bide-a-Wee, a hunter's inn outside Harpers Ferry. Business was slow and the inn was struggling. Honest Jim thought maybe the name was to blame. The catchers sat in the lounge beneath antler chandeliers, listening to the tick of the clock in the lobby and the lash of rain on the glass. The chestnut floor at their feet was the color of bourbon. A man might drop to his knees, lick the grain and get high.

"Take your hat off, for Christ's sake," he told the rookie, because appearances were important, even at the Bide-a-Wee. They were not punks from the city. They were gentlemen. They were swells.

"A Mole in the Ground," said Rinaldi. "Explain that one to me."

"What's to explain? Some they like and some they don't."

"Sure, but that piece specifically. What's to like? It's a joke."

He knocked ash from his cigar. "Whoever played it, Mr Coughlin says. Which is true. Which is fair. But keep in mind, kid, that most hill-country pieces are old. They got no owners, no parents and they keep on changing shape. Each time you hear one it's just a little bit different. So try again, who's responsible? Who decides this version, not that one? This shape, not the others? Who is the real creator here?"

The rookie nodded. "OK, I get it."

"He gets it, Jim."

"It's the catcher who makes the song," said Jim Cope. "It's the fellow who caught it. Which means us, by the way." He had his smoke and his drink and a cushioned footstool for his heels. He was getting comfortable now. He was settling in for the night.

Some catchers were grifters—it was a piratical trade and it attracted all types: con-men and crooks, snake-oil salesmen and pimps. But Honest Jim Cope by and large played it straight. He paid thirty dollars in cash for every side he laid down, a straight square deal with a bill of sale thrown on top. You got the money and he got the song and afterwards you were quits, it was a sweet, clean exchange.

"Shook your cherry tree the Friday before. Shook out your blossoms 'til the branches got sore."

"Sex," he said. "At the root it's all sex."

"Sex, sure, so why the dance? Why the costumes and the coyness? These are simple people so say it plain."

"Tommy," he said. "You want me to sit here all night and unpick every line?"

In the hills of Appalachia he was always Honest Jim Cope, glossy and handsome, come to make people rich. But he'd been born Shem Kopl—premature, underweight—and he had spent the first years of his life beside the tanneries in Trebic. Even today he retained a vivid memory of his arrival in New York—incredible, given that he could barely recall what he'd eaten for lunch or whether he had turned left or right out of town. He remembered the crush of the children being funneled single-file through the pens; the bored medics and deckhands playing bocci on the wharf. The sunlight so blinding and the sea-breeze so fierce that it felt that all of those bug-eyed urchins were about to be whisked into egg-white or dissolved into foam, which is maybe what happened, it was as good an explanation as any. He had been clutching a woolen rabbit, his cherished toy, but when he brought up his hands he saw it had gone. Belongings get lost, said his mother, not turning. So stop crying, keep walking, don't hold up the line. Not everything survives the Atlantic crossing intact.

He was Kopl in short pants and he was Jim Cope in his twenties and he lived his life on the road, with the footwell of his van filled with maps and notebooks and hotel receipts that blew up like confetti when he cranked down the window. This was how the world turned and American men were made new. Shem Kopl, God help him, had been a ham-and-egger at best. Whereas Honest Jim Cope, general manager at Victor Records, was regarded as the finest catcher in the country. His salary last year had been just shy of $13,000.

"You have a goodly number of Jews in New York," a dignitary's wife had once remarked, solicitously touching his wrist inside some mildewed town hall, and he had replied that yes, this was true, a great number of Jews, most of them quite harmless, never gave him any trouble. Whenever the subject of his own background was raised—which was a little more often than he would have liked—he'd explain that he was raised Presbyterian and kept a doting wife, Glad, and three boys at home in Hoboken. A man in the field has to do his best to fit in, and never mind the fact that his birth name was Kopl and that he was unmarried and childless and most nights amused himself with loose women and whores. This was one of the curious quirks about Virginia, he'd found. It contained as many loose women as Manhattan and Brooklyn combined.

"Women," said Rinaldi. He kissed his fingertips and steepled them as though in prayer. "Please God, let there be some women on this trip."

"Wine, women and song. But songs first, always the song first and foremost. It's the songs that pay for the other two."

"Songs first," said Rinaldi. He gestured with his cigar. "Except that the songs and the women are all thataway."

"Over the river."

Rinaldi nodded, lost in thought. "Over the river and into the trees."

They called it the Far Corners, that part of Appalachia, because it seemed so remote to the paymasters in New York, like a fairy-tale kingdom, utterly foreign and strange. Thick forest, blue mountains and crossroad company towns that didn't show up on the map. The first time Cope went down—summer of '24—he'd been like some pith-helmeted explorer landing on Galapagos, or Adam in the garden, trying to name all the birds. One day, picture this, he had scared away a black bear. The musicians had barely begun playing when the bear wandered up, hips rolling, bold as brass and that might

4

have been that—everyone either fled or dead. But he had clapped his hands and faced it down and the beast had paused for a moment, then back-pedaled and ran.

"That's because you didn't know any better. Soft boy from the city. You wouldn't pull that shit now."

"Who says that I wouldn't? It worked, didn't it?"

"Thing could just as easily have eaten you."

"Yeah, but it didn't. It didn't, that's my point."

Rinaldi pivoted in his chair. "I hope you're taking notes, kid," he said to the rookie. "He's breaking out all the old war stories now."

"Oh I got a stack of them," Cope said. "Tales of black bears and dragons." Because privately he believed that the first trip was the greatest, when it was just him and the music and nobody else to contend with. As opposed to these days, right this moment, when he was running with the pack, lumped alongside Rinaldi of Talking Machine, Canter from Columbia, other sad hustlers from the lesser outfits; a victim of his own success, so-called. And while most of these pygmies would soon fall by the wayside, it was a bother to have to be constantly looking in his rear-view mirror, meeting at joints such as the Bide-a-Wee every trip to ensure that everyone was on the same page and no one was targeting another man's patch. The code of the catchers, Rinaldi liked to call it. You agreed your routes in advance, circled your town and shook hands. That way you avoided any unpleasantness down the line.

"Now take the kid here," said the Italian. "His first trip to the Corners. Maybe his first time out-of-state. A new guest at the table and so what? The more the merrier. Plenty of food to go around." He turned again to face Coughlin. "But I swear this to you, kid, with my hand on my heart. If I get wind you're catching anywhere close to Lynchburg there's going to be hell to pay, believe me, and nobody wants that."

"He's serious," Cope said. "Matter of fact, we both are."

"I get it." The rookie cleared his throat. "I mean, don't worry, I won't. I'm fixing to head all the way down to Sutton."

"Well then, that's fine. Thinking big, that's the catcher's way. The way I see it, Tommy, this kid will go far."

"Literally so," said Rinaldi. "All the way down to Sutton, Tennessee."

That day it had rained in a dismal, unremitting gray mist that softened the roads and filled the potholes with water. Only now around dusk did the rain start in earnest and they could hear it dripping through the trees and drumming on the hulls of the three vans in the lot. The night would be ugly. Tomorrow might be worse. "Bad weather a-coming," announced the innkeeper with relish, and he did not seem a man naturally geared towards relish. "Bad weather a-coming," as though he was laying a curse. This, joked Rinaldi, was because he saw rough weather as his friend. If the innkeeper had his way it would rain into next week, it would rain all the way until June. When business is slow you cling to your guests like grim death. Keep them marooned at the Bide-a-Wee. Keep pouring out the produce; keep running up the tab. That way—maybe only that way—the hotel might cling on until fall. Shooting season, salvation. A gaggle of fresh huntsmen beneath the antler chandeliers.

"Is that shooting season? September, October?"

"November, December. The truth is, I'm guessing. I'm a city boy like you."

"Babes in the woods. Jesus Christ, look at us."

Rinaldi nodded. He said, "I looked down the road just as far as I could see. A man had my woman and the blues had me."

"Hill-country music." Honest Jim smiled. "What can I tell you? Some land and some don't."

Outside in the lobby, the grandfather clock struck eleven. The rookie went to bed. The two catchers remained. Probably the innkeeper was sleeping by now, too, but he'd left behind the decanter and it was still a third full.

The fire burned low. Shadows twisted on the wall. Cope yawned and shifted and lit a last cigar.

"Still raining?" asked Rinaldi.

"Yeah. You can't hear it?"

The Italian crossed his heart and tapped the side table three times.

"You think that'll help?"

"It might," he said. "Ain't no harm in trying."

He was an odd fellow, Rinaldi: animated and tetchy, in thrall to quaint superstitions. He wore paperclips on his tie and duck-feathers in his hat-band and he never caught on a Wednesday because this only invited ill fortune. His eccentricities were so conspicuous, Cope thought, that they must surely count against him in the field. And yet the man did all right and had scored some sizable hits this past year, which suggested that at least some people liked his oddness or were comforted by it. It made the interloper less threatening if the locals felt able to look down on him a little. There was room for all sorts. Every party needs a clown.

He said, "The trouble with you, Jim, is that you see music as science, or a puzzle in math. The trouble with me is I see it as magic. Neither of us is exactly wrong, but both those approaches only take us so far."

Cope shrugged. "We're riding our luck. That's all we can do."

"Talking of which, here's a question. What's the best side you ever landed? The juiciest fish you ever caught?"

That was easy, Cope thought. "Did You Ever Dream a Dream? by Yodeling Jack Flatt. Bought for thirty dollars. Shifted half a million copies."

"I didn't say the biggest. The juiciest one. The side you loved best."

"It sold half a million. What's not to love?"

"This proves my argument, see? The trouble with you, you're all bottom line."

In the field they were loners. At the Bide-a-Wee they were friends. They could pore over their maps and trade their tales of great catches. They prided themselves on their achievements so far. They pitied the chancers who came trailing in their wake. The Irish rookie, they agreed, would not stay the course. You could tell right away. Some had it, some didn't.

"Did you hear where he's headed? Sutton, Tennessee."

"He won't get there," said Cope. "And if he does he'll get nothing."

"Poor bastard. Poor kid. He'll catch a cold, nothing more."

Outside it was raining. Inside it was warm. Rinaldi stood up to put another log on the fire only to become distracted by the hunting prints and the enormous mounted elk's head. He embarked on an unhurried, unsteady circuit of the room. He said, "What do you think he makes of it all?"

"The kid or the innkeeper?"

"The moose. The elk. Whatever it is. What is he thinking of us right this second?"

Cope had grown tired. He looked around with an effort. "He's wondering where it all went wrong, how he ended up on that wall."

Rinaldi snorted. "Of course he is. Poor bastard, look at him."

"Big, good-looking beast like that. He's thinking, 'Why, this can't be right. I lost to these jokers? These shit-heels?'."

"Meaning us?"

"Absolutely meaning us. He's an elk, for Christ sake. He wouldn't see any difference."

If catchers had a failing, it was that the good ones—the great ones—never knew when to quit. A three-minute song might very well last forever, but each success has a shelf-life and only makes a man feel more hungry. No treasure, no catch, was ever quite big enough. There was always something better up around the next bend. Yonder, they called it, the people of Appalachia, as though it were a physical place that a man might eventually reach. Yonder village, yonder town. Yonder mountain, yonder stars. Good catchers were drawn yonder, wherever yonder might be. This of course is what made them good catchers.

It was barely an hour past dawn when he set forth for the hills and the warmth of his breathing made the windows mist up. His head was aching and his eyes were sore. His rear wheels fish-tailed on the damp dirt road. But when the van crossed the river and ducked into the woods, the image that swung into his mind was of a sun-blasted wharf and whisked white-capped foam, and he experienced a sense of release so profound that it felt like oxygen from a can. The light rain turned to snow and this gave his tires more traction. He drove for an hour without seeing a soul. The branches around were all etched in hoarfrost.

Sometimes on the road a sheriff would flag him down and demand to know who he was, this sharp-suited roustabout from New York, and where he was going and what line of work he was in. And on such occasions Honest Jim Cope would explain that he was a field recordist, a talent scout, sent out to source and collect songs from the local hill-country musicians. He'd step from his vehicle and open the back doors to show the recording lathe in its cases and the wax masters in the rack, and he'd say, "Here it is, sheriff, my field recording machine," because men understood the concept of field recording even if they were ignorant of its details, and more often than not they would then leave him be. When the truth was that no one in the business called it field recording, or ever referred to themselves as talent scouts. They were song-catchers, pioneers, and they spoke their own language. So among themselves they would say that they were riding around the fairgrounds, or cutting about the Far Corners. They were panning for gold and diving for pearls, spearing the big fish, trapping fireflies in a jar. All of which was to say they'd been out on the road catching songs.

And now here came the snow, folding and dragging in a motion that felt almost tidal until it glued to the glass and made the wipers squeak and stutter. He passed an abandoned farmhouse, a barn, and the shell of a Model-T truck, and he fancied that his grip on the road had become a little less certain because the van kept jinxing to its left and he had to turn into the drift before gently correcting its course. And even then he was unconcerned, unafraid, because the land in those days rewarded the men who ran through it and penalized those who ducked their heads and took cover. Up ahead, around the bend, lay the wild, open country. It was a treasure chest, a casino. You relied on your wits and rolled the dice every day.

The snow blew sideways. The tires spun and caught. For an instant he feared he had lost sight of the road, but he aimed for white space, for the gap in the trees. Up ahead lay the fairground, the first of the hills. Behind that lay another, and then another hill beyond that. The man sang to himself as he wrestled the wheel. He sang, "The moon so bright, the gentle stream. Oh tell me, sweet Annie, did you ever dream a dream?"

2

FOR SEVEN DAYS it rained non-stop across the southern states. Rivers broke loose and ponds overflowed and the farms became useless; the livestock swam in mud. Nashville underwater, Chattanooga submerged. At the weather station at Cairo, the engineers tapped the gauge and left sweaty smears on the glass. Eight separate flood crests crawling down the Mississippi.

It rained from Illinois all the way to the Gulf. It was the first blast of God's trumpet. It was the end of the world. Inside the Greenville Baptist church the preacher quoted Genesis 6:17. "Behold, even I am bringing the flood of water to destroy all flesh which is the breath of life, from under Heaven. Everything that is on the earth will perish."

In the hills of Virginia the rain fell as snow. Snow stuck to trees and stone walls and to barn sides and fine houses. Milled to fine powder, it blew through keyholes, under doors and down flues. Nothing moved on the roads and busy towns became still. Bad weather a-coming: the innkeeper was right. Cars were buried and cabins were flattened and men lost their way on land they'd worked all their lives. The snow was so deep that it leveled the grounds of the Roanoke states' war cemetery. Anyone passing would think there were no graves there at all.

If music was played during that worst week of the spring, it was played in private, indoors, for an audience of family members. There were no try-outs or buy-outs; there was no travel of any kind. Instead men lived as their grandfathers had lived: alone in the woods and shut off from the world; lit by kerosene lamps and heating melt on the stove. The previous summer, a cowpuncher,

Pete Janowicz, had pocketed $60—a king's ransom—for the sale of two songs. Now those same sides (Deep Down Mountain Blues on the A; Pretty Polly on the B) were selling by the thousands in Boston, Philadelphia and New York, with the singer rechristened as Great Uncle Joe Suds. Hibernating, Pete Janowicz never knew the first thing about it.

The skies cleared on Monday and the snow froze where it lay, so that people slipped on its surface like skaters on a rink. A local hunter, Clem Pritchard, buckled his snowshoes and set forth through the woods, but the crust cracked underfoot and gave away his approach. He spotted fresh tracks all the way up the road. Deer and bear and fox and rabbit, as though the animals had absconded from a party upon hearing human steps. He pressed on for an hour, thinking he might at least bag a squirrel.

Right-side of the road, the ground dropped away to reveal the tops of tall trees. Below lay a stream just as solid as glass, with a silver cascade frozen hard up against it. As a boy he'd assumed that cascades froze in a flash, of a sudden—that they were crashing water one second and an ice sculpture the next—until his mother had told him that this wasn't nature's way.

She said, "Bless you, Clem, no. It happens gradual, it takes its time. Most freeze from the top and that's how you get the long icicles, see? But it never happens all at once, no sir, what a notion." He even remembered where she had been when she said it, out on the buckboard, indicating the Clover Fork with a switch. Bless you, she said. That isn't nature's way.

He found a break in the bushes and eased himself down the slope, testing the snow with each step and using the branches for handholds. The climb back would be awkward and he was no longer a young man.

Halfway to the stream he paused to take stock. "Hello!" he called, feeling foolish. He did not anticipate a reply.

The light was softer in the woods than it had been on the road. The breeze had dropped; the sense of solitude was intense. Which meant that the only thing moving was him, clumsy fool, with his cumbersome shoes and his breath like a bellows and his Winchester rifle perpetually catching in the branches. He more skidded than walked the last yards of descent before wedging himself between a pair of ice-cold boulders. He hollered his greeting a second time now, but only to check for an echo and establish himself in the scene.

The vehicle had cut a ragged path through the frozen growth. Its chassis was crimped and the tires had burst and the snow had matted its side panels in dalmatian markings. The van had either sat there for days or for a matter of hours. Clem couldn't say; there was no way of knowing. The cold snap pinned and preserved everything that it touched.

Gingerly, his breath fogging, he crossed to the front of the motor, conscious that his shoes were now crunching on beads of glass as well as ice. The impact of landing had concertinaed the hood and put out the windscreen and peeled back a section of the van's metal roof. And yet on bending his knees to peer into the cab, his impression was one not of violence but of peace. A column of sunlight had found its way through the canopy to illuminate the interior, so that the driver, half-turned about in his seat, glowed like a saint in a stained-glass window. Snow had collected in the lines of his suit and crystals of glass glistened in his thick hair, and his posture was that of a man who had decided to pull off the road for a doze, and who might at any second stretch out and continue on his way.

How long did the hunter stand beside the wrecked vehicle, transfixed by the sight of the young driver at rest? Again, there was no way of knowing, but afterwards he figured it must have been a considerable while, because when he eventually straightened it was as though the season had broken and an icy enchantment had lifted, and he saw a pair of sleek white-tailed deer foraging for acorns nearby and heard the drip of running water coming off the cascade. Springtime, Clem thought. Well, thank heavens for that.

3

MOSS EVANS WAS a hooch boy in Washington County, Mississippi. He had a stoppered flask strung over his right shoulder and a Stella guitar strung over his left, and his mud-spotted glasses were mended in two places with twine. He poured drinks and played music like an all-round entertainer, except that he performed for the convicts out of Parchman prison and they'd rather have been almost anywhere else. "You know what you got?" joked the bootlegger, Old Duke. "You know what you got? An honest-to-God captive audience."

This was the year that he turned eighteen and the ideas for the songs came for him every day, some days every hour, as if they were people—assailants—crowding him on the street. One minute he's walking and the next he's been collared and they're tugging his apron and shouting mischief in his ear, wanting him to raise up his guitar and make some sense of it all. Archimedes, he'd heard, sat in the bath and said Eureka. He says, "Quit your clamor. Leave me be, I'm at work."

This was the year that he turned eighteen and came by the Stella that made the bullfrogs explode. He hadn't wanted to make the bullfrogs explode (he had nothing against bullfrogs; what had they done to him?) but once he found the right chord it was like the guitar steered his hand and it became almost funny, everyone grew excited. Some of the cons were yelling at him to stop while others were yelling to keep going, goddammit, and why not try to make the prison guards explode too? Split the storm-clouds, kill my wife. Break my chains, I'm out of here. The guitar cost $2, it was a real piece of shit. But the guitar didn't know this, it saw itself as the boss.

This was the year that he turned eighteen and taught himself to play music or something like music, when he wrestled with phrases and changes, tunings and slides. Try as he might, he could never make the songs come out right. They started out fine, but then would crab-walk and change costumes so that they became unrecognizable, and he blamed the obstinate Stella or the angry ideas in his head or—most likely—a combination of both. Moss Evans was maybe not the best hooch boy in Washington County, Mississippi. But he was widely considered its all-time worst musician.

In March '27 it rained every day. Rained like God had turned the faucet, rained like the angels took a piss, so heavy it clattered like gravel on the roof of Duke's truck. Moss grew to detest those fraught trips out and back. The roads half-underwater; the wheels spinning at different speeds. If you asked Duke to slow down, though, he'd only cackle and accelerate.

Parchman prison lay some distance to the north, but it tended to send its work crews south. In summer the boys were put on the road pouring pitch. In the fall they were sent to pick cotton bolls in the fields. Now all day, every day, the crews were at work on Mounds Landing near Greenville, forming the first line of flood defense. Folk joked that it was only the convicts who were stopping the levee from falling down. The fate of civilization, they said, in the hands of the scum of the earth.

"Is this on account of the river?" he'd asked the first day they drove out and the bootlegger had laughed and said that no, it was on account of his maiden aunt who had the mumps and her parakeet that had molted; of course it was on account of the river, pinhead. "Every fuckin' thing's on account of the river," he said.

From the road, closing in, Mounds Landing looked like a circus, with big tents and gennies and light bulbs strung on wires. Each time he came up, more tents and more men. The pot-bellied guards leaned into their rifles and smoked. The self-styled levee captains played games of dice under canvas. And more often than not, the sheriff's deputy, George Piper, would be on hand to greet him, lounging in his deckchair as if he hadn't a care in the world. He'd say, "Well, if it isn't our hooch boy, our picker, our prince. God bless your heart, Mossy, you get over here now," except that his broad, sunny smile never once touched his eyes.

If this circus needed a barker, it might as well be George Piper, at least for the time being, until his duties called him elsewhere. It was Piper, in his loose, easy fashion, who oversaw the various comings and goings. And it was Piper, he recalled, who had seen off the pastor when he objected to Duke's barrels. The pastor—a youngish fellow but old inside—couldn't see the sense of loading colored convicts up on liquor. Come to that, he didn't like to imagine that any white folk drank it either. The Christian thing to do would be to push every one of those barrels downstream.

Piper had whistled, evidently fascinated. He said, "Well gosh, there's a thought. Just roll the barrels downstream."

"It would be an act of mercy, Mr Piper."

"No doubt about it. No doubt that it would." But it had reminded the deputy of a tale he'd been told by his cousin Benjamin over in McGehee, Arkansas. He said, "You ever been to McGehee, pastor?"

"No sir, I have not."

Moss stood by the barrels, waiting to see how the conversation played out.

"Oh," Piper said. "Well now." Unhurriedly, he patted his pockets to locate his cigarettes. "Well, you're going to like this one, pastor. Let me see if I can't get it straight."

"Mr Piper . . ."

"Terrible scene over there in McGehee. Most everyone drinking. Most everyone drunk. McGehee, Arkansas, though, so what else can you do?" He had raised his voice by this point, performing for the men who had gathered behind the men. "Now the preacher, well, he's like you, he's had enough. And so the next Sunday in church, he draws himself up, all high and mighty like, and he says, 'After the service we're gonna take all the whiskey in town and dump it in the river, as God is my witness. And now please rise for our closing hymn.' And the old choirmaster . . ." At this, Piper leaned forward to slap the pastor's shoulder, cuing him up for the punchline, including him in the joke. "And the old choirmaster, he says, 'Today's closing hymn is Shall We Gather at the River'."

Moss walked the barrel into the tent, his head blissfully empty for once, his guitar case tapping against his hip. He filled the flasks and prepared to set out on his rounds. A mouthful of hooch for every con every hour. An emergency dose if one passed out or pitched a fit. A moderate mouthful was all that was required, Piper said, in the same way that a small amount of chili powder can help a tired horse win a race. Put a little smudge on its ass and the beast perks up and runs faster. Any more than a smudge and it loses its mind.

The deputy made as though to ruffle Moss's hair. "You just leave that barrel with us, my boy. We'll guard it with our lives and give it a good home." And this, Moss knew, was how it went every time. The con got his mouthful and the white men drank the rest.

"Small smudge on the ass," Piper said. "Itty bitty dab will suffice."

A circus, he thought, yes, although not the fun kind. On the western slope, a hundred prisoners had been put to work making mudboxes. Why they were called mudboxes Moss hadn't a clue, given that they contained no mud and weren't boxes at all but planks of wood laid end-to-end. The cons teamed up to set each plank on its side and then shoved sandbags behind so as to hold it in place. It was like they were fitting the levy with a wooden topcoat

He moved up the line. The closeness of the men stirred his senses. Some of the cons stood out from their neighbors. Some he would have liked to stop and talk to for a minute without the guards waving their rifles to order him on. This one time a fellow had asked him for a kiss. Most just asked for more hooch, or whether he knew a song called Jacob's Ladder and if so could he play it in a way that sounded something fucking like it.

This far down the slope you couldn't tell what the problem was. You weren't aware of the thing that had everybody so scared. You saw the willows and the canebrake. You heard the noise of the workers and the drag of the rain through the grass. A man could go about his business for hours and never know any better, wondering what was the point of all those sandbags and planks. That was human nature, Moss thought. If you can't see it or hear it, a thing might as well not exist.

At that time on the levee there was a man named Miles Craven, who was rumored to be just as cracked as an egg. Miles Craven worked as an engineer down in Vicksburg although he supposedly came from back east, out of state, and Moss suspected that this is partly what people held against him. That and his manner, which could be lordly. Mr Craven knew everything there was to know about pressure and erosion, sand-boils and spillways, which was all well and good and what one would expect of a River Commission engineer. But Mr Craven also had a tendency to talk people down and broadcast his opinions too loudly, and these opinions, it was said, were always full of gloom. The levee captains pointed out that the river was still away over there, across the batcher and past the willows. The way Miles Craven carried on, you'd think it was dressed up for dinner and knocking at the front door.

Most mornings when he drove up from Vicksburg, Miles Craven brought with him a fancy Gibson guitar. The young man enjoyed music, which was taken as further proof of his strangeness. Specifically, he enjoyed Moss Evans' music, all those unearthly noises, and wanted the boy to teach him a new song or two. Most white men would never have dreamed of passing the time of day with a colored, but Mr Craven didn't care. He'd beckon Moss over as if he were requesting a favor.

The captains hurried over. "Is this boy bothering you, Mr Craven?"

"Not at all," he told them airily. "But I dare say, boys, that you are just a little." Deputy Piper enjoyed playing to the gallery and Moss thought that in a queer roundabout way Mr Craven did as well. It was as though he saw his friendship with the hooch boy as a stick to beat the captains with.

"Now run along, please. Moss and I have some work to do."

Duke was supposed to pick him up every day at five. But Duke, being Duke, preferred to keep his own time which meant that it was often close to sundown when his truck—the Good Luck Buggy—came limping up the track. And it was during those doldrums at the end of the shift that Craven would have him sit under the canvas and go back and forth over this song or that one until Moss thought that the stress might make him start screaming. It had got so he couldn't say what he hated more: the captains or Miles Craven or that bastard, Old Duke, for not rescuing him sooner.

"These songs," Craven said. "I am trying to think of the word."

Moss stared at the ground. He was listening out for the truck.

"I want to say ridiculous. But I also want to say beautiful. So it's a quandary, Moss, you understand what I mean?"

"Yessir."

"You don't need to sir me, Moss, remember. I am not a knight in shine armor."

"No sir," said Moss, and this made the engineer miss his stroke. It was funny, Craven said. When he missed a stroke it was a mistake, nothing more, whereas when Moss missed a stroke it sounded rather interesting. It rather made him think there might be something halfway sentient behind all the mistakes the boy made.

The engineer smiled. "All these songs that you play. The old ones and the new ones. I'm not convinced that they are coming out wrong, exactly. One might even go so far as to describe them as a different version of right."

The drumming of the rain had grown less insistent. Moss took this to be a good omen. It meant that the day might not be all bad.

"Talk me a little bit through the process. You sit down and start playing This Little Light of Mine, say. And then what? Tell me how you do it."

"I don't know, sir." Because the last thing Moss was about to do was tell this white man, Miles Craven, of how the ideas were wont to grab him on the street and how the Stella guitar had a mind of its own. Yessir and no sir them to death, said Old Duke. Yessir and no sir until their eyeballs roll back and they start pleading for mercy.

"Well, try to think. Help me out." By the end of the day Mr Craven's voice had become strained from arguing with the captains and Piper and the men from the levee board down in Greenville. He said he had no great desire to quarrel with the hooch boy as well.

"Rain looks to be stopping."

"Don't change the subject, Moss." He choked the strings of his Gibson. "Or wait: is it me who is guilty of that? Changing the subject and distracting myself? I mean, good heavens, the rain certainly ought to be the subject. You are entirely correct."

"Yessir."

"Yessir." Craven laughed mirthlessly. "Absolutely yes sir."

The Army said that the Delta was safe, and most likely it was. Mounds Landing wasn't like the small earthwork levees up-river, apt to go with the flow at the first sign of trouble. Mounds Landing meant business. Mounds Landing was federal. Six miles long and four stories tall. The immovable object, Greenville's lord protector. It was simply that the harder it rained, the more the river gained steam. All that month it had been leaning its weight on the levee, pushing at its shoulder, seeking a weak spot to break in. Think of the levee like a tooth, Craven told him. As with a tooth, you've got to keep it maintained at all times. Check the surface for cracks and holes. Check for rotting driftwood and crawdad nests. Because if the levee gets a cavity, the footing is compromised and the very ground turns to sponge. Then like a tooth it gets pulled, except that it's the river that pulls it.

This explained all of the frantic activity on the levee. The wheelbarrows and earthmovers and sandbags and planks. The work crews and guardsman and half-drunk levee captains. Obviously it explained Craven's own presence as well, much good as it did. It seemed to Miles Craven that he spent the majority of his time telling people things that they didn't want to hear, bussing about and making a nuisance of himself. "And now I'm doing the same to you. Do tell me if I am detaining you against your will."

"Yessir," said Moss. "I mean, no sir, you ain't."

The captains never liked Miles Craven so well, Moss thought, as when he went down the east slope in search of sand boils. This was because the man's gumboots had no tread and he was constantly falling down. He only had to say, "I'm going to check on the boils" and a ripple of excitement would pass through the white men in the camp, and you could see them break off from whatever they were doing and gather about to watch. The boils made small fountains and showed where the river had already found its way through the levee. So long as the water was clear, Craven said, there was no great cause for alarm. But he made a point of inspecting them several times every day—slipping on the wet grass, flapping his long arms for balance—while the fellows at the summit covered their mouths with their hands. Moss did not believe he had ever met a man so graceless as Miles Craven. What made matters worse, he used to get so angry about it. He'd sit on the grass and start punching the ground as though it had deliberately tripped him. That was the kind of man Craven was. Nobody liked him, maybe not even his kin.

They shouldered their guitars and stepped outside. The rain had paused but the clouds looked bruised and the wind was thundering in the canvas sheets. An apron of wet farmland rolled away to the east. To their backs lay the barrow, the willows and the river. "Avert your eyes," the engineer said, mostly joking, which of course had the effect of making Moss turn about. The whip of the gale was so vicious that he thought in that second it might be enough to lift him. Then, squinting west through his mud-spotted spectacles, he saw the treetops and the trouble and a portion of Arkansas, too. "What did I tell you?" the engineer said in his ear. "Cover your eyes, Mr Moss, there's nothing to see over there."

Old Duke liked to say that the reason the Mississippi was so wide was because it was fed by about one hundred other rivers to the point where it wasn't one river but many—a braid of disputatious streams, each one doing its own thing. Look closely and you could see them clashing, warring, jockeying for position, one current pulled taut and its neighbor gone slack, while a third did its best to muscle in between them, cross-stitching over and under like a sewing thread, stirring the surface into whirlpools and white curd. The sight put Moss in mind of the sick man in the Bible who ran to Jesus for help and when the Lord knelt down and asked for his name, the man said, "My name's Legion, because there are so many of us."

The wind snapped the tent flaps. He could hear Old Duke's truck on the track. But the view had him pinned and refused to let him go. Already the water had crossed through the wetlands to the woods so that from a distance it gave the impression of being as much land as liquid, heaving with fence posts and barn-sides and uprooted, stripped trees. The old monster, he thought. The cause of all the bother. Yellowed and swollen and rising two feet every day. One hundred rivers all with the same name.

4

THE FIRST LAW of business is that the boss doesn't know about business. He's stuck in an office with a gramophone in the corner and 9th Avenue at his back and that's the extent of his knowledge, his horizon, his world. The second law of business is that the boss doesn't care. When you think about it, that follows—the first domino knocks the next. The boss can't understand a business that operates five hundred miles from his desk in a place he's never been, so the boss has no concept of how the product is made. Send a fellow off to the Far Corners, he says, as though hill country starts about three blocks downtown. Go pick up some songs, like he's ordering coffee.

The boss doesn't care because the boss doesn't know. He's middle-aged and out of touch, a working stiff who got lucky and has no understanding of why. Let's say he started as a sheet-music salesman on Tin Pan Alley, or selling tone arms and motors out of a Cherry Street warehouse. Ten years later, kapow, he's got his name on the door and a secretary on his lap and he's ticking along, his life's pretty swell. Waltzes and foxtrots keep the accounts in the black. But suddenly, out of nowhere, he's got the New Southern Series—authentic American music recorded in the field on the cheap—and it's boom time, a gold rush. Thirty bucks buys a song and then the company owns it forever. But what are these songs? Why should he know what they mean? The average record company chief has no grasp of southern music. He has no idea how it's made and no idea how it's caught, and honestly, speaking frankly, he couldn't give less of a shit. The way the chief sees it, his duties have been stripped back to the essentials, which is to bang on his desk and shout for more every month. More of that stuff that did so good the last time. More of that stuff I wouldn't listen to anyway. That's now become his entire job, shouting "More". And he only fails at this job if he shouts for more and gets nothing.

"All right," said Rinaldi and coughed into his hand. "Now picture this man, this boss, sitting at his big desk. Lee Teltscher, Victor Records. He hears about Cope and what's his first reaction? What is the primary emotion that Lee Teltscher feels today?"

"He's upset," replied John Coughlin.

"Sure, he's upset. He's distraught. He's in pieces. This is the worst thing to happen. This could bring the company to its knees. But what's the first thing that goes through his head when he's told? The very first thing Lee Teltscher wants to know."

The question was rhetorical. Rinaldi pressed on:

"He thinks, 'What about the recording lathe? Was it damaged in the crash?' Those machines cost a fortune. He needs to know it's OK. The second thing that he thinks, 'So wait, where's my more? We gotta send someone else out to the Corners right away'. One man dies and it's a pain in the ass. Miss a delivery and it's a full-blown fucking tragedy." He grimaced. "The best catcher in the business. The man who unlocked the mountains. None of that matters. They'll have replaced him already."

Rained-in at the Bide-a-Wee. Rinaldi had a habit, on waking each morning, of checking the ground in the lot with the ball of his thumb. Coughlin, the rookie catcher, who was usually up a good hour before him, would sit on the porch and observe this daily ritual, watching as the little Italian strode purposefully out to where the vans were parked. Probably it wasn't the best test of conditions, sticking your thumb in the ground, but he deferred to Rinaldi, who knew how the Far Corners worked. Rinaldi said that the last thing they wanted was to get stuck fast in the mud twenty miles from town.

"We're stuck fast right here," Coughlin said. "I ought to be down in Sutton, Tennessee."

"Listen to him, the Irish Rover. Raring to set sail and hasn't learned a damn thing."

There were two other guests at the hotel that week: a pair of wiry old hunters who kept their own company. Periodically Coughlin would hear them blasting away in the woods, although they never seemed to return with anything beyond grouse. Probably that's what they came for. Maybe birds were their specialty. But these mangled feathered corpses would then be laid out on the walnut table in the lobby, arranged side-by-side in a stiffly formal display. Displayed for who, Coughlin wondered. Surely this wasn't for his benefit. He was a Mott Haven street-rat; a one-time thief, now reformed. He knew the Bronx and Manhattan. Everywhere else, not so much.

Rinaldi looked him up and down. "Jesus, kid, take your hat off. I shouldn't have to keep saying it."

"You're right, I'm sorry."

"What outfit are you with anyhow?"

"Humpty Records. Tenth Avenue."

"A lightweight. A mayfly," Rinaldi said, not unkindly. "Another Johnny-come-lately trying to crack the hill-country market. Wait, wasn't it Humpty that put out that Spider Joe song?"

"That was me. I mean, I found the guy. I arranged the song."

The Italian's eyes narrowed. "Well, don't sound so perky. You ought to apologize for that song, not the hat."

Bad weather incoming, the innkeeper had said. But, on testing the ground on the fifth morning of their stay, Rinaldi decided that by tomorrow he might finally think about chancing his arm, heading out. But heading out as in back, he explained to Coughlin over breakfast. The trip was a bust, he couldn't stress that enough. The expedition was jinxed; they should have waited a month. His revised plan was to return to the city, dry off and try again. It's not like the musicians were fixing to go anywhere. The songs would sound just as sweet in April as they would have in March.

The rookie frowned. "If it's dry enough to drive back, it's dry enough to go on."

"Trust me, kid, it's not. The roads get worse the further south a man goes and you're fixing to go to—Jesus Christ—Tennessee. I don't know if that even counts as the Corners. I never went that far down."

"Too far, you think?"

"Hey, that's your business. If you want to run before you can walk, be my guest." He shook his head. "But don't run tomorrow, that's all I'm saying."

Rained-in at the Bide-a-Wee. It was an occupational hazard, he explained. It was part and parcel of the catcher's life. When the weather turned rough, you sat it out or you died. And then when it thawed you added another two nights for safety, because the last thing you wanted was to drive through the spring run-off. Every wagon-trail like a river and snow-melt pouring off the hills. He put his faith in St Christopher, but even then there were limits.

He indicated his necktie, his pockets and his hat on the table. "I put my faith in this, this, and this. But even then there are limits."

Rinaldi's superstitions, no question, had served him well in the Corners. His rivals might laugh at his stones, his duck feathers and his sprigs of jasmine. His tarot cards and his thrice-tied shoes. The intricate arrangement of paperclips on his tie. But the joke was on them, because he was still catching, still breathing. Also, as he liked to point out, it was paperclips and the tarot which had steered him in the direction of an impoverished old cattleman, Pigeon George, who swore blind that his fiddle was a Stradivarius copy. Pigeon George used his fiddle to mimic local birds. Each tune was made up of birds chirping back and forth in the trees. Anyone else would have passed, but Rinaldi thought what the hell. Hill-Country Bird Blues. It had sold by the boxload.

"Explain that one to me. Explain Pigeon George."

"I guess I can't."

"Nobody can," said Rinaldi, which was the final truth of the business. Because he could sit and berate the bosses all he liked. He could say they were dumb, out of touch and didn't know what they had, and he stood by every word: that was exactly what they were. But catchers in the field were likewise in the dark. The business was young and the market was fragile, which meant that nobody could say that they knew what they were doing. There were no rules, only guidelines, and no clear path to success. But that was catching, that was music. You might as well try to throw a purse seine around smoke.

"Guidelines are good," Coughlin said. "I need all the help I can get."

"Did I say there were guidelines? Maybe there's not even those."

By the fifth day of their stay it was warm enough to sit out. Coughlin could hear gunshots in the woods and the distant growl of a motorcar. The land, he thought, was waking up from hibernation.

"Guidelines," said Rinaldo. He appeared to give the subject deep thought. "First is obvious. Give the company what it wants. The boss shouts for hill-country pieces, that's what you deliver. No race music, no jazz, nothing that steps out of line. The boss wants a fish, so don't bring him a cat. Also hill-country music, my God, that's a broad enough church as it is."

"Sure," Coughlin said. "Like your Pigeon George."

"Second guideline, also obvious. You record in the field and you get out right away. Pay your thirty bucks for a side and then it's over, it's done. We're buyers, not managers. It's about the song, not the singer. So suck out the juice, pay your money and throw the pulp to the curb."

"And third? Give me one that's less obvious."

The catcher regarded him shrewdly. "The third guideline's the joker. Third is trust your gut, trust your instincts. Nobody knows what will sell but the good man, the smart man, always knows what he likes." He plucked at his shirt-cuff to dislodge a beetle. "And maybe that's the wrong word. Maybe it's not even your taste. But when you hear it, you know it. And there's your firefly, your big fish."

Coughlin leaned forward. "That's what I want. I want to bring back the big fish."

"Music," said Rinaldi. "The best thing in the world. Also the worst. When it's bad it's the worst. But then you know all about that, Irish Rover. You've got to love music, otherwise you wouldn't be here."

"I do," Coughlin said, although that wasn't quite right. He had drunk too much produce and it had loosened his tongue. "I mean, everybody says that they love music, don't they?"

The catcher accepted that this was so.

"What they really mean . . . what they really want . . ." He clammed up, embarrassed.

"Out with it, kid. It's only you and me here."

He tried again. "What they really want is to feel like the music loves them back."

And just like that, he thought later, he had broken Rinaldi's third guideline or commandment or whatever it was, because he should have trusted his first instinct and kept his mouth shut instead of blurting something so stupid and exposing his idiocy.

Rinaldi blinked and looked away. It would have been better if he'd laughed. He said, "Yeah, maybe, who knows? It's a pretty thought, I guess."

It was a historic inn, the Bide-a-Wee, insofar as the original structure was 150 years old, an awkward arrangement of brick and stone. It had a wraparound porch and eight guest rooms upstairs. A century before, the innkeeper explained, the building had been the home of one Henry Quirke, personal physician to President James Madison, although it had not been called the Bide-a-Wee back then, no sir, he did not imagine it had a name at all. It stood on a rise half a mile from the Potomac—as isolated a spot as Coughlin had been in his life yet positively congested compared to the land beyond the river. The town was close by. The view was quite pleasant. It was only on crossing the bridge that the traveler became aware of the country turning strange, at once opening out and crowding in, as though the windscreen had curved like carnival glass and a man could no longer trust the evidence of his eyes. Oh, went the song, all of the places we'll go. Over the river and into the trees.

Honest Jim Cope loved Appalachia and believed it loved him back. That was his nature. That proved to be his mistake. The man threw himself at the mountains as an excitable farm boy might drop into a mound of loose straw, viewing it as a country of soft landings and warm pockets. Appalachia with its good, simple men and pliant, sun-bronzed women. Appalachia with its docile black bears and whitewashed Baptist churches. He saw the Far Corners as paradise, his happy hunting ground, when of course, he was wrong, it was nothing of the sort. It was a savage country, pitiless and arbitrary, ripped by foul weather, red in tooth and claw. You went for the music, nothing more, and you came back exhausted, assuming you came back at all. And the more times you went down, the less good music you found, which meant that the next time you had to go deeper and look harder. The chiefs didn't care so long as they got the music. They didn't know what was out there. They would struggle to locate the place on a map.

All day long Rinaldi had been trying to picture the scene. A man leaves the Bide-a-Wee first thing in the morning. Steals out like a thief without saying so much as goodbye, figuring he's got the jump on his competitors, that he's won this particular round of the game. Ahead of him, though, is the void: hundreds of miles of mountain country. He's reduced to a flyspeck and swallowed by the land. It was a miracle that Cope's body was found as quickly as it was. Any other time it would have lain in the wreck for several months, by which point the animals would have squabbled over it at their leisure, fussing for the choicest cuts.

Rinaldi had his cigarette alight. He gazed past the lot at the low line of damp trees. "The worst part," he said. "You know what the worst part of it is?"

"Worse than him getting eaten in the woods?"

"The worst part of it is that we got along pretty well. I liked Jim Cope and he liked me. And still the first thing I thought was that this was good news for the rest of us, that I'd gained an advantage before I'd even got out of bed. One less catcher in the field, more ground for us to mine for gold. How's that for human decency? How's that for the catcher's code?"

"Oh," Coughlin said. "Well, yeah, I don't know."

"Truth of the matter, I'm glad he crapped out. Probably I hope that you crap out, too." Rinaldi grinned at the woods. The cigarette burned in his fingers. He said, "I'm being honest with you, kid. It's not nice but it's true. This is the reality of the business we're in."

The previous night he'd sat up late. He'd lit the lamp and read the tarot and it was this that had made up his mind to turn back for New York. Rinaldi had built his tarot deck piecemeal over several years and to his own specifications, so that it now contained a number of regular playing cards: several clubs, a brace of diamonds and the image of a bare-breasted young redhead to represent the Queen of Hearts. Probably no one other than Rinaldi could decipher the deck's meaning. No one other than Rinaldi could tease out its peculiar twists and turns. But he had read it last night and hadn't liked what he saw. Images of ruination. Lightning strikes and broken towers. Rivers running backwards. Men hung upside-down. He said, "Do yourself a favor and forget about the guidelines. Forget about Sutton or wherever it is that you're going. I'm serious, Irish Rover. Turn around and go home."

5

HOME WAS MANHATTAN, before that the South Bronx, although he had never quite felt that he belonged anywhere. Probably that's how it went with most people, he thought. Modern men spend their lives scurrying between situations, reluctant to settle yet scared of being moved on.

He worked as a plugger, placing Humpty records downtown. It was a good job in warm weather and a grind when it rained. New York in the winter, that was the worst time of all, when the January air felt as dry as a bone and the snow was so bright it burnt the eyes just to see it. Shoes slipped on frozen trolley lines; bare palms stuck to railings. Everyone on the street pinwheeling their arms for balance. Every car at the curb sealed fast like hard candy. The drivers had to crack the ice casing before they could get their keys in.

The job took him all over. He walked from station to station and store to store, switching his satchel from side-to-side as he went. "New music!" he'd shout, blowing steam in the doorway. "New music, hot wax!" and by and large this was true because the boys up at Humpty just ladled it out, the whole industry did. Thousands of records thrown into the city each month in the hope that one would land right side up and justify all the rest.

He knew a Bronx girl, a nurse, who said that out of every ten babies delivered on any given day, eight will live and two will die. Only with music, he'd told her, the ratio is reversed. Eight recordings will crash while two might claw back their cost, which was a lousy business model and hardly seemed worth the effort. Except that every once in a while—a blue moon, a leap year—a song would catch fire, and the money it earned kept everybody afloat. These were the freaks, the fireflies, the big fish. Bye Bye Blackbird, Did You Ever Dream a Dream, the ones that leapt from the depths and gave no clue as to why. So it was an inexact science, the recording and publishing game. The entire business relied on the periodic appearance of monsters.

"That's what I want to do," he had confided to Rinaldi, sitting out on the veranda and too drunk to know better. "That's what I want to do. I want to catch the big fish."

At nine in the morning, the merchants of Cortlandt Street set wooden pallets on the ice and placed electric goods on the pallets. Then for block after block there was nothing but music and he'd work his way west from the shadow of the El, past the illuminated signs for Leotone, Digby Auctions, Heins & Bolet, Arrow Radio, past the portable phonographs, Valencias and Victrolas, and the pure noise of the place was enough to make his teeth buzz. Cortlandt Street played foxtrots, jazz, opera and jigs, and as Coughlin picked his way from one awning to the next, the melodies blended and blurred so that it seemed to him that the machines were somehow talking together as one.

Now out of the glare, in tinsel and sequins, stepped Miss Downtown Radio, who was paid an equal sum by all of the Cortlandt Street merchants and was therefore owned by none of them. Miss Downtown Radio: a vision, a mirage. Her office was the road and she was outside in all weather, gesturing to this store and that store with her palms pressed together; swinging out from a central position so that the act of pointing became a dance and the accompanying patter a kind of song. She cried, "Well hello, handsome sailor, Heins & Bolet, Heins & Bolet. I see you walking like a jungle cat, Digby Auctions to your left right there."

At the end of each month, Miss Downtown Radio would vanish. At the start of each month she'd reappear, born anew, so that where once she'd been blonde she was now a brunette, with a bonier figure behind her colored sash. Instinctively, though, she recognized the salesmen coming through. Sashes or satchels, they were in a similar line of work.

"Here he is, the Humpty man. If it don't kill you, it makes you stronger, right?"

"So they say. I hope it's true. How are you doing this morning?"

"Freezing my tail off, thanks for your concern."

With her forefingers steepled, she indicated the row of Victrolas outside Wild Electric. The crosswind dragged her skirt's tassels and put gooseflesh on her arms. But her smile was unshakable; it was built to withstand hurricanes. She said, "I'm getting a fucking migraine, too."

"Say again?"

"Migraine." She beamed. "Like anyone gives a shit."

One thing that surprised him: when he first landed the job at Humpty Records, he had thought, here it is, a new world, transformation at last. No more thieving and fighting and loafing outside the drugstore. He was running with the fancy crowd and had better stand tall and speak smart. Right away, though, he saw it really wasn't so different. The song-pluggers from the other outfits were just versions of the kids he'd observed every day in Mott Haven, all of them hustling and every one of them hungry. Street rats in fine hats. Grifters with pocket squares. They dreamed of being catchers, of reaching the top rung of the ladder and spoke as if it were already so, as though by talking they'd somehow make it happen. "We're trapping fireflies," they'd joke, shielding their cigarettes from the wind. "We're off to the Far Corners," they'd say, when what they really meant was downtown.

When the weather got up inside Radio Row it lifted the powdery snow off the crust and stirred it so that it might have been a fresh fall. You had to be tough to stomach Cortlandt Street after Christmas. You had to be as cold-blooded as a lizard and to love music more than most.

"I used to love music," Miss Downtown Radio said. "I thought that I did. Then they stuck me out here."

Once he had stood with his satchel not far from this spot and watched a brawl play out on the snow-blown street. Three rival song-pluggers grappling outside the door to Digby Auctions, their breath fogging in the frozen air, one kid blowing bubbles of blood from his nose and open mouth. The combatants went at it in a dogged, unhurried fashion, throwing their punches with such an air of detachment that it made him wonder if this were a regular occurrence, the latest installment in a long-running dispute over which plugger had dibs on the shops of Radio Row. And as he stood curbside he was aware he'd been joined by several onlookers and that the middle-aged vendors had abandoned their tills and were watching the fight with a placid interest. The Valencia beneath the awning played This Fine Man of Mine and Miss Downtown Radio maintained her distance, her tassels streaming sideways as she swung from the hips and pointed left and right. Coughlin could hear her above the din. She said, "Right this way for Leotone. Now kick him, kick him, don't let him get up. Your home from home, it's Leotone, and break his balls, it's Leotone."

Rinaldi was right—Humpty Records was small, precarious, barely breaking even. For years it had operated as an ethnic importer, trading in Yiddish, Italian and Chinese music. Now it employed a house-band that worked out of a draper's warehouse on 10th Avenue. The musicians put out cheap copies of authentic hill-country recordings. If Columbia had a hit with My Mother the Mountain, the Humpty house-band would quickly run up a piece that was either about mountains or mothers. When Victor scored big with Did You Ever Dream a Dream, quick as a flash there was Humpty with Did You Ever Dream of Jean.

Mornings, to warm up, the boys would work their way through the same loose instrumental. The melody was flimsy, no more than a doodle—a creepy piano refrain that left space for the comings and goings of whatever instruments were to hand—but Coughlin quite liked it. He thought with some effort it might be coaxed into a song. "Stranger things have happened," Oncins, the bandleader, said—and Coughlin chose to take this as an official commission of sorts.

He wrote the piece out one night after Christmas, sitting at his drop-leaf table, looking out on King Street. It would work best, he'd decided, as a haunted-house song, like a piece of musical theater, so he rigged up some words about a traveler who seeks shelter at an abandoned farm only to realize he's not alone in the dark. He thought Oncins might be persuaded to sing the part of the traveler. He already knew who he wanted as the ghost.

Spider Joe was a beggar out on Radio Row. You could find him most days outside the Cortlandt Street El, angling to carry people's bags up the steps. Typically Spider Joe demanded a dime for this service, figuring that if he asked for a dime he might come away with a nickel. If you paid him a dime, it made him feel he'd been crooked. He'd wish that he'd asked for a quarter instead.

Spider Joe, what a character. Coughlin was compelled. The man suffered from a mild palsy. Ordinarily this would have lent him a tragic air. And yet Spider Joe had taken the decision to lean into this frailty so that he walked with a rolling asymmetrical gait, throwing an arm out wide and occasionally stopping to curtsy, like a drunken John Barrymore playing King Richard III. His years on the street had graveled his lungs and reconditioned his voice so that it sounded scarcely human. You could hear Spider Joe from a hundred yards out. You heard him over the scream of the train and the din of the music and the groan of the ferries pulling into the depot. Men heard him cry out for business and it stopped them in their tracks. His speaking voice was unearthly; his laughter purely hellish.

Coughlin waylaid him on the metal steps. "I want to book you for the afternoon. Easy job indoors, in the warm," he added. "Sitting on a chair. Singing into a horn."

Spider Joe shook him off. He half-turned on the steps so as to give the impression that he was addressing someone else. "Singing at a what?" he said.

"Singing into a horn. I can pay you ten bucks all in."

That got his attention. He said, "Who says that you can?"

They recorded in the windowless little room that the boys called the chokey. Velvet drapes on the wall. Thick carpet underfoot. Spider Joe perched on a stool, singing and cackling on command. He veered off the script but mostly kept in tune. The whole thing took an hour. Coughlin handed over ten bucks.

"Dammit," said Joe. "I shoulda asked for twenty."

Outside in the corridor, Oncins lit a cigarette. He felt obligated to point out that the song was a joke—not least because the rummy had kept on forgetting his lines and introducing himself as Spider Joe instead of the Farmhouse Ghost. The song was a joke but that was just how it went. If Humpty could make back its money on Did You Ever Dream of Jean, Oncins saw no reason why they shouldn't chip a few extra dollars out of this one as well.

Coughlin nodded, embarrassed. All things considered, he thought the recording had gone well. "We'll put it out as Only Me and Spider Joe. And I was thinking, how about we credit it to the Lonesome Pioneers?"

"Whatever you like," Oncins had said with a shrug, because the boys didn't care, they changed their names every week. In the past month they had been the Orangutans and the Pie-Eyed Troubadours, the Happy Valley Doughboys and the Coldstream College Quartet. This was the nature of the Humpty Records' house-band. The week after that they'd be called something else.

"Only Me and Spider Joe," the catcher, Rinaldi, had scoffed. "You made that record? You ought to be ashamed." And yet he wasn't ashamed, he was pleased, because the record had sold. Children adored it. Adults were amused. It made Coughlin think he had, for once, done something worthwhile. Towards the end of February he even got wind that one of Spider Joe's nonsensical ad-libs—"I'm gonna kill you all your life"—had been adopted as an insult by the kids in Mott Haven, hollered at motorists or the elderly ice-man on his wagon. "Hey, watch where you're going or I'm gonna kill you all your life!"

The piece was a joke. It was an affront to good taste. No one liked Coughlin's record apart from all the people who bought it.

The song sold 8,000 copies in the first half of the month and nearly 20,000 in the second—small beans when compared to something like Sleepy Time Gal but more than sufficient to be considered a hit. The rain-drenched wayfarer shaking himself dry in the house. The malign farmer's ghost cackling from darkness. "It's only you and Spider Joe and thirty miles of big bad woods. Get over here and shake my hand, I'm gonna kill you all your life."

How much money did it make, Only Me and Spider Joe? It got so that Coughlin felt bad, only paying the man his ten bucks with nothing else thrown on top and no royalties pending. Except that the next time he dropped by Cortlandt Street, meaning perhaps to top him up a little, the stairway was unoccupied and a fresh panhandler was working the corner of Church, and he concluded that Spider Joe had gone wherever the Spider Joes of this world went. Another street, another station and eventually, probably, the city morgue because the rummies of Manhattan tended to live brief, torrid lives. All the same, he wished him well, and hoped the man might beat the odds. He thought that without Spider Joe the side might not have landed and he might not have been taken off the song-plugger beat and put in charge of a panel delivery van and a field recording machine and sent off to the hills to see what else he could find. Without Spider Joe he might still be hauling his satchel of copies up Radio Row, shouting "New music, hot wax," while his bones turned to glass.

He had fancied the Far Corners to be a few miles away: across the bridge and through the trees, after which the blue mountains would pile up all around. But beyond the woodland, instead of mountains, the road led through miles of sodden farmland. He saw red barns and white churches and a distant line of pale hills. Again, he imagined these hills to be close. But he drove for an hour without appearing to have gained any ground.

The country was larger than he realized; it would take some getting used to. Drive a mile in Manhattan and you might pass a million people. Drive a mile in Virginia and you'd be running through the same small swatch of land. The same post-and-rail fencing, rolling out like sheet music. The same band of trees hanging on the horizon. He longed to go faster but the graveled road felt unstable. Press too hard on the gas and a pothole might snap the axles, blow the tires. Brake too vigorously and the ground-water would surf him right into a ditch, his adventure over before it had begun. So he proceeded with caution, hunched over the wheel, aware of the recording lathe in its cases dragging at the vehicle's hindquarters.

He thought of Rinaldi, who would now be on the road back to New York. He thought of Jim Cope, who pulled up lame, came up short. He knew he counted for nothing, John Coughlin, and had mostly wasted his life before now. In that moment, however, he felt he had both those great catchers beat.

"Sutton," he said. "Tennessee. The Far Corners." He was off the fairground. He was off to catch fireflies.

The sky was clear and the day was warm but some hours later on a lonesome stretch of road, the van ran into a light, steady hail of coppery flakes that he mistook at first for burning embers. Slowing, he was able to reach out, his hand cupped, only to find that these were not hailstones or coals but floating flecks of straw, evidently shed from the back of a farm truck up ahead.

Coughlin resettled and put a little more weight on the gas. He figured that before long he was bound to see the culprit and overtake it; some laggardly behemoth with its bed heaped with bales. But it seemed to him that he drove in this manner for mile upon mile as the copper pieces danced across his windshield, like colored confetti at a wedding or the sparks from a fairy godmother's wand. He didn't mind, it was good. The copper flakes and green trees; the land thick with sunlight. That long day of travel was one of the best of his life.

6

THE HOOCH BOY, Moss Evans, had once made the bullfrogs explode, so why not the pig that the river washed up? Frog or hog, what's the difference aside from the matter of size? So hit the strings harder and see if that does the job. Little pebble killed Goliath. Two dollar guitar bursts the hog.

Now it seemed that each time Duke drove him out, there were more men on the levee, which meant more loading of barrels, more pouring of hooch. Everywhere you looked, motors and earthmovers and pyramids of damp sand. The Landing was no longer a rackety circus. It more resembled one of those western boomtowns which hatch overnight and promptly fill up with residents. The week before it had only been convicts loading bags and building walls. Now the word had gone out to bring every colored in the county. Didn't even matter what other work they had on. Wake them up and load them in the trucks. He saw fellows out here he'd known his whole life. Sam Tucker, making mud-boxes, tipped him a wink as he passed. "Hey Moss," he said lightly. "How d'you like this little picnic?"

It had rained Monday and rained Tuesday and no surprise it was raining on Wednesday as well. Did the river still count as a river at all? It had become like the ocean, full of swells, wells and trenches. Already it had pressed through the willows and the canebrake, filling the air with a roaring, crackling sound that put Moss in mind of a forest fire. The Mississippi was rising. Maybe it was speeding up too; the current gouging away at the soft outer bank, gnawing into the western side of Mounds Landing. Nowadays he fancied he could feel it moving underfoot; the very earth turning liquid and everyone's boots sinking in.

"What did I tell you, Mr Moss?" said Miles Craven. "Our molar is rotten. Do you think our dentists can save it?"

"Yessir," he said. "I hope that they can."

Craven flicked a fly from his shoulder. He said, "I'm bound to say that I have my doubts."

He drove up from Vicksburg a couple times every week, the well-dressed young dandy from the River Commission, though lately he didn't look quite so young any more. It used to be that Mr Miles Craven was constantly on at Moss to pick out a fresh tune so he could learn it himself, like he had all the time in the world and assumed that Moss did as well. He'd say, "Relax, simmer down. If anybody objects, you send them straight to me." Then more sand-boils appeared on the eastern slope—like bubbling springs except that the water was dirty—and the sight of the boils had a big effect on Miles Craven. It was almost as if he had become dirty, too, because for the past few days he hadn't said a word about music and was too busy shouting at the other white men who were there—the fat levee captain with the broken veins in his nose, or the irritable engineer from the Army Corps. It was obvious that the man was coming apart at the seams. If it hadn't been the dead hog it would have been something else.

The sheriff's deputy, George Piper, gestured for Moss to bring over the flask. But then he dangled it by the handle, in no hurry to drink, which meant that the hooch boy had to stand to one side and wait.

Piper spat and wiped his brow. He was gazing out at the laborers. He said, "If we shot one of them, would it make the others work harder? And let's say it did, would it be enough to compensate for the loss of that man? These are the questions that run around in my head."

"It depends, though, doesn't it?" said the red-nosed levee captain. This subject piqued his interest; he spoke with great authority. In the captain's view, there were several factors to consider. If you have a crew of ten men, then one man down is a loss. On a crew of one hundred, however, it matters less. Added to that, you had to consider the particularities of the victim himself. By which he meant that if you shoot the laziest worker, that's fine, it sends a message to the rest. But if you shoot a good worker, it creates more problems than it solves. The others can't see the logic and now have more slack to pick up.

Hungrily, he eyed the flask in Piper's hand. "Shoot the laziest, that's my advice. It's not like we haven't got plenty of layabouts to pick from."

"No doubt," Piper said. "Even so, hear me out. You shoot the laziest and yes, that's logical, that makes sense. Maybe it motivates his friends to work harder."

"Gentlemen," interrupted the Army Corp engineer. "Can we have a little less talk about shooting today?"

"But shoot a good worker, or simply a worker at random, and what does that mean? That makes no sense at all. The world has gone mad."

The captain was stumped. Piper had brought him up short. "Well, sure" he said. "Sure."

"So now the other workers are spooked. They're scared out of their wits. I think that maybe they work harder still, because all of a sudden they understand what's at stake."

"Or they mutiny," said Craven, who had been standing close by. "They decide that they're dead either way and have nothing to lose. They run up the levee and tear us limb from limb."

The mental image appeared to amuse the deputy. He admitted that this was a distinct possibility. "These are simply questions—scenarios—that I'm going over in my head."

"That's because we're stuck," said the captain. "How much longer have we all got to be out here anyway?"

"Until the river level drops," the engineer told him. "Or the levee falls over, whichever happens soonest."

"Levee ain't gonna fall over."

"It might," Craven said. "It is—let us say—a distinct possibility."

Left to their own devices, the men might stand about jawing for hours on end. They had little to do besides watching black workers make boxes and trying to make themselves look important. Deputy Piper was still swinging the flask as though he'd forgotten he even had it. The last time this had happened, Moss left him to it and simply went to fetch another, except that the Deputy had made a big song and dance about this. He play-acted being sad and sighed that Moss had forgotten all about him. He said that maybe holding a flask meant that he was a hooch boy himself. He'd called over to the engineers to involve them in the joke and said, "Good news, fellows. Young Mr Moss just made me his assistant hooch boy." On balance, therefore, Moss thought it best to stand by.

"Like the Big Bad Wolf," Miles Craven was saying. "It huffs and it puffs and it blows them down, one by one. Laconia Circle just last night and that's what, less than ten miles upstream?"

"Laconia Circle was old and spent."

"It was old but it was sound. The river huffed and puffed and knocked it down."

"It was put up by dirt-farmers. It wasn't federal."

Craven was amused. "You think the river cares that this is federal?"

"Yes, sir, Mr Craven," said the irritable engineer. "That's a fair summary of our thinking, yes."

From his place on the sidelines. Moss could follow the argument's twists and turns. Piper, he could tell, was keen to side with the Army Corps engineer. Piper viewed every criticism of Mounds Landing as a criticism of Washington County itself and therefore, indirectly, a criticism of the sheriff's office down in Greenville. His feeling, he said, was that there was nothing wrong with the Landing that a few black boys couldn't fix. The Landing was strong, nothing to worry about there. The only aggravation was having to be up here every day, keeping the show on the road. Each morning, it seemed, brought more people to manage, what with the Corps and the captains and the prison guards and what-have-you.

His gaze fell on Moss. "Not to mention our little hooch boy here, getting under everyone's feet. Run along, boy," he said. "Quit bothering us. If I wanted you to take the flask, I'd have said to you, 'Boy, take this flask'."

"Yes, sir," said Moss.

Piper turned away, seeking again to involve the engineer. "See what I mean?" he said. "This is what I have to deal with every day."

The way Moss saw it, there wasn't a great deal of difference between the deputy, the engineers, the prison guards and the captains. They all carried shotguns. They all drank too much hooch. They all liked making themselves feel important by rounding up men and setting them to work filling bags. These days it seemed to him that everybody was constantly shouting over one another. No room to move and no space to think. If the river didn't take the landing, the sheer weight of the men was liable to collapse it.

He fetched a fresh flask and moved off up the line. His guitar slapped at his side, demanding his attention although he hadn't played it all week and didn't know when he would again. Five hundred laborers and one hooch boy between them and still it was mostly the captains who demanded a gulp. "Where's my drink? Don't you be wasting it on your kind. How come he gets a drink when I'm fucking dying right here?" No sooner had he set off in one direction than he was being called away in another or scurrying to the tent for a refill. The ground strewn with empties and the drunken captains waving their shotguns for balance and the songs piling up in his head, one after the after, hollering to get out until he thought that they might send him crazy. So it was an ugly scene on the Landing that day. Everybody on edge and perhaps himself most of all.

Halfway up the line, he saw it happen. A bushy piece of wet ground detached itself from the slope. Moss watched it slide off and turn soggy, a floating island of grass. Then straight away, a line of men was sent to patch over the damage. Sandbag it, mud-box it, whatever it takes to stop the bleeding. The red-nosed captain was shouting for the workers to huddle tighter together and to pass

43

the bags and boards quicker, but the mud was so wet that several men slipped and fell, and this struck the captain as funny until he fell over himself. And it was in the midst of all this—the clatter of boards, the pinwheeling of arms—that the worker who had been stationed at the head of the line pulled back the rushes and saw what lay behind them.

"Stop that noise!" yelled the captain. "Christ sake, shut up." But now the line lost its shape and the panicked men broke for cover. And standing on the slope, rainwater on his glasses, Moss could see something bloated and ugly at the river's edge.

An engineer clambered past him, nose wrinkled, eyes squinting. "What in hell is that?"

"Dead body," said Piper. "Some poor bastard washed up."

"No way that's a person."

"Pig," said the captain. "Big old monster pig."

"Feral hog." Piper whistled. "Holy God, look at that."

The men stood together, barely three feet from the river, with their pant-legs drenched and steam rising from their shoulders, bracing their hands on their knees so as to lean forward as one. Moss watched with interest. Were the ground to crumble, he thought, all three would be swept away, just as quick as you could draw a breath.

The hog lay on its side, half-hidden by the rushes. Its uppermost tusk had been sheared off near the root. Flies buzzed and crawled in the folds of its ear. Its mouth was hooked open and its tongue had gone black. The very sight of the thing made his stomach turn over.

"Luckiest pig in the county," said the captain. "Eating its body weight in corn every day until the river came along and ate him up with one bite."

"No arguing with a flood."

"That's right. However big you get, the river's always bigger."

Now here came Piper again, elbowing his way through the onlookers, meaning to reassert his authority. It was a pig, he confirmed. Nothing to be scared of. Except that when he ordered the thing to be rolled into the water, a fresh ripple of unease went through the laborers standing by. No one stepped forward to perform the task.

"Roll it," he barked. "Right into the drink." But Moss could see that the problem was not the weight of the beast but the state of its body. Intestinal gas had inflated the carcass like a balloon. The skin around its middle had turned almost transparent. In life the pig would have been a fearsome thing. In death it might turn out to be more dangerous still.

"So the sausage leaks a little," Piper complained to the engineer. "So the skin splits and tears."

The engineer thought that it might do more than just split. He puffed his cheeks and threw his arms out wide.

"God damn it," scoffed Piper. "It's a pig, not a bomb."

The captain's idea was for Piper to take out his handgun and put a hole in the side. Buckshot risked making an awful mess, whereas a single bullet would release the gas and reduce the swelling after which they could roll the remains off the edge. Piper, though, disagreed. He said that he wasn't about to waste a good bullet on a dead pig because a few coloreds had decided they were too hoity-toity to touch it. He added that if he was going to shoot anything, it would more likely be one of them, the coloreds, and as if to prove his point he unholstered his Smith-and-Wesson and flicked the safety with his thumb.

"Whoah," said the engineer. "Point it that way, Christ sake."

Tempers were fraying, which meant it was best to steer clear. So Moss sidled up the slope, fixing to fold himself in with the huddle of laborers, fixing to make himself invisible again. Only this happened to be the worst move he could make because there in the throng stood foolish Benny Gibbs, who was about the only convict that he knew by name and reputation. Benny Gibbs spoke too loudly on account of being silly and was always landing himself in trouble as a result, always bouncing in and out of prison, always getting knocked about the head. This of course made him more silly still and more likely to land himself in trouble the next time. Round and round, so on and so forth, the bone-chipping, teeth-loosening Benny Gibbs roundelay.

Benny saw the hooch boy. Lights switched on in his head. "Moss!" he bellowed. "Moss!" even though Moss was practically pressed right up against him. "Why don't you play your guitar and pop the pig like you done the frogs?"

Moss spun away but too late, because the white men had heard and ordered them both to step down. And now Benny was stricken, on the verge of tears, figuring that he was bound to get hit again. In Moss's opinion, the kid shouldn't have been on the Landing anyway, least of all Parchman Farm, because his brains were fitted wrong and he pitched a couple of fits every week. He felt sorry for the kid, poor old Benny Gibbs. In that moment, however, he could have happily strangled him.

"Get out here," Piper said. "Do I have to say everything twice today?"

The guards knocked Benny down and rolled him in the mud, although Moss had the impression that this was mostly for form's sake, or as a way of lightening the tension between them. Benny's wails, too, struck him as just a little performative. The kid probably thought that if he pretended they'd hurt him, they'd let up on him sooner.

"Who's Moss anyhow?" asked the engineer. "The hooch boy here?"

"Yessir," bellowed Benny. "Yessir. Moss Evans."

"Just played his guitar and the bullfrogs burst?"

Piper guffawed. "Bullfrogs," he said. "Bull-crap more like."

And yet the mention of Moss's name had worked a magic on Craven. He stirred from his stupor and picked his way up the shoreline, moving like a wading bird, craning his neck for a better view. He said that he knew Moss Evans very well, yes indeed. He counted Moss Evans as a personal friend. Some of the boy's songs had to be heard to be believed.

The red-nosed captain opened his mouth to say something. He

stared at Craven a moment and then shut it again with a snap.

"This boy," Craven continued, pointing at Moss. "This boy is a marvel. Not much to look at, I grant you, but that's the wonder of music. And the music he plays—I've never heard anything like it."

Deputy Piper had been enjoying watching Benny being rolled in the mud. He wiped his nose with the back of his hand, the revolver still in his grip. One false move and he'd have shot his own ear off. He said that he'd never heard anything like the boy's picking either. The bullfrogs, he added, most likely popped themselves to escape.

The levee captain chuckled a little at that.

Piper said, "God bless your heart, boy, I've got to tell these fellows the truth. You might pour hooch well enough, but you can't play worth a spit."

Moss, with faint hope, had been attempting to edge his way back into the crowd. Craven, looking over, motioned for him to join them. The well-meaning white man, Moss thought. The deadliest creature on earth.

"Go ahead, Moss," Craven said, "I'm interested to see whether you can do this. No harm done if you can't."

"Sure," said the captain. "Only hurry it up."

Moss fumbled for the catches and eased the guitar from its case. He thought the feel of it in his hands might be a comfort. Instead, it was as though all the bits of songs that had been crowding the inside of his skull this past week suddenly snapped to attention, more insistent than they had been all day. Convulsively he turned himself to the river, because it wouldn't do for the men to see his face in that moment, not with all of those songs rushing in front of his eyes.

At his back, Craven called for him to play the same chord he had played for the frogs. He said he shouldn't worry if it didn't work. It was an experiment, or a joke, nothing more. But then Deputy Piper pitched in, at the end of his patience, to say that he wasn't about to stand about all day arguing about dead hogs and banjo pickers when they still had mud-boxes to make. He said he was coming around to the captain's way of thinking and reckoned that he might use his pistol after all. A bullet for the pig and after that back to work. He'd had about as much foolishness as a man could stand.

Moss clutched the guitar. Melodies ripped through his head. A fly had got in his mouth; another put itself behind the left lens of his glasses. He stood in the rushes, breathing through his nose. He stared at the swollen gray body and the coiling brown water. The dead pig, he decided, had become a makeshift levee itself. It lay right on the river, the last line of defense.

Craven said "Moss" and the captain shouted "Boy!" and he bore down on the strings as the gun went off in Piper's hand so that afterwards he was never able to say for sure what had done it: the gun or the guitar or something else altogether. He hit the strings to break the earth and open the sky and to pop the veins in the deputy's head and the carcass tore open like a mound of dry leaves in the wind. The beast's long-jawed head leapt into the air and its big body collapsed and a second later a band of rust-colored rain hit the men and caused them to cry out as one. Piper sat down in the mud. The pig head landed in his lap. The captain stepped aside, scratched his cheek, and was sick.

His head had been ringing from the stroke and the shot and so it took him a moment to register that Miles Craven was laughing. Moss would have sworn he'd never heard Craven laugh before, but he thought probably the man had been storing it up, because once he got started he couldn't stop. Not when Piper, still winded from the pig's head, shouted at him to shut up. Not when the Army Corps engineer seized his collar and shook him, just like a dog would worry a stick. If anything, the shaking only made the man laugh all the more.

"Craven!" the engineer shouted. "Look at me. Craven. Craven, look at me." And sure enough, all the laughing and shouting set Benny Gibbs off as well. Such was the din on the levee right then that if Old Duke had chosen that moment to steer his beat-up truck up the track, Moss wouldn't have been able to hear it. Not above the whip-crack and rolling thunder of the Mississippi river going by. Not above the laughing and retching and the raised voices of the guards. Not above the sound of simple Benny Gibbs on the ground, bloodied and dizzy from the licks he'd received and mimicking the engineer in a hysterical cracked falsetto.

"Craven!" shouted the engineer. "Pull yourself together, God damn it."

"Craven!" Benny shouted. "Craven, pull yourself together! Look at me, Craven. Look at me. Look at me."

7

BUCHANAN CASEY GARNER was the most well-liked and respected fellow in the city of Sutton, Tennessee. Hardly an hour went by without someone seeking his counsel on this matter or that. He couldn't walk more than a handful of paces without tipping his hat at a passing acquaintance or planting a kiss on the brow of a colicky child. It was a wonder the fellow ever got where he was going. It was a wonder a person ever got anything done.

Coughlin was made aware of Bucky Garner's reputation in the first minute of their meeting. He was made aware of this reputation because Bucky Garner, in person, was at pains to point it out. He bobbed his head and said, "You step outside and ask the first fellow you see. Stop him on the street and just ask him outright."

"I'll take your word for it."

'Well, that's what I'm saying. You can take it on trust."

He was near Coughlin's age—twenty-three or thereabouts—but the similarities ended there. The local agent was healthy-looking and handsome, with a mouthful of white teeth and a spray of freckles across his nose. The one possible imperfection Coughlin could identify was a disproportionate broadness to his hips and his lap, which suggested that sunny Bucky Garner might one day run to fat. Every physique carries clues to its eventual destination. Bucky's midriff knew something his head and shoulders did not.

"Old ladies," he said. "Schoolboys, schoolgirls. White folks and coloreds. They all come to me."

He was based in Sutton, on the border with Virginia, and he covered the southwestern corner, placing recordings in Roanoke and Knoxville and all the points in between. Coughlin couldn't imagine he earned much more than a retainer, but this was fine, because he held down other jobs, too. He wrote daily news for the Sutton *Bugle* and read the weather reports on the King Biscuit radio show. Tuesdays and Wednesdays he sold neckties in a department store. On weekends he managed the faltering fortunes of the Carousel, a girls' baseball team. Bucky said that the girls were better at pitching and catching than their male counterparts. The difficulty lay in persuading the other teams to compete with them. "So I'm sitting in the bleachers at the Little League games, trying to get the crowd to join in with a chant. 'Come on, boys, take the Carousels for a spin'. Sure enough, everybody's singing along, even if most of them don't know the Carousels from a hole in the wall."

"That's good," Coughlin said, but he was struggling to keep pace. "Is it good?"

"Oh sure, it's good, it's crackerjack. Everyone's going to know about the Carousels now."

He had pulled into Sutton shortly after sundown, rocking and bouncing down the deserted main drag. His eyes were bloodshot and he was in need of a shave. The girl on the desk at the Bedford hotel glanced up from her ledger.

"You the recording fellow from New York?" she said.

"John Coughlin, that's right."

She looked him up and down. "You?" she said, unimpressed.

He had slept fitfully and awoken feeling sluggish—and now here came Bucky Garner with his loud voice and extravagant friendliness. Couglin had pictured the men of the Far Corners as placid, leisurely types. The local agent, though, was as frisky as a colt. He could have run rings around Coughlin without breaking a sweat.

"You don't talk much, do you, Mr Coughlin? I got to learn to do that, you'll have to give me some pointers. Actions speak louder, that's what people say." Bucky blinked and beamed and held out a cigarette. "Smoke?" he said. "Me neither, it's a dirty habit. But I'll tell you, sir, I never leave the house without a pack all the same. I'll give a cigarette to any fellow I meet and I couldn't begin to guess the number of times that's helped me out. I reckon that what I lose in cigarettes I make back in goodwill."

"Yes, sure. Very smart."

"Cross my heart. I couldn't even begin to guess."

Hatless, in shirt-sleeves, they turned onto State Street. The town was livelier that morning, he saw. The stores had opened, flags snapped in the breeze and the housewives gathered outside Jenkins Meat Butcher. Motorcars pawed the road and honked wheezy greetings. Their gasoline fumes cut the resiny mountain air.

"Now you'll say that I'm partial and well, sure, you'd be right," Bucky said. "But you won't find a finer base of operations than Sutton. First up, you've got the modern conveniences of a city like New York. And second, we're surrounded by Appalachian hill-country people. And hill-country people means hill-country music. But you know that, Mr Coughlin, you know it better than me."

"And you figure they'll come? For the try-outs, I mean."

"Hundred percent they'll come. Whole town's fit to burst." He stopped to shake the hand of a dilapidated old soldier, bent at the waist by the weight of his medals. "You'll come won't you, Wilbur?"

"You bet," said Wilbur.

Chuckling, Bucky turned back towards Coughlin. "He don't even know what we're talking about."

Wherever you went in Sutton, the mountains went too. Whatever direction you faced, the scenery turned in sympathy: round-shouldered, thick with trees, full of mink, deer and bears. Appalachia. The Blue Ridge. George Washington rode his horse through the woods north of here, back in the days when he was a colonel in the militia and the hills were a stronghold for the Iroquois and Tutelo. After that came civilization, so-called. Wave upon wave of European settlers. Coal-mines and quarries, sawmills and roads. And yet still the place struck him as impossibly wild. In the states' war, the hill-country people had fought on both sides—north and south—because it was said that they hated Confederates and Yankees alike and simply took aim at whichever soldiers were closest. Everyone was an outsider, everybody a threat. The rich upstate farmer; the genteel Dixie planter. The people of Appalachia wanted no part of either world. Mainly they wanted to be left alone, hidden in the woods, living in the same dog-run shacks that their great-grandfathers had built, sleeping ten or twelve to a room, drawing water from the well. Plank floors underfoot. Oiled paper serving as window panes. "I can see why they call it the Far Corners," Coughlin had said, but the local agent had explained that it was only strangers who called it that. Men like Honest Jim Cope who came into town from the north.

"You go ask Wilbur what the Far Corners are and he'll say it's New York and Chicago. Hell, he'll probably tell you it's Lynchburg and Richmond."

"Everybody's Far Corners is different, you mean?"

"Sure," Bucky said. "Except I'd never be able to say it as pretty as that."

They turned off the street and into the cool darkness of Hank's Food & Drink. The agent took a seat in the booth and smoothed down his pant-legs. He said he had something special to show Coughlin, an item in that day's paper, but that they should at least order first because his stomach was growling. The radio rasped and chattered. Horseflies tapped the glass. Bucky waved for the waitress and demanded ham and eggs twice, brown toast on the side. He said, "Della, out of interest, are you selling much of that calamine tea?"

"Chamomile," she said. "Not calamine."

"You know what I mean. How much are you pouring on an average day?"

"I don't know." Her eyebrow twitched. "It ain't so popular."

"Yeah, and that's because you keep hiding it on the shelf, like the ugly girl at the dance. You got to place it out front and make a big old fuss. 'Ooh, look at this. Ain't she a dandy?'. That way you get folk interested."

The waitress looked to Couglin for help. She said, "Customers don't want it. So what am I to do?"

"God damn it, Della," said Bucky and slapped the table in disgust.

He had only been in the job a few months and was still learning the ropes, befriending the storekeepers, trying to understand what they liked so as to better provide it. That's why he was so excited to meet the new catcher, John Coughlin, who had produced the scary ghost song. Certain songs sold well in certain towns; Bucky was still getting to grips with the various regions. But everyone liked Spider Joe, didn't matter who you were. Imagine putting out a side like Only Me and Spider Joe or Did You Ever Dream a Dream. Put out a song like that and a man could die rich and happy, which he supposed was what happened to Honest Jim if the recent stories were true, that he died rich and happy in his car on the road, although Bucky had to say he didn't believe it for a minute. Jim Cope dead? Not a chance, no sir. Not buying it.

Coughlin was finding it hard to get a word in edgewise. "No, it's true, he's dead. He ran off the road in the blizzard, only last week."

"So they say. I reckon he'll surprise us."

"Christ sake, Bucky. They found the man's body. It's over. He's gone."

"Mercy." Bucky stared out the window, allowing this news to settle. "Mercy," he said. "Well, that's clouded the day."

When breakfast was served, the local agent perked up. Through a mouthful, he said, "I nearly forgot what I wanted to show you. Della, run fetch me the *Bugle*. You're gonna love it. Page three."

"You placed a notice?"

"Better." He chewed and swallowed. "I placed a story."

Coughlin made space on the table and peeled back the front page. The headline read, 'New York City Contest Seeks Finest Hill-Country Musicians'. Below this was a byline: 'BC Garner'.

The catcher raised an eyebrow. "You wrote this?"

'The great city of Sutton this week commences a never-be-fore-witnessed search to determine the finest musicians and singers from the beautiful Blue Ridge Mountain region. The top prize for the winning contestants—a life of guaranteed fame and fortune in the form of a music contract with the world-famous Humpty Recording Company.'

He opened his mouth to protest, but the agent flapped a hand to urge him on.

'The inaugural Hill-Country Music Contest will be held in the ballroom of the beautiful Bedford Hotel on State Street on Saturday April 9 between the hours of midday and 4 p.m., with the contestants all judged by the famous Mr John Coughlin, creator of the much-loved and best-selling record Only Me & Spider Joe. Ahead of his arrival in Sutton, Mr Coughlin told the Bugle: "I've heard a rumor that musicians of the Blue-Ridge Mountain region are the finest on the planet. I plan to gather as many as I can find and take them with me to New York."'

Coughlin started. "I said no such thing."

"Yes, but that's OK, I wrote it in. It's all about tickling the public's buying bone. Once you've got their attention, they're more likely to show up."

Della dipped to refill his mug of coffee. Coughlin fortified himself with a mouthful and returned his gaze to the page.

'Upon hearing the news of the contest, scores of Hill-Country musicians were reported to already be on the road towards Sutton, driving just about as fast as their wheels will carry them. Preparations are underway to provide them with the warmest of Tennessee welcomes. Local resident Bucky Garner told the Bugle: "I've lived in Sutton my entire life and this is the most major event the city's had in years. I don't know of a single soul who won't be lining up outside the Bedford Hotel before noon on Saturday April 9."'

Bucky by now was fidgeting with excitement. "What did I tell you? How's that for a story?"

Coughlin stared. "You can't write a story and be in it as well."

"Sure I can. It was the best quote I could find."

"But." He rubbed at his temples. "But no, Bucky, look at this. People see your name up here and your name down here. You think they're not going to make the connection?"

"Oh," Bucky said. "Well, I guess you're right." And it was apparent that the agent's confidence was not quite unwavering, because he took criticism hard and flinched when he was scolded. All at once he appeared to be on the brink of tears.

"Hey," Coughlin said, embarrassed. "I'm not saying it's a bad story. And it's much better than a notice."

Two middle-aged women were strolling past the glass. The agent spun in his seat to wave at them with gusto, although Coughlin had the sense that this performance was mainly for his own benefit and was a means of restoring his equilibrium. If so, it had the desired effect because when Bucky turned back from the glass he was his old self again. "Della," he called. "When are we getting some more toast over here?"

He plucked at his pant-legs. He smiled at his fork. "The trouble with me, I go at everything full-steam. A man asks for moonshine and I think I've got to bring him the moon. Which isn't what the man wanted, what he wanted was moonshine. I keep making the same mistakes. You asked for a notice and I gave you a story. So you've got every right to be put out. That's strike one against me."

When Coughlin motioned for him to slow down, Bucky agreed that this was his problem exactly, the catcher had put his finger right on it, exactly. He needed to slow down and listen and not be leaping about like a fool. He was grateful to Coughlin for putting his finger right on it. "And I swear to God here and now, with Della as my witness, that I'm never going to let you down again. You can count on that."

"Enough," Coughlin said. "It's not a big thing"—and no doubt this was true. But over the course of the following week it seemed he could not open the *Bugle* without encountering another story which bore the local agent's byline and contained supporting quotes from him, too. BC Garner wrote—in a tone of stern disapproval—about a logging truck which had shed a portion of its load near the schoolhouse. He wrote with lavish affection about a deceased states' war hero, Captain Clayton Peerless. He reported on the damage caused by the winter floods and wrote about the surging popularity of herbal tea among the more forward-minded citizens of Tennessee and Virginia. He profiled the hill-country musicians who had camped on Gatlin's farm outside town. Local resident Bucky Garner, he wrote, had already heard them rehearsing at night in the fields and had been for several minutes convinced that they were God's own angel choir.

Half-a-century ago, Sutton must have been pretty grand. Its brick-fronted downtown retained an air of old-world respectability, while the porticoed homes looked more dignified than tired. There was a department store, a county courthouse, and a foursquare limestone bank with a water fountain out front. But these six stately blocks were being slowly squeezed by the times. Beyond the cemetery, the road became an avenue of telegraph poles and wrecking yards. Big wooden hoardings proclaimed the virtues of Benzol Gasoline, Cherokee Parts and Royal Baby Powder. On approaching the town, misdirected by a road sign, he had become briefly lost on the gravel tracks of an extensive stone-cutting plant. This, he learned later, was Sutton's largest employer. It milled rock from the quarries for table tops and stone floors.

Jim Cope liked to say that when he first came to Appalachia nearly two years before, he had been like an explorer landing on an uncharted island. The place was wild, untapped, ripe for exploitation. Wolves and raccoons enjoying free run of the roads. Bald eagles perched on every rooftop in town. As many musicians as trees; a song for every firefly. Not once but twice, he said, he had to chase away bears that had intruded on the open-air try-outs; clapped his hands to scare the beast off so that the performance could continue. That was the measure the man Coughlin followed. These were the shoes which he now had to fill.

"You too," he told Bucky as they strolled back to the hotel. "It's you and me here. This is a big chance for us both."

"That's right," said the agent. "I mean, the try-outs, that's bully. I reckon Honest Jim must have done a few try-outs in his time."

"Sure he did, but probably not on this scale. Nothing this far south anyway."

"Honest Jim, what a life. All those songs that he found. Did You Ever Dream a Dream. The one about the blue mountain. Rock Our Babies to Sleep. That's what I want to do, Mr Coughlin, catch myself some big fish, just like Honest Jim."

Coughlin stood to one side to allow a girl with a pram to go by. "It didn't end so well for him."

"So they say," Bucky said. "But I reckon he'll surprise us."

Aside from their encounter at the Bide-a-Wee hunting lodge, Coughlin had known Cope mainly by reputation. The downtown New York song-pluggers were beneath the man's notice. Catchers, moreover, spent most of their time in the field. But that night Coughlin dreamed of him. In the dream, Honest Jim emerged from the door of a hotel not dissimilar to the Bedford into the revitalizing daylight of Sutton's main drag. He was dressed in the off-white white suit of a Southern Baptist preacher and his hair was perfectly pomaded, he had never looked more handsome, and he clapped his hands crisply as he descended the short run of stone steps. Out on the street, a trio of bears reversed course and took flight, moving in unison, their hindquarters swaying, and in the curious manner of dreams it seemed to the catcher that he was simultaneously the bears and the brave man in pursuit and that all of these players—the lone man, the three animals—were somehow not adversaries but a band of happy adventurers and he laughed in delight and shook himself awake in the bed only to discover with dismay that he was John Coughlin again.

8

THEY PLAYED DEEP Down Mountain Blues when he took his seat for breakfast. They played Did You Ever Dream a Dream as he gazed out at State Street. The music made him self-conscious. He wished they'd cut it out.

Already he had grown accustomed to the hotel's daily rhythms. Picking at his omelet, he could see the manager making his customary rounds of the tables, straightening the settings, rearranging the flowers. In the evening he would watch him again in the lounge, pouring measures of scotch from a bone-china teapot. The manager of the Bedford was named Hermann Stubb. He went about his duties with a dignified, tragic air.

If Coughlin was embarrassed by having the Valencia wheeled into the dining room for his benefit, then Stubb took responsibility and was positively mortified. He had been led to believe their guest would like his own music played. It had been suggested that this might make the catcher feel at home.

"But it's not my music. It was done by other outfits. Other catchers."

"Of course. But they are all hill-country pieces, yes?"

"Maybe it's not even theirs, come to that. They just, I don't know, helped it along a little."

Like Coughlin, the manager was an outsider. He kept his German wife and three children in the Richmond suburbs and made an effort to visit one weekend every month. But this arrangement was flexible, dependent on various factors. The more time he spent in Sutton, the more he felt himself taking root. He liked the city. He liked his job. He liked the people, too, especially Mrs Rose Cornish, who chaired the Thursday evening meetings of the Humane Society. Mrs Cornish was a widow and nearly twelve years his senior. Moreover she suffered from a number of sensitive health issues. So their friendship, he stressed, was innocent and platonic.

"All that being said, this is not a sizable city and certain women like to gossip. When Mrs Cornish and I set out on our afternoon stroll, I am convinced, Mr Coughlin, I can hear the distinct sound of tongues wagging."

"No doubt."

"Jane, for example. The girl on the front desk." He moved off through the dining room, straightening the napkins with a rigid ceremony, before circling back to pick up the exchange.

"Sometimes, it's true, Mrs Cornish stays the night. This is because she lives several miles from town. Her vision is poor when it is dark on the road."

"She stays at the Bedford?"

"She stays in 4C, which is the suite next to mine. There is a connecting door, yes, but it remains locked at all times."

Coughlin's table had been set for two. Stubb finessed the unused knife and fork so that each ran perfectly parallel with the folded napkin.

Abruptly, he said, "Mr Coughlin, I know what you're thinking."

The catcher shook his head. "Who cares what I think?"

"You are thinking, 'Why, this big oaf won't admit he's in love'. You are thinking, 'Why, this looks like a marriage'. And in this respect you're correct. Except that this is a marriage without a physical side. Because, you see, I am already wed."

For weeks through the winter the weather had been fearsome. Gales lifted roofs and toppled billboards. Dumps of thick snow buried the town five-feet deep. At the end of his day, his duties complete, the sad hotel manager would unbutton his waistcoat and light a fire in the grate of his sitting room in 4B. He sat with his back to the connecting wall, listening to the squeak of the sash, comforted by the presence of Mrs Rose Cornish next door. Stubb had never loved the Bedford so well as he did on those vicious nights. He never slept so soundly as when he knew that his friend was close by.

Mrs Cornish, for her part, was alarmed by the weather. She saw it in Biblical terms, as a judgment from on high. Not so, he would tell her. These troubled times are explained by science, not God. Everything is accelerating, probably more than is healthy. Model T Fords spilling off production lines in Detroit. Smokestacks pouring filth into Ohio's blue skies. Release too much energy into a system all at once, he told her, and it will overheat and break down. It results in more rain and snowfall, more ruin, more deaths. Ultimately, though, it didn't matter what he thought or what Mrs Cornish thought. God's wrath or Mother Nature's, the end result was the same.

He said, "Would you say that the world is doomed, Mr Coughlin?"

Coughlin frowned. "No," he said. "No. We just had some weather, that's all."

Outside town, Stubb had heard, the land remained unstable. Winter was over and the skies had cleared. But the ground would be boggy and a number of roads were washed out. "Where do you plan to go from here?" he asked. "I mean, when you have completed your project. When you have recorded your music."

"Maybe back to New York. Maybe a way further south. It depends on the haul. If I get enough decent sides."

The manager saw his job as an almost spiritual calling. He prided himself on tending to his flock and hated the thought that one might go astray. He said, "My advice to you, Mr Coughlin, is to stay with us for a spell. One can do an awful lot worse than Sutton, you know."

On Saturday morning the country people came in. Coughlin had expected a trickle; what he received was a flood. The visitors poured along State Street past the onlookers and beneath the cherry trees. They sat five-deep in the beds of farm trucks, or lined shoulder to shoulder on the benches of woodie wagons, or piled in ramshackle buggies pulled by skeletal mules. He saw the men in overalls and the women in sackcloth and all their mismatched relations who'd been dragged along for the ride. Owl-eyed urchins with dirty brown feet. Toddlers enthroned on their parents' laps. Straight-backed old women with windfall-apple faces. The catcher attempted a headcount and quickly gave up. The medium-sized Bedford ballroom would not hold them all.

Buchanan Casey Garner had joined him on the steps. He had a carnation in his lapel and a newsboy's cap on his head. "Turned out good," he said.

"It did."

The local agent grinned. "I'm not going to say it was the newspaper stories that did it. I ought to leave that for other folk to say."

The hard road spooked the mules: they lifted their hooves in alarm with each step. The big hotel spooked the country people. They filed through the lobby like tourists at a cathedral, ogling the corniced ceiling and the gold brocade wallpaper. A pair of burly farmhands waved their hats under the chandelier, trying to make the glass droplets tinkle. They nodded at the catcher but gave him a wide berth. Coughlin was as alien to them as they were to him

He crossed to the front desk to fetch a notebook and pencil. "Hillbillies," said Jane. "Looky there, what a sight. Billie-boys and billie-girls."

"Is that what you call them or what they call themselves?"

"Don't matter," said Jane. "Hillbillies is what they are."

Inside the hall, Stubb had instructed that the chairs be arranged in tight rows. He had borrowed twenty-five from the courthouse, another ten from the cafe, and had propped two hand-printed signs on either side of the stage. One read, WELCOME! PARTICIPANTS OF THE HILL-COUNTRY MUSIC CONTEST and the other read, ABSOLUTELY NO ANIMALS, LIQUOR OR GUNS. Once the room was at capacity, the door was open and wedged so that the music could be heard by the spill-overs; by anyone who was left in the lobby or who had gathered on the street.

Coughlin moved through the crowd, scribbling names in his book, roughing out the running order. He drew Bucky aside and lowered his voice. "We've got about thirty acts to get through in four hours. So we have to keep the performances short. In and out. No dawdling. No encores."

"Sure," Bucky said. "Sure, sure, that's bully."

"I'm guessing we can't cut a couple from the list."

The agent's eyes widened. "They'd skin us," he said. "They'd kill us, no kidding."

Afterwards, taking stock, Coughlin would decide that the day contained only one disappointment. The Copeland Christian Ladies College quartet had bused all the way from the city of Danville. The singers were devout and well-dressed and so awed by the occasion that they only spoke in whispers. Coughlin thought them perfectly harmless, but Stubb had been scandalized and refused to let them in. And while this was a trivial matter when set against everything else, it bothered the catcher and weighed heavily on his mind.

"If it were up to me, I'd wave them through," Stubb had told him. "But I'm a stranger here, Mr Coughlin, as you are yourself. Both of us, interlopers. If one wants to be welcome, one makes sure to follow the rules."

"Yeah, I guess so," he said, staring out at the street. Almost certainly he would have decided against recording the quartet. Sacred songs—race songs—weren't Humpty's bag. Still, he hated the thought of the girls coming all that way across the state and then having to turn around and go home without singing so much as a single note.

The clock was ticking, his palms were moist and he was more relieved than exasperated when the local agent jumped the gun and bolted on stage several minutes before time. Bucky lived for moments such as these—the big occasions, the chance to grandstand—but the excitement undid him and his opening remarks became a torrent. Turning his cap in his hands, frequently losing his thread, he thanked the Bedford hotel and the famous John Coughlin from New York. He thanked Jesus Christ, Calvin Coolidge and the Carousels baseball team. Had the catcher not gestured for the first act to go on, he worried the kid might have talked right through until four.

Don't sweat it, Coughlin told himself. Take a breath and relax. At its worst it's just music, so how bad can it be? Even bad music was music and there was nothing better than that.

The Bedford hotel try-outs began at noon, overran by two hours and featured the work of thirty-two separate acts. The musicians brought banjos and fiddles, washboards and mouth organs. Dulcimers chattered. Stovepipes groaned. The catcher pinballed in and out of his seat, supervising entrances and exits, trying to keep the show moving smoothly. He had planned to write detailed notes on each performance. In the event he caught himself writing YES for one and NO for the next, throwing in a question mark here, an exclamation mark there. It was an inexact science. He had to go with his gut.

Inside the hall, the atmosphere had loosened. The spectators grew merry. Several were now on their feet and attempting to dance, hemmed in by Stubb's seating plan and scraping chairs with every turn. Bucky had drifted towards the back rows, but Coughlin could hear his honeyed voice booming out. The agent was wanting his newsboy cap passed around. The hall, he kept saying, was only booked until four. He said, "If we want to keep this show running, we need to raise twenty bucks. Small change in the hat. Every nickel and dime helps."

Stubb had lowered himself to one knee by the chair. Coughlin cupped his hand to his ear. An acapella quartet was singing I Plan to Praise Him Forever.

The hotel manager drew a breath. He said it was entirely acceptable if the try-outs ran late and that there would be no extra charge. In actual fact, the ballroom had no further bookings that day.

Coughlin nodded distractedly. "Thanks."

"Perhaps you could relay this information. Your friend is laboring under a false impression."

"Sure," he said. "Sure."

But during the next change of performers, Bucky was back on his feet, bobbing in the rows like a hare in the corn, intent on conducting his own ancillary event. He cried, "Friends and neighbors. Friends and neighbors. I've just got the word that they mean to shut us down. Twenty bucks, can you believe it, is the figure they're demanding. So what can we do? We've got to raise that money right now." He began to say something else, but this was buried beneath the uproar.

Coughlin crossed the hall and pulled the man to one side. Bucky accompanied him willingly enough, but his hungry gaze was still on the crowd and he was clearing his throat as though to shout out once more. Out of the corner of his mouth, he said, "This is bully, they love it. Look at them, look at them. They're having the time of their lives."

"The manager's not loving it."

Instinctively, Bucky motioned for the cap to be passed on. "No, but that's OK, it's a knock-out, we can give him his cut at the end. Split the purse three ways? Is that fair or too much?"

"It's a lousy grift. It's not fair at all." And now Coughlin saw the agent's smile collapse. The effect was so sudden as to be comical. The hare had been leaping. Now the hare had been shot.

"For Christ sake," Coughlin said. "Pull yourself together."

Bucky, distraught, rubbed at his eyes with a sleeve. "I've done it again. I got carried away."

"All right. Enough."

"Honestly, John. It's like I'm possessed by the devil."

"Never mind that. Just get the fucking hat back."

Mr Abraham Fisk was an elderly farmer, so stooped and infirm he had to be helped to the stage. He cuffed his guitar with an arthritic wrist and sang a homage to the three fields which comprised the extent of his land. Fisk sang of these fields as if they were his daughters, or conceivably his ancestors, gone on before. Each had its own character, its own emotional weather. Each was singularly precious in its way. And Coughlin—who was not altogether sure he had ever stood in a field, much less farmed one—pictured himself on a high rocky bluff, surrounded by eagles and elk. Emboldened, he placed a pitchfork in his hand. Emboldened still further, whiskers on his chin.

He was so bewitched by this mental image that he remained in his chair after the final chord died and so it fell to Stubb to supervise the arrival of the Blue Grasshopper Dirt Band. What a name, what an act: the Blue Grasshopper Dirt Band. Six drunk musicians, plus a hairless boy singer, no older than fourteen, who they introduced as the Cue-Ball Kid. The Cue-Ball Kid appeared to be missing an eye. He clutched a corncob pipe in one hand and sang angry scat versions of primitive folk pieces. And now Coughlin became aware of the chairs being moved to clear space for a dance. Stubb protested, but it was no use by this point, nobody could hear him. The Blue Grasshopper Dirt Band were in unruly full spate, tearing into an Irish jig that Coughlin dimly recalled from his youth. And he rose from his chair to see that the whole room was in motion: the men swinging their wives; lone farmers stamping their boots; children turning circles in order to make themselves dizzy. He thought that maybe a fight had broken out, too, where the dancing was at its most intense. But in craning his neck for a better view he spotted more shady business away in the back rows. Bucky's newsboy cap seemed to be in circulation again.

The local agent bobbed and ducked at the rear. His voice wove in and out of the music so that it almost became a song itself. He cried, "Friends and neighbors, good people, we got to raise twenty bucks! I've begged on my knees but the hotel boss, he won't budge! He wants his twenty bucks now or he's putting us out on the street!"

The manager was clawing his way through the throng. Years of stiff dignity had been thrown to the wind. "Mr Coughlin," he pleaded. "This is simply untrue."

"That fellow right there! Hermann Stubb is his name!"

"Bucky!" roared Coughlin. "Bucky, what the hell?"

The Blue Grasshopper Dirt Band careened to a halt, leaving the dancers in disarray: some demanding an encore, others berating the hotel manager while a third group tussled at the center, hurling insults and throwing punches. Bucky Garner found a chair and leapt aboard it, splay-legged, so as to make himself better heard. His collar was open and his hair stood in spikes and he was so precariously balanced that a breath of wind might dislodge him. Lifting his voice, he shouted, "'What the hell?', Mr Coughlin says—and yes sir, who can blame him? He's as mad as I am. He's angry, you're angry. God in heaven, we're all angry."

"Bucky!" Coughlin shouted, but it was no use. Hoarse with emotion, on the brink of tears, the local agent would not be stopped. He cried, "These people want to keep playing! We want to keep dancing! And it's only Mr Stubb there—that German fellow right there—who says he's putting us out on the street right away. So dig deep, all you got, small change in the hat. We need to raise twenty bucks or they're going to shut us down!"

9

THEY DECKED THE walls with blankets. They propped a mattress at the window and strung bed-sheets across the ceiling. Even then, holding his breath, he could hear the noise of State Street through the glass. He's rigged a portable studio in a far-flung mountain town. The acoustics were as good as they were ever going to be.

For half the night he'd lain awake, doubting his ability and second-guessing himself, reversing all of his yeses and nos, mentally projecting himself out of a job. But that morning, splashing cold water on his armpits, he felt his head clear and his heart-rate steady. He knew what needed doing and dared to believe he might do it. Having removed all the recording parts from their cases, he surprised himself by the ease with which he then slotted them together. It seemed that every piece he reached for connected seamlessly to the next.

Now here it was in all its glory: the Truetone recording lathe, one of only about a dozen in existence. Put it together and it was like a cuckoo clock. Knobs and levers, weights and pulleys. So sweetly calibrated it could catch the fine-grain of a murmur, a sigh and a breath. So highly strung that it picked up the buzz of the city itself.

Bucky Garner hung in the doorway, awaiting further instruction. After the scene in the hall, Coughlin would have preferred to cut the kid dead. That would be self-defeating and foolish, he knew. The catcher required all the help he could get.

"For the next few days you're my assistant engineer. How's that for a promotion? Assistant engineer."

Bucky grinned happily. He stared at the lathe as though he

would quite like to eat it. "The Bedford's fully electric. How come we can't just plug it in?"

"The supply's too unstable. A surge could cook the circuits." He pointed. "That's why we use the batteries, see?"

No sooner had Coughlin answered one question than the agent came back at him with another. What's that do? What's that thing there? He liked the idea of the weight at the top of the tower. "Looks like the strongman game at the county fair. Hit it with a mallet and whoosh, up it goes."

"Yeah, kind of. Except this weight starts at the top and drops slowly. That gives us three minutes to record a whole song. Any longer than that and the lead weight hits the floor."

He gestured for Bucky to pass the small metal screws. Bracing the amplifier rack with his knees, he eased it carefully into place.

"The song becomes a patty of wax," Bucky said. "Patty of wax becomes a gramophone record."

"Pretty much."

"It's like we're cooking up an experiment."

"Well, yeah, we are."

"It's like we're doing magic."

Magic, he thought. Maybe magic, why not? Jim Cope likened the process of recording to trapping and preserving a butterfly. Except that this wasn't right, Coughlin decided, because the wax pressing was not a killing jar. The captured song lived on and traveled; therefore one might even call it free. A record moved through the country. A hit song played to more people than the singer would meet in his life. In the end, he supposed, it would outlive the singer himself.

Into the second-floor suite came Abraham Fisk, the elderly farmer who was in love with his fields. He walked gingerly, his gray eyes darting, his stubbly jaw in dispute with his dentures. Coughlin demonstrated how he should sit facing the horn and begin playing the instant that he saw the catcher wave. If he were to quicken the tempo by a degree or two, well, that would be good for safety's sake too.

The farmer tapped his strings. "Three minutes ain't much to make a song," he said.

"That's all we've got. One minute for each field."

Fisk nodded but his face was pained. "One minute for each field," he said, like an echo. And when the weight hit the floor what would become of the man? He'd gingerly shake hands and slip his cash payment into a pocket. He'd climb into his truck, or untether his mule—and after that, what then? He'd slide out of town and take a wagon trail west until he dropped from sight in some distant green hollow, which meant that the only trace of Abe Fisk so far as the wider world was concerned were the wax pressings he'd left in the Bedford hotel.

Or what about Peggy Prince, eighteen last birthday but possessing a tenor voice that was seemingly several decades her senior? Wholesome, pretty Peggy Prince delivered wholesome, pretty tributes to the joys of first love and family and Sunday mornings in church. But she sang with the hard, banked fury of a woman for whom first love was a joke and who was estranged from her kin and who woke hungover on Sundays and lay in bed until noon. It was this friction, he decided, that gave her music its power. But what would Peggy Prince think when she listened back to the recordings? Would her life by that point have caught up with her voice? Or would she sit back and marvel at how young she'd once been?

Hermann Stubb, ever helpful, brought up lunch on a tray. They sat together in the gloomy suite.

Coughlin said, "It's the strangest thing. It's like they come through the door and pass across something precious. Put it in my hands. Turn around and walk out."

Stubb had been frowning at the arrangement of blankets and bed-sheets. Unconsciously, he twisted the wedding band on his finger. "Is it a large company you work for? Humpty Records?"

"Nothing like. Small potatoes."

"Ah. I see."

"That's why I've got to get this right. If I don't . . ." He let the sentence hang.

Stubb was nothing if not sympathetic. He said, "It is interesting that you regard it as precious, this music. To me it sounds brutal. To me it sounds strange and wild, but then I'm not an expert. And I have faith in you, Mr Coughlin, just as I know that your employers do. You think you have found some good music here, yes?"

Coughlin thought about it. "I hope so, I don't know. In the end it's all guess-work."

Magic and guess-work. Superstitions, dark forces. Riding around the fairgrounds, catching fireflies in a jar. Of the thirty-two acts that had played in the hall, he'd selected the ten best to record their songs upstairs. New Versions of Old Familiar Tunes. That's what Humpty had ordered; that's what the bosses thought sold. But how new were the versions? How familiar were the tunes? Jim Cope, he knew, had favored the old and familiar. He liked earnest, upright, traditional pieces. Yodeling farmhands and barrel-chested baritones. Brothers and sisters who play-acted the roles of young sweethearts. If Coughlin had been smart, he'd have been on the hunt for those, too. Instead, he caught himself rejecting the acts Honest Jim would have signed in favor of new versions, original compositions, anything that hadn't been performed note-for-note a thousand times in the past. But was he right or was he wrong? If a man is minded to throw out a winning formula, he'd better pray for dear life that his replacement works better.

Ten separate acts. Some cutting two sides, some four, others six. That was $30-per-side. What was four times thirty? Six times thirty? He'd had the accounts desk at Humpty wire the funds to the bank. The payment had arrived without complaint. All the same, the numbers made him nervous. He felt as if he was juggling with live rounds of ammunition.

"Lot of money," Bucky said.

"Lot of money," he agreed.

Coughlin had not even had time, that first day, to be annoyed with Bucky Garner. He was working flat out. Evidently the local agent was, too. For hours he slalomed between the lobby and the suite, steering in fresh arrivals. He stoked the fire and repositioned the patties, ensuring that the wax retained the right consistency. He was a tireless assistant, Bucky Garner. The kid wanted nothing more than to beguile and impress.

"Too much money." It was not quite a question.

"That's the company's call. The market rate."

"Sure," he said. "No doubt about it." But the question of money was a constant fascination for him. "I mean, how much did we pay that young girl? Peggy?"

"Four sides. So that's $120."

Bucky whistled. "One hundred and twenty," he said.

Coughlin had been wadding the rack to damp down the vibrations. "Fine," he said. "What's your point?"

"Only that it's a big fat figure. In New York City maybe that buys you a Coke and a sandwich. But throw that kind of money around Sutton and it scares folk half to death. Scared Peggy Prince half to death, that's for sure. She nearly didn't take the full amount."

Coughlin looked at him sharply. "She did take it, though, right?"

"Sure she did. It's just a big pile of money, that's all that I'm saying."

Coughlin considered the matter closed. The agent, though, quickly circled back. Ostensibly testing the patties with his thumb, he said, "This Peggy Prince, see, she's only eighteen years old. If one of those sides sells a bundle, is she due much more money?"

"No, she's not. We bought her out."

"$120 today and then that's it forever?"

"That's it."

"Poor little girl. Now you've got me feeling sorry for her."

Coughlin flummoxed. "You're sorry for her because we paid her too much, or you're sorry for her because we didn't pay her enough?"

"I don't know," Bucky said. "I don't know, maybe both."

He'd chosen ten acts. He might have chosen ten others. I'm like a blind man, he thought, tossing darts at a board. Most would miss. Maybe all would miss. It was guesswork, a gamble; nobody knew anything. If a song was a hit, did that make it good? Plenty of hits he disliked. Plenty of misses he loved.

"Jim Cope used to say that he could right away tell a good song from a bad song. He said it was all about bone structure. He said that this is what he looked for, when he was out in the field. Like the song was a face and had its eyes, nose and mouth all in the right place."

"Bone structure. Yeah, I like that."

"But I don't know," Coughlin said. "I think a good song sounds like something that has always been there. It's new and it's fresh. It's the first time you've heard it. But it feels like something that you've known all your life."

"Bone structure," said Bucky, as though he was taking notes in a class. "The song's like a face. Also, it sounds old."

The Cooper sisters rode in from Mechen, West Virginia. They played rough-hewn mountain songs built around simple ingredients: squabbling banjos, basic stanzas, criss-crossing harmonies like two swallows in flight. The Truetone alarmed them and the dropping weight made them rush. Mindful of bringing their songs in on time, the sisters set about each recording with such breathless violence—their fingers a blur, beads of sweat in their hair—that Coughlin had to spin his finger to make them go back and repeat the opening verse. Even then, every side was wrapped up with a full fifteen-seconds to spare. Common sense told the catcher that he should have the songs done again. But he went with his gut and left them as they were.

What would later be referred to as the World-Famous Sutton Sessions ran for two days and yielded forty-four sides of music—although later, thinking back, trying to recapture it, he would find his mind snagging on the little details and distractions as opposed to the thing itself. The mug of coffee he'd spilled on the rug. The discarded tack in the restroom that he had trodden on in bare feet. He remembered the heat and humidity. The lack of fresh air and the smell of old sweat. And he remembered the end—after the Cooper sisters were shown out and he had walked the mattress back from the window and seen the lamps glowing orange along the length of State Street and realized that the time had gotten away from him again. There had been a solitary couple out for an evening stroll and in his memory this couple became the hotel manager, Stubb, and his cherished Mrs Cornish. In reality, he suspected, it had not been them at all.

The fire next door had been allowed to burn out. Bucky lolled in the armchair. He grinned out of habit when he saw the catcher limp in.

"Tired?"

"No, sir," Bucky said. "Just the warmth made me drowsy for a second."

They had both worked hard. They had both earned their rest. But tomorrow at the latest, Coughlin must decide. New York or the mountains? Assuming there was anything still out there worth recording.

He ran his fingers through his hair. "It would mean you taking the pressings to the Humpty office. They'll want the songs right away. When it comes to me, they can wait."

Bucky knitted his brows, not quite understanding. "The Humpty office, where?"

"New York City. You'd have to take the train."

"New York City." It was as if he'd never heard the words before.

"You know what's funny? I keep asking myself what Jim Cope would do at this moment. Would he think, 'OK then, my job's done' or would he keep going and try to find something better?"

"New York City," said Bucky. Every time the man smiled, it was like Christmas lights coming on. "Well, yeah, New York City. Good gracious, you bet."

"I'm chewing it over, though. I haven't decided yet." But he was like the drunk at the party who can't bring himself to go home. The assignment was finished. Accept it, move on. Business hours were over, the street had been cleared and the city of Sutton was closing for the night. Standing at the window, he wondered what the world further south could offer up anyway. Higher mountains. Thicker forests. More shuttered towns like this one. The prospect made him blue, but this was only because he was tired and lacked confidence in his haul. It will be fine, he thought. Stop wallowing. Most of the men who consider themselves sad are simply in need of a decent night's sleep.

It may have been that these thoughts showed on his face, because when he turned from the glass he caught Bucky watching. The local agent was not the type to feel despair. But he was sensitive enough, it turned out, to recognize the condition in others.

Smiling shyly, he said, "I'll bet I know what you're thinking about."

"I'll bet you don't."

"No shame in it. Stands to reason."

Was that what he needed? Was that what he wanted, too weary and soul-sick to even know his own mind? It took a man such as Bucky Garner—a low man despite his shows at gallantry—to name his complaint and then hold out the cure. What a mess, Coughlin thought. I really ought to go to sleep.

"It's no great thing. It's human nature. Somebody comes in and takes care of it all. Next morning it's like you dreamed it, only you also feel better."

Was this what he wanted? For that moment it was. He stared at the glass and his pale face stared back. "Not through the lobby, though. I don't want Stubb knowing."

Bucky nodded. "It's Jane's night on the desk. She knows how things are."

A dreadful thought hit him. "It's not Jane, is it?"

"No," Bucky said. "Don't worry, it's not Jane."

But when not a half-hour later he heard the tap at the door, he knew that yet again, like a compulsion, he had chosen wrong. She came in rust-red heels and a cream woolen coat, and her marcelled hair held the glow of the bedside light, and afterwards he would struggle to recall whether she had been his age or much older, a respectable woman in her middle years, perhaps with children, or a crippled husband who was suddenly unable to work. Her name was Joy, or so she said it was. He stood by the bed and she arranged herself by the dresser, not quite putting her full weight upon it and it seemed that neither party looked directly at the other. By what means had she arrived at the Bedford hotel? Not on foot, surely. Her red heels would have rung all the way along State Street.

Eventually, ruefully, she said, "You want to help me out of this coat?" and he replied that it was a fine coat, elegant, a big city coat. It was not a coat you see very often in a smallish town like Sutton.

"Thank you, yes, the coat is fine. You want to help me out of this fine white coat?"

A lone motor went by on the road. The engine was loud. Head-lamps raked the room. Receiving no response, she dug into a pocket and removed a case of cigarettes.

"I'm sorry," he said. "It's not going to happen."

"Don't be sorry," she said lightly. "A big-shot New Yorker like you."

Midway through her cigarette, he risked lifting his gaze from the floor. If the woman felt offended, she appeared keen not to show it. What would he have made of this Joy were they to pass on the street? No doubt she was more composed—more refined—than the girls he was used to. But did that therefore make her his superior, too?

He mentally willed her to finish smoking and leave. "I guess this doesn't happen often."

"Actually, it happens all the time," she said. "A fellow doesn't know what he wants, or doesn't think he can do it. The woman then tells him that he does and he can and we go on from there." She stubbed out her cigarette and mimed consulting an invisible wristwatch. "So far I would say that we are roughly on schedule."

His legs had turned heavy. He sat on the bed. "Probably I'm just tired."

"Yes," she said. "That's plain to see."

He shook his head, which she read as an invitation to draw near. Her marcelled hair smelled of smoke.

"I'm undecided," he said.

"Yes," she replied. Serious, practical Joy. "Yes," she repeated. "That's exactly how it goes." She was on the bed with him now, still in her coat and red heels, and Coughlin could see that she bit her nails and had recently removed a wedding ring. Crippled husband, he thought. Waiting for her at home. Won't allow himself to sleep until he hears the creak of the screen door and her tread on the stairs.

Joy lay back and smoothed her dress. "The man doesn't know what to do, or what he wants, or where to go. But the woman knows and can tell him. And that's what this is, this little business between us." She patted the coverlet like she was burping a baby. She said, "Close your eyes, mister, and try to think happy thoughts. I'm going to tell you exactly what happens next."

10

THE NAME OF the town was Kowaliga, he said, and it stood in the woods down in eastern Alabama. Kowaliga was colored; it was a town for freedmen. It contained a gin and sawmill and a sizable private school and was considered a good place, a safe place, leastways for a while. The year before he had been working as an engineer for the Alabama Power Company, supervising the completion of the Martin Dam and the eviction of the residents who made Kowaliga their home. The valley was flooded; the streets and buildings submerged. But it is said that on stormy nights the lake turns the bells of the Methodist church so that they still seem to be calling the faithful to prayer. Miles Craven didn't know whether he believed this story or not, but it was an arresting image, he had to admit. The drowned black township. The church bells turning. Kowaliga, he said. He thought about it a great deal.

"Yessir," Moss said, deliberately hanging back at the mouth of the tent. Rain drummed the canvas and steam rose off the ground. The white captains called orders to the black men passing bags. "Yessir," he said, his regular evening ritual. Saying yessir to Craven and listening for Duke's truck on the track.

"May be a little late picking you up today," the bootlegger had said on dropping him off that morning. "But that don't matter, does it? You just hunker down in the tent."

"You're a little late every day," Moss told him, and Old Duke had guffawed, even though it hadn't been meant as a joke.

"Well, that's what I'm saying. It's just a normal day like the rest."

The radio claimed it was raining across every acre of Mississippi. More than that, even—across the whole South and Midwest.

Each day the levee felt frailer and thinner. Each day the roar of the river increased. The big bad wolf, Craven called it. Huffing and puffing. Knock-knock-knocking at the door. Anyone who still had a brain—anyone who had an ounce of commonsense—would be scurrying out the back by this point, hoisting up their skirts and running like hell for higher ground, which is what he was doing himself, pretty much. This was likely the engineer's last day on the Landing. Either tomorrow or the day after, he was taking the train east, out of state, and could not honestly say when he'd be back, if at all. The way Craven told it, this was mostly his decision. But Moss had his doubts, he thought the man had most likely been pushed.

No one had liked Craven to begin with. Since the day with the pig, he'd been more messed-up than ever. Time and again Moss had seen him accosting the fellows, saying that the levee wouldn't hold and that they should be thinking about evacuating the entire city of Greenville, no less, until the Army Corps' engineer had thrown up his hands in disgust. He said that maybe Mr Miles ought to lead by example. Quit the levee, quit town and see if that don't start a trend.

Moss ducked his head and edged into the tent. He said, "You want I should teach you a song or two?" because he hadn't played a lick on the levee for the past three or four days and his fingers were itching and his heart cried out for some music. Previously he'd hated performing songs for Miles Craven. Now he found that he longed for it. It only went to show how quickly life turned around.

He was on the camp bed, a blanket round his shoulders. The man must have caught some kind of chill in the rain. He said, "In a different world, Moss, we might have spun you into gold. Taken all your crude compositions and buffed them to a shine. You'd have liked that, I think."

Moss frowned. "Yessir."

"I might have been your . . . your manager, let's call it. I'd have billed you as Mississippi Moss Evans, guitar picker extraordinaire. Or better yet, Blind Mississippi Moss Evans, because of your spectacles. A noted promoter . . ." He coughed and drew breath. "A noted promoter once told me that blind musicians sell better than sighted ones, don't ask me why. Blind Mississippi Moss Evans, now how about that?"

He tried again. "You want I should play some music, sir?"— almost pleading for permission to get out his guitar and never mind if this meant that he might not be able to hear Old Duke's truck on the trail. Where was the bastard anyway? Off visiting with his women. Off getting high on his own supply.

Already it was growing dark outside; the wind going up and the temperature going down. Moss had heard that the captains now had the men working shifts through the night, which meant that the levee never truly went to sleep. It made him uneasy, the thought of everyone digging sand and passing boards in the dark, half deafened by the noise of the river at close quarters and straining their eyes so as to identify solid ground. How would Benny Gibbs be coping with that? Or had Benny Gibbs already bowed out? Stepping to the left when he ought to have stepped right. The black water closing over his head so completely that no one on the shoreline—the cons, the guards, the laborers from the fields—was even aware that he'd gone.

Craven was watching him. "You realize by now that he's not coming back."

"Yessir." For an instant he thought the man was referring to Benny.

"The bootlegger fellow. The man you're waiting for. He has given you up. He has skedaddled, he's run. That means, I'm afraid, that you now join all the rest."

Involuntarily, Moss turned for the tent-mouth, as though by staring hard he might yet be able to summon Duke's truck into being. His stomach turned over. He needed time to think this through. If he could only play guitar, he might clear his head and see straight.

"No one is coming to save you," Craven said at his back. "This is difficult to accept but there it is, it's a fact."

The previous evening had been dry. The engineer had dined alone in the town. There were so many fine restaurants in Greenville to choose from—French and Italian, Spanish and Chinese—and he tended to bounce between each establishment like a tourist on vacation. And then afterwards, strolling past the illuminated shop-fronts, through the milling crowds, it was possible to think that the world was secure and that all his fears were unfounded. The city of Greenville, the Queen of the Delta, had seemed the epitome of civilized society that night, which on one level was true, inasmuch as that counts for anything. Because what's civilization, he asked, but a sandcastle on the shore, or a flickering light in the darkness? Men build a campfire and huddle beside the flames to keep warm. They call this their city, their family, their home. And yet beyond the ring of warm light there is only the forest, the dark.

"Mississippi Moss Evans," he said—and this made him laugh. "Kowaliga," he said, and this made him laugh harder still. Moss turned back to face him, but he was still listening for the truck.

"Do you understand what I am saying, boy?"

"Yessir."

"The church bells under the water, that's you."

It might happen tomorrow. It might happen next week. Not the end of the world, no sir, nothing quite so grand and final as that. But a significant and irrevocable event nonetheless: the end of the world as they saw it and knew it. The campfire extinguished. The fortress leveled. Society, so-called, ripped away like a cobweb.

Miles Craven, Moss thought, looked almost as flimsy as a himself. The man sat on the camp bed in his stained linen suit with the stink of sweat in its creases and his pale hands bunched into fists. The second before he had been doubled over with laughter. Now just like that he appeared close to tears. He said, "I'm sorry, Moss, I must confess that I have let you down. No one is coming to rescue anyone."

81

11

SOUTH OF TOWN lay a mountain valley, thickly wooded on either side, crowded with red oaks, sugar maple and tulip poplars. In the morning the hills were cloaked in a swirling gray mist, like a scene from a German fairy tale. Then the land brightened and the mist took new shapes, descending in corkscrews and columns to touch the valley floor. The light was soft and the air was warm and he drove for an hour without seeing a soul. The world felt strange and lovely that morning, as though it had been born overnight and he was its first visitor.

There was a rushing stream in the valley, but it was as elusive as the mist. It bounded from the woods to track the right-side of the road before ducking beneath his wheels to reappear at the left. The road zigged and the stream zagged and they maintained this exchange for several miles with him as their patsy, suckered at every turn. Even so, he liked the stream and had grown fond of its crafty comings and goings, so that when it finally turned back for the trees he was left feeling lonely all over again.

Most of all he missed Sutton, which made no sense at all. Sutton with its department store, schoolhouse and stone-cutting plant. Sutton with its amiable citizens and drowsy midweek afternoons. Just a week before the place had felt as foreign to him as the Russian steppes. Today on the road it had become the home that he'd lost; more homely somehow than Manhattan or Mott Haven. Sutton with its hard roads and soft beds. Sutton with its electric lights and Victrolas and pots of warm coffee. Civilization's last gasp, before the Far Corners turned wild. It bothered him, the fact that he had nothing to prove he had ever been there at all. Even the recordings he'd cut were now several miles behind him, left in the charge of Bucky Garner, who was under strict instruction to transport them by train to New York. Bucky in the city: the place wouldn't know what had hit it. He pictured the kid blowing into the tatty Humpty office, introducing himself with a flourish, a carnation in his buttonhole. *I come bearing gifts*, he'd tell the bemused secretary. *A crate-load of new music. A box of chamomile tea.*

The road climbed from the valley in a business of tight turns. The lathe in its packing cases bumped and slid on the bed. He ran through a village, but it was there and gone in a moment. A distempered sawmill. A shuttered general store. Maybe the place was a ghost-town; maybe the land around was deserted. But no— because here and there he spied half-concealed tracks leading off the road, and figured that these must be access routes to whiskey stills. Bootleggers, then, would be somewhere close by. What would they do if he were to walk up to their camp? Invite him to sit down and gather around him with banjos? Put a knife in his belly and coolly watch him bleed out? Or fly on soft feet the second they heard his approach? The last one, he thought. Almost certainly that.

The mountains were grand. They made him feel rather mighty. He wound down the window and took in big breaths of clean air. One day someone more clever than himself would find a way to bottle those drafts of uncut wintergreen and sassafras. They would sell it from a stall beside the steps to Penn station. *Appalachian Mountain Air, only $3 a can.*

One measure of good music, it clung to you like a burr. The recordings were gone, already boarding the train to New York. But the songs remained with him, as though they had opened the case and slipped free. Upstairs at the Bedford he'd had hard-voiced Peggy Prince put down a mountain staple that she'd spun her own lyrics around. The song, she'd explained, was called Young and In Love, except that either the words wouldn't scan or the phrasing was wrong. Finally, with a worried eye on the clock, Coughlin had suggested she substitute the word "and" for "animals" and when she did it that way the entire thing was improved. Young Animals in Love was a better title anyway.

Afterwards he hadn't thought much more about it. But today, behind the wheel, he found that the song kept returning—Young Animals in Love—and he supposed that this meant it had some value after all. The moon so new, the morning dew, like something being born. And in the mountains, sure enough, young animals in love.

He recalled the clattering fury of the Cooper sisters' How Long is This Shortcut? He hummed Abe Fisk's cranky ode to the three fields that he tilled. On the second day of the sessions, more out of pity than anything else, he had cleared space for a cadaverous lay preacher named Philander Jones who dealt in sacred songs and had brought along his two daughters to provide back-up vocals. Philander Jones—what a name—had his girls repeat every line of each song while he gathered his breath for the next, except that they kept being caught out and eventually got the giggles. Coughlin eventually realized what the problem was. The addled old preacher was improvising, barking the first thing that came to mind, so that the girls had to regroup every time in order to follow his lead. They went through several takes and each one was a wreck. Except that now, inexplicably, several of these songs came back, too.

The forest was dense and the going was hard. Potholes rocked the van from side to side. He passed a black bear; it nodded hello as he passed. But that afternoon the scene changed again. His ears popped and the sky expanded. He could see other green ridges beyond the nearest green ridge, further far corners beyond the one he was in. His right foot ached and his shoulders had knotted. He needed to get away from the wheel and stretch his limbs for a spell.

At the crest of the hill ran a low stone wall. This in turn gave out on a parcel of land: meadows, an orchard and a handsome farmhouse. And beyond that was arranged the full glory of the west, or at least as much of it as Coughlin was able to process.

Out in the field, men were at work planting trees. First they dug out a small square of turf. Then they inserted a sapling and staked it in place. The men looked like lumberjacks, Coughlin thought, but these were lumberjacks in reverse because they were creating a forest, not cutting one down.

He was so engrossed by this operation that it took him a minute to realize he was not alone at the wall. A young man sat in the long grass, looking west. He had his back against the stones and a pair of crutches at his side. Evidently he had been conscious of Coughlin all along because he spoke to the catcher without turning his head. He said, "By the end of this week this field will be replanted. Clear across to the wall over yonder."

Coughlin grunted, embarrassed. After a moment, he said, "Replanted?"

"This used to be wooded. It was cleared for grazing. Presently, God willing, it will be woodland again."

With a painstaking slowness, he got to his feet and propped the sticks at his armpits. Coughlin could see that the young man was lame down one side. His left foot dragged; the arm was withered. At first glance, the cripple cut a sad and sorry figure. But his features were lively and his clothes were well-tailored and the hand he extended was soft and clean to the touch. A city hand in a rural place.

"John Coughlin. Passing through."

The young man raised an eyebrow. "From a good distance."

"New York City. I'm a long way from home."

"And Coughlin. So before the city, the old country."

"Not me, my parents. Before I was born."

The cripple, for his part, had lived his entire life in the mountains. As a boy he'd tracked deer, climbed trees and swam in every stream he could find. Then he'd come down with polio and now required a leg-brace and two sticks. Much of the time he was confined to his quarters. Still, he liked coming up to these hills, the rocky balds. He liked to feel the wind on his face and observe how the seasons left their thumbprint on the land. The mountain air was a tonic. All mountains, probably, but these ones in particular.

They stood at the wall and gazed at the laborers, the orchard and the red-roofed farmhouse with its wraparound porch.

"Whose land is this? Who lives down there?"

"This land? This land is the property of a man named Brodie, insofar as anyone can be said to own the land. It belonged to his father and his father before that. Before that, I don't know."

"And he's easy with people coming and going? Trespassing on his turf?" Worrying the livestock, he was going to add, except that there appeared to be no livestock on this particular farm. The fields had gone to seed. Wind moved in the grass. The laborers had turned their backs and were working at a distance. The noise of their mallets didn't quite correspond to the movement of their arms.

"What line of work are you in, Mr Coughlin? If you don't mind my asking."

He slapped at a fly. "I'm a song-catcher. So this is what you might call a fishing trip. I find musicians and record them. Old-time pieces. Mountain songs. Whatever I think people might like."

"And do you play music yourself?"

"Not a lick. I'm a listener."

Whatever the state of the farm itself—if indeed it was a farm—the house below appeared to be in good order. He could see hanging baskets on the porch. White linen twisted on the clothesline in the yard. Like the onlookers at the wall, the farmhouse faced west towards, well, what exactly? One green ridge followed by another. Forests and lakes. Eventually a mighty river.

The cripple had been speaking. The wind had dragged his voice.

He smiled and tried again. "I asked if you had caught your fish, or if you are still out with your net."

"I've caught some good ones. No giant so far."

"And, as you say, you're a catcher. You would know one if you found it."

"Yes," he said firmly. "I'd know a giant all right."

It was a curious thing, the march of progress. When Brodie's ancestors first came to this country, they cut down the forest and forced out the wolves and put cattle and sheep on every hill they could find. The expectation therefore was that Brodie would do the same, simply continue the tradition—and for several years in fact he had. Now, though, he'd turned in the opposite direction. His plan was to replant and restore; to return the ground to its virgin state. This, Brodie said, was a man's last obligation. To clean up and set right. To cover his tracks so completely it was as though he had never existed at all.

The wind had lifted the cripple's hat. Coughlin stooped to retrieve it before it had time to take flight. "I don't know," he said, handing it back. "Shouldn't a man try to leave something behind when he's gone? Something big, something good. Otherwise what's the point?"

The cripple didn't know either. He said he was merely relaying what Brodie would say. "But I'll admit that it's pleasant to picture those saplings there fully grown. The field would look much as it did in the days of Thomas Walker or Daniel Boone. This is what our ancestors would have seen when they first climbed the hill."

"Not my ancestors."

He laughed. "Well, perhaps not yours specifically. But these mountains were settled by the Scots and the Irish. My people and yours. On your travels you must have seen some Irish traces here and there."

"In the music, sure." He remembered the jig performed by the Blue Grasshopper Dirt Band. The crowd in motion; the Cue-Ball Kid's loose-boned, liquid dance. "But even then it's not the same. It was Irish once but it's American now. It's like . . ." He scratched at his neck. "One thing that's always bothered me. People call it old music. Old-time pieces. Old familiar tunes. I guess I do it, too, because it puts the customer at his ease. But it's not old music, it's too lively for that. It's young music, if it's anything."

The cripple had repositioned himself on his crutches. His attention was back on the distant farmhands with their spades and mallets. He said that if a tree isn't felled it can survive for centuries. Then, towards the end of its natural life, it lowers its thickest limbs to the ground for support. In its final years it resembles an old man with a stick. Or a young man who's clock is running just a little too fast.

"Talking of clocks," Coughlin said. "Talking of time going by."

They'd shaken hands across the low stone wall. The catcher had introduced himself. Had the stranger done likewise? Coughlin didn't think he had.

He said, "This Brodie fellow that owns the land. That's you, right?"

"No," said the cripple. "I'm like you, passing through." And yet afterwards Coughlin would reflect on the lack of a car or a horse and wonder where this man had emerged from if not the big house and how far he could travel on that dragging right leg and would conclude that the cripple at the wall had likely been Brodie, watching his servants from a distance as they made the land new again.

Tomorrow or the next day he would turn his wheels for home. But for the time being he drove and slept and drove on again, hanging west where he could in search of an alternative way back, because why retread old ground when you can find a fresh path? He was looking for his giant, his treasure, whatever form that it took.

So it was a curious route, the one that he took, along the southern spine of Appalachia and through a Christ-haunted country of tumbledown churches and undressed dog-run shacks. In Virginia the signs at the roadside had said, CHECK YOUR RADIATORS and CHECK YOUR BRAKES. In Tennessee they said, GET RIGHT WITH GOD and THE LORD IS MY SHEPHERD. They asked him, ARE YOU BOUND FOR HEAVEN OR HELL? and DO YOU HEAR HIM CALLING? IS HE CALLING FOR YOU?

Tomorrow, he swore, he'd turn around for New York. But today he consulted his creased and grease-stained map and moved from one town to the next. At night he boarded in mildewy guesthouses or purpose-built cabins set back from the road. These cabins were interchangeable, every unit the same, and on pulling into the forecourt he would see the same indistinguishable gaggle of salesmen smoking and drinking and taking the evening air. They tipped their hats and said 'How-do', but this was the extent of their interest in him. The salesmen were tribal and nomadic people. They spoke their own language and had no time for outsiders. Lying in bed, Coughlin could hear them joking and laughing into the small hours, discussing the merits of women who were not their wives. And then, on stepping outside in the morning, he would find them already gone, the place deserted and his van alone on the gravel amid a scatter of butt ends.

Every morning, the same routine. Dawn banged at the screen. April yanked the bedclothes. And by now—not yet a week out of Sutton—he had grown to love the thrill of riding out in the van every day, with the sun at his back and the mountains arranged in his windscreen. Spiderweb hammocks hung out in the grass. The morning mist rising like spirits bound for heaven. The trees around here were a thousand years old, the cripple said, and Coughlin had nodded politely, because who the hell knew for sure? But suppose he had been right—about the trees and the world and all the rest of it. And suppose the young cripple had been Brodie all along after all. It made him think of John's account of Mary Magdalene, who met Jesus beside the empty tomb and took him to be the gardener.

Inside flyblown cafes, over eggs and grits, he heard that west of Appalachia the land was underwater. The rains of the winter had returned from the Gulf. The rivers had burst and flooded a number of towns. In rough weather, he knew, the mountain roads ran to mud. Cars spun their wheels or stuck like bugs on flypaper and nothing moved for days on end. Whereas Tennessee, thank heavens, remained reassuringly warm and dry. The sun still shone and the wind had dropped and what traffic there was threw up plumes of dust. And then that afternoon, on a straight ribbon of road, he came across the wrecks of those who'd passed this way before. The buckled hubcaps and torn lengths of tire and sometimes an entire car that had been spun about and abandoned at the verge. And maybe this was what became of all those salesmen who set out before dawn. They'd ridden so hard that their motor vehicles collapsed—and then such was their haste that they had simply detached themselves and ran on. Coughlin pictured them shrugging off their armor or shedding their skins and becoming like ground-fog or green saplings, planting themselves back in the folds of the hills.

12

THEY SET UPON him at the end of his fifth day out from Sutton. He should have seen it coming but had allowed his guard to drop. All those hours spent watching the trees for wild animals, checking over his shoulder each time he stepped out of the van for a leak. He should have known they'd come for him in a crowded, well-lit place. That's how it happened on the streets of Mott Haven. That's how it happened in the Far Corners as well.

At some point he thought he must have pushed beyond Appalachia. The land was less rugged, the midday heat more intense, and this was surely his cue to take the next northbound turn. But that afternoon he passed a hand-painted sign that for once wasn't shouting about hellfire and damnation. HATCHING THIS EASTER— THE HERBIE LAX CARNIVAL. And then another, two miles on. HERBIE LAX CARNIVAL IT'S EASTER EGG-CITING. And another, barely two hundred yards beyond that, UNCLE HERBIE SAYS STEP THIS WAY LADIES & GENTLEMEN—& JUNIORS IS ALWAYS WELCOME TOO!!

The carnival spread across the grounds of Comfort Hall, a historic plantation house, still in operation. Coughlin caught a glimpse of the place as he eased off the road, in the few seconds before he was swallowed by the tents and stalls and the tidal surge of the crowd. Herbie Lax's traveling carnival promised THRILLS and EXCITEMENT and SYRUP FOR THE SOUL. It contained a George Ferris wheel, a fifty-foot-high helter-skelter, plus a dancing automaton that was prone to catching fire. A final sign at the turn-off read HUMAN ODDITIES, CLOWNS & TUMBLERS,

LASHINGS OF OLD-TIME MOUNTAIN MUSIC and this was what did it; that last line sealed his fate.

He figured there must be a large town close by (Birmingham? Tuscaloosa?) because the grounds were thronged, a man had to move edgewise and clasp a hand to his hat. He saw more people in a minute than he had seen in a week; more people, most likely, that had been at the Bedford try-outs and everyone packed so tightly that it was difficult to say who was related to who. Young mixed with old, white folk with black. Children squirmed between legs and crawled out from under-skirts. Shouldering his way up the central aisle, he was briefly stalled by the passage of a white-haired woman in a wheelchair, borne aloft by unseen hands as though she were an Egyptian princess inspecting her subjects. She waved him a curt greeting as her conveyance lurched by.

Piecing it together afterwards, it would seem to him that every-thing had been fine until his encounter with Donny the Dummy. He weaved contentedly between the stalls, inhaling the smells of cotton candy, cologne and spit-roast. The hills remained bright but the field was already darkening and the electric bulbs left blotchy after-burns on his lids when he blinked. For a time he fell in with a thin, studious youth named Morton Haines, who had arrived with his sister only to lose her in the crowd. Morton Haines had ink-stained hands and wore thick-framed spectacles and he spoke in a rush to outpace a mild speech impediment. He said, "One upside to losing Susan is that I can sneak off and watch the hoochie-coochie."

When the catcher moved on, the kid matched his stride.

"Over yonder, Judie Bonville. She's a showgirl—flamingo feathers and tinsel, like this—and her specialty's the hoochie-coochie. But if I watch it with Susan, she'll drop it into conversation with Ma and I don't need that runaround, I prefer the quiet life. So it works out better for everybody concerned if I see Judie Bonville on my own."

Coughlin nodded. "I'm interested in the old-time pieces."

"Oh sure, the Alabama Doughboys, they're not on until late. You'll like them, though, they're worth the wait. My Uncle Clifford plays guitar with them, so might say that I'm partial but even so, never mind."

"What time are they on?"

Morton Haines's face clenched. A tendon jumped in his neck; he might have swallowed a stone. "Cousin," he said on a violent outbreath. "Cousin, not uncle. Excuse my mistake."

There really was a Herbie Lax, but he was like Miss Downtown Radio: a performer, a front. He sported a stovepipe hat and a candy-striped waistcoat and his job was to keep the show moving and direct the visitors to this stall or that. Disproportionately he directed them towards the herbal laxative stand, which had given the carnival its name. It was said that, back in the early 1900s, the business had been a straight horse-and-buggy affair. But in '08 its owner had patented a range of flavored syrups and the money this earned had allowed him to hire a juggler and a strongman, a whirligig, the full works. These days the original stand formed the centerpiece of a large traveling show, tucked in amid the barkers, exhibits and rides; the titular head of a rambunctious, sprawling family.

Herbie Lax had grown hoarse from shouting the merits of his softener. He said, "It cures, cleans and sanctifies. It blesses your pipes and washes your soul. You can put it on ice-cream or stir it in your coffee. It's your friend in the morning and your nursemaid at night. It's ninety-nine cents a bottle and that buys perfect peace, guaranteed."

There was a battle royale to the left and what appeared to be a static electricity globe to the right. Coughlin's view was obscured by a knot of children. Morton explained that the year before there'd been a female impersonator, a man got up as a lady, and he'd been popular too, except that this one bunch of fellas took against him for some reason. So in the middle of the act they ran up on stage and opened him up there and then, opened up his whole face, like they were fixing to pull it inside-out. "This was about the most awful sight I ever seen in my life," he said. "Couldn't shake it from my head for weeks. But then at breakfast the next day she doesn't ask about that, not a word. Instead it's all about the hoochie-coochie, asking what was I thinking, watching a showgirl do the hoochie-coochie." His Adam's apple twitched. "So that's why I give up. Seems the entire country ought to get its priorities straight."

Sex hung in the air and hid in the wings, but it found an outlet of sorts at the Healing Hands of Dr Tibbs. This was because Dr Tibbs' hands had a tendency to wander—and over time this had become the central feature of his show. The physician preyed on respectable, bored women. The respectable, bored women by and large played along. They explained to the doctor that they suffered from cricks in their necks or swollen feet, or that they were prone to migraines or gassy stomachs. Then with a frowning solemnity, Dr Tibbs would lay his palms on the afflicted area and make comforting noises for a moment or two, after which his left hand would go roaming in search of a buttock, breast or thigh. Invariably, the onlookers would howl in protest at each transgression, while the physician restrained his left hand with his right. Whatever properties the Healing Hands of Dr Tibbs had once possessed, the clinic was now a pantomime. At the end of each appointment, the patient was discharged, flushed and disheveled, to be fussed over by her friends.

When he wasn't proclaiming the virtues of the acrobats, the herbal remedy or the Ferris wheel, Herbie Lax called the names of lost children and the plates of motor vehicles which were found to be poorly parked. Lifting his voice, he announced that this spectacular event, this glittering carnival, was only made possible thanks to the generosity of Colonel Bird, who had thrown open his doors and turned over his fields. Not only that, added Herbie Lax, but he had just received word of their host's grand arrival. "A round of applause, ladies and gentlemen, for Colonel Bird of Comfort Hall". Craning his neck, Coughlin caught sight of a raised arm in white linen, but this was all he would see of the famous Colonel Bird. And on turning back he noted that Morton Haines had gone, too. The kid had seized his chance and sloped away to watch the hoochie-coochie unobserved.

Night struck like a hammer in this part of Alabama. The sky was bright, then the sky was black. He spied the crone in the wheelchair making her precarious return trip up the aisle, her blue-veined shins gleaming, her hair like a halo. He hoped that she might wave again and felt downcast and dismissed when she passed him by without a glance.

If there existed a genuine marvel among the performers and exhibits at the Herbie Lax carnival, it was surely Donny the Dummy, whose antics were so wild they even spooked his owner. When Coughlin drew near, Donny snapped to attention. He said, "Ahoy there, Big City. Yes you, pal, Big City. I'm talking to you."

He was dressed as a swell, in top hat and tails with a jet-black bow-tie. But he sat in the lap of Wilfred Peters, whose suit was worn and whose Brillo-pad mustache smelt distinctly of rye. While the partnership had its uses, theirs was not a happy union. Once, when Peters had decided he could stomach no more, he'd driven hours into the piney woods before tossing the dummy into the grass at the roadside. Afterwards, though, he felt idiotic and sad. The next day he drove back through the woods to retrieve him.

He said, "That's right, Big City, ain't you a long way from home? What do you want with us country folk?"

Wilfred Peters said, "Donny. Leave the man alone."

The crowd was thinner at this end of the field. Either the families with children were already heading home, or else Donny could not compete with the more gaudy exhibits. Coughlin half-turned towards the stand. He was reluctant to give the ventriloquist his full attention.

"Attaboy, there we go. What's your name, Big City?"

Coughlin hesitated. The New Colonial March played on the calliope nearby. Addressing the ventriloquist, he said, "You tell me. Seeing as you seem to know where I'm from."

"Come on, Big City, I'm not clairvoyant."

Wilfred Peters winced in anticipation of the joke. "No," he said in the space of a breath before Donny piped up. "You know Claire Voyant? Sweet girl. Great kisser."

The catcher grinned. "You're pretty good at this game. I can't see your lips move at all."

"Thank you," Peters said. "But money speaks louder, if you take my meaning."

Coughlin dug in his pocket. Up close, beneath the electric bulbs, the ventriloquist looked especially forlorn, with his yellowed mustache and one eye pink with blood.

Donny's molded face turned his way. A horsefly had alighted on the hard brim of his hat. He said, "Jeepers, Big City. D'you want to help me? I'm drowning."

"All right, Donny, that will do."

"But I'm drowning. I can't breathe. Big City, I'm drowning." The dummy's head spun full circle. The horsefly took flight.

"Donny," said Peters. "Donny, shut your mouth."

Coughlin stepped back, at a loss. "Fine," he said. "Fine. Good speaking to you." But it was at this point that Donny, determined to cling on to his audience, dashed through his repertoire of tricks. He made his tie rotate and crossed his big painted eyes. He had his owner bring up a glass so that he could mime drinking water.

He gargled; he gurgled. He said, "Help me, Big City. Please help me, I'm drowning. I'm a poor little dummy and I can't swim worth a damn."

"Donny! Donny!" Peters jerked convulsively and the half-filled glass of water—assuming it even was water—rolled into the aisle. And in turning to fetch it, Coughlin was swept up in the traffic coming off the exit ramp from the Ferris wheel and by the time he'd detached himself he found that the last thing he wished to do was retrace his steps. When the dummy called for him once more—"Big City! Big City!"—he put down his head and pretended that he hadn't heard.

At the coconut shy he ran across Morton Haines. The kid had picked his own path through the throng and managed to reconnect with his sister. Coughlin wondered if he'd also found time to catch the hoochie-coochie dance show. Given the presence of Susan, he figured it was probably safest not to ask.

Morton regarded him with some concern. "You ought to sit down, you look all juiced out." He cocked his thumb. "That ventriloquist, shoot, he's the honest-to-God worst."

"Oh yeah, Donny," Susan said. "There ain't nobody likes Donny."

She was built like her brother, as long-limbed as a wading bird, but her speech was more natural and her coordination more certain. She felled two coconuts in quick succession and only missed the third because she was talking as she threw. She said, "Sometimes, though, they stick them down with glue. Not all of them, not most of them. Only enough so you can't say for sure."

He turned to Morton. "You were saying earlier about your cousin Clifford."

"Cousin Cliff, you bet. But he won't be out for another hour or so. The band is all limbering up 'round back."

"How about you introduce me? I can watch them rehearse. It might be a good thing for them."

"Why might it be a good thing?" Susan asked.

"You mind your own," said her brother. "That's their business, not ours."

They escorted him to the far side of the trailers, past a couple locked in a drunken clinch and a pair of boisterous dogs which had got their chains in a tangle. The roar of the gennies was louder back here and the electric lights laid milky eggs in each lens of the boy's spectacles. Morton screwed up his face. His Adam's apple jerked. On an outbreath, he said, "Here he is, Cousin Cliff" and swung from the hip with his fist closed and a dimpled duster on his knuckles, and if Coughlin had learned anything from his years in the Bronx it was that if you were hit you had to hit back without thinking because the longer you left it the more time you allowed for the pain to sink in and take root and the greater likelihood you had of getting pegged worse the second time. So he struck back on his own outbreath and put skinny Morton Haines on his back and it was only then that his wits caught up with the situation enough to inform him that his eyebrow had split and his balance was off and that, furthermore, his right hand had gone numb.

Were it not for the duster, he might have been in better shape. But when he wound up, meaning to kick Morton Haines before the youth could get up, his legs betrayed him and he had to steady himself against the side of the trailer. Dimly he was aware that the drunken lovers had fled and that the tethered dogs were in uproar. From afar Herbie Lax was shouting something about dancing. He said that he loved to dance and couldn't believe that there was anyone alive on this planet who didn't love to dance, too. He shouted, "Ladies and gentlemen, do you love to dance?"

In a heartbeat they were on him, Morton Haines and his sister. And while it was true that the boy did most of the damage, the girl played her part. She had some kind of cudgel—conceivably a nightstick, more likely an ax handle—and staged her own small performance at the edge of the fray, seeking to land it on his head, elbow and hips. He defended himself as well as he could, backed up against the trailer, swinging with his left first and his tender right, and in this way was able to put Morton down for a second time. But now his eye had closed and his head was ringing and it was all he could do to keep his feet planted and his hands up. And the thought that came to him, trapped in the wings of the Herbie Lax carnival, was that history repeats, that it plays like a record and that reckless men are stupid men and stupid men meet violent ends. God knows, the warning signs had been there all along. It had happened to Jim Cope. It was his turn tonight.

13

A FULL SACK of sand weighs about the same as a woman. That's what the men said and it made ugly work that bit sweeter. They weren't hauling bags, they were handling pliant, pretty girls wearing sweaty sackcloth dresses. This one is named Beulah and that one is named Blanche. They passed the bags one by one up the line. They said, Hey, mind if I cut in and dance with Blanche? Send me down Constance now, I reckon I can tackle two ladies at once.

How many women came up the line every day? Hundreds of them, thousands of them, each passed from man to man before joining the others at the water's edge. And how many would still be resting there the next morning? Not a single one, sad to say, that was just how it went. The river rose in the darkness and washed all those ladies downstream.

He still had his guitar slung over his back. He didn't want it on the ground; didn't want it washed away, come to that. One time Deputy Piper walked up the line, scared out of his wits and shouted, "You put that fucking thing down," and he had begun to comply because he also didn't want to get killed. But then Piper had walked on and been distracted by some poor old fellow who had stumbled, and so he decided to keep the guitar on his back and hope for the best until the next time he was told.

All yesterday and into the night, trucks roaming the bottomlands, zipping in and out of the colored neighborhoods, rounding up every man and boy who could work, except it was never enough, they always needed more bodies. And now the Landing, it seemed, had become as crowded as the town; the black men digging sand and passing bags through the mud; the white men arguing back and forth by the tents. He could see the fellows in dirty suits from the levee board and commission. He could see the cons and the captains and the men from the National Guard. He could see June and Velma and Pearl and Pam, all of the ladies getting unceremoniously swung up the line.

It was going to happen, Miles Craven had said. The ground had gone rotten and the sand-boils came up dirty. It was going to happen, the only question was when.

Now more than anything Moss was aware of the river. The noise of it; the speed of it. The enormity of its presence on the far side of the bags. The men had roped an army barge to the jetty, but the crew were still on it with the engine still running, so as to prevent it being swept off alongside all the other streaming wreckage. The chicken coops and sides of barns. The cabin roofs and the full-grown trees. One time Moss had looked up from his work to see a hay-bale slide by with a live goat standing, brace-legged, on the top. The goat looked in good spirits, all things considered. It had a glossy coat. It had a healthy bleat. It was riding down the river on an adventure of its own.

The previous summer, when he was pouring hooch for the road crews, he'd drive up Highway One with Old Duke. The bootlegger's still produced so many barrels that the man must have been as rich as a riverboat gambler. And yet there he was driving the same beat-down delivery wagon he'd owned for ten years, a T-truck so ancient that you could hear it for miles and smell its fumes on your clothes hours after you got out.

Old Duke called the T-truck his Good Luck Buggy. He said that in all the time he'd been driving his Good Luck Buggy he'd never—not once—been pulled over and searched. Moss thought this maybe had more to do with him greasing Deputy Piper's palms every month, but he did not point this out, because Duke had a temper and you never knew what would set him off. So they would sit together on that sweltering drive up Highway One, with Moss having to shout at the top of his lungs to be heard and the judder of the engine so violent he feared it might loosen his teeth. And he knew that one day quite soon the Good Luck Buggy would blow, exploding on the road in a pillar of flame with Old Duke shot through the roof before he even knew what had happened. Shot through the roof with his skull gone to splinters. It made him think of the joke about the bird that flew into an airplane propeller, and the last thing that went through the bird's mind was its ass.

The land ahead became liquid and the wall of sandbags disappeared. Stationed halfway up the line, Moss felt the rupture in his blood before he heard the ground break, the way one is aware that the fuse box has shorted an instant before the room is plunged into darkness. His foothold had been stable and then all at once it was not and he watched the men nearby become weightless as they were lifted and spun and sucked into the crevasse. One second they were working. The very next they were gone.

Now the river was loose and came pouring through the breach. The barn-sides and rooftops pivoted in midstream. And all at once the whistles were blowing and the bells were turning and he heard the man beside him screaming, "You're dead, you're dead, you're dead, you're dead!" The man was pointing from the guards to the captains to the soldiers by the trucks. He seemed overjoyed that they would all soon be dead.

It had rained in February and it had rained in March. The weather front stalled over the south-central states. The Mississippi rising by two feet every day, the Arkansas river forced backwards; the flow so intense that it knocked out the defenses. Mounds Landing toppled, the Delta laid to waste. And that was that, it had happened, just as Miles Craven said it would. Blame the corner-cutting engineers who built the levees in the first place. Blame the hellish bad weather, blame the corkscrew river bends. Blame all of the loggers in the Upper Midwest. Blame the draining of wetlands and the pulping of forests because it's true what they say, when the North soils the bed, it's the South cleans the sheets. Blame God, too, while you're at it, because this is his work in the end. Every great disaster, said the pastor, is in essence divine.

The line went to pieces. Panic took hold. Piper had his bullhorn and was shouting to be heard above the commotion, ordering the workers to remain right where they were; ordering a path to be cleared so the white men could reach the barge. Except that no one was listening to him anymore, not when the levee had broken and the sandbags were useless. Not when the rest of the Landing might be swept away in a heartbeat.

Now it seemed as though the whole place was in motion. The laborers massed around the makeshift jetty, slipping in the mud and pressed up against one another. Several of the captains, it seemed, were tangled up in the throng, and at least one of these was intent on shooting his way to the boat. The guardsmen called for order and aimed their rifles at the sky.

"All coloreds stay put!" Deputy Piper was shouting. "All of you boys, goddammit, you still got work to do here."

Most of the white men had reached the jetty by now and they took the gangplank two abreast, jockeying with their elbows, their meaty hips swinging. The barge fought the current with its engines in reverse. It sank low to the waves as the officials climbed aboard. Only one laborer dared to run at the plank. The red-nosed levee captain lifted his handgun and fired.

"Drop back! Drop back!" one of the soldiers bellowed. And Moss, who was nowhere near the front anyway, figured that it was probably safer to do so. Anyone storming the jetty was only going to get himself killed. Given the choice, he reckoned that he would rather be taken by the river than shot down like a dog. At this stage he figured it might be the only choice he had left.

The barge bumped in the water. Passengers steadied themselves on the deck. He had lost track of Piper amidst all the confusion but he could see him again now, still clutching his bullhorn as though it were his most treasured possession. Moss thought of the man who'd called out, "You're dead and you're dead," with such violent glee, as though simply saying it—wishing it—could ever make it so.

The current had pulled the rope so tight that the crew couldn't get purchase and had to saw through it instead. The rope's severed end reared up like a snake. The barge sloughed off from shore and was hit from all sides, spinning almost full circle and he thought that anyone who hadn't had a hand on the railing would have been pitched overboard and dragged under. Dead and dead and dead and dead. Except that they weren't: they had escaped the wrecked levee.

Moss abandoned the jetty and crossed to where the trucks were parked. A small dug-out canoe lay on its side on the grass. He stared at it, frowning. His back and knees ached from hours of hauling bags. But his mind was alert and his thoughts jumped like rabbits.

Sam Tucker, the sharecropper, materialized at his shoulder. Moss could tell who it was by the thin squeak of his breathing. He was a strong man, Sam Tucker, but his time on the levee had hit him hard. The rain and the cold had wormed its way into his lungs. He said, "How many men could fit into that thing?"

"Three," Moss said. "Maybe four all bunched up."

"Three or four, it don't matter. It's three or four dead men as soon as that boat meets the water."

"There's a paddle, too," he said. "Over there, see?"

"A paddle." Tucker almost laughed. "Oh sure, in that case."

They each took an end and dragged it to the waterline, not far from the spot where the feral pig had washed up. Moss sat in the rear, assuming the farmer would take the front end. Their efforts, he saw, had already drawn a small crowd.

Tucker hung back. "This is crazy," he said.

"The white man gets a boat. Why can't we get a boat?"

The farmer shook his head.

There had been a rush for the barge. There was no rush for the canoe. Moss sat at the tapered end, feeling foolish, staring at Tucker and trying to think what to say. Then out of nowhere, in climbed Percy Hart, who couldn't have been much more than thirteen and was therefore too young to have known any better. For a moment that looked like it might be it, until one of the Parchman convicts—a small, light-footed character—detached himself from the onlookers and clambered in without so much as a word of greeting.

Three in the canoe. Moss held the oar out to Tucker. "Sam," he said. "C'mon, last chance."

Several minutes had passed since they turned up the canoe. The army barge ought to have been some distance down-river. But there it was, still worrying at the water, holding its position near the jetty. Such was the violence of its movements that Deputy Piper had not yet relaxed his grip on the rail. With his free hand he brought the bullhorn to his face.

"You boys!" he shouted. "Yeah, I see you there, hooch boy. You get out of that thing."

It was funny, Moss thought. Piper had used to play-act being kind. He had said, "Oh, bless your heart" and, "Well, if it isn't Mr Moss" whereas now he said "You boy. You bastard. You nigger," all sorts. He had put all his sweetness away in the dressing-up box.

At the sound of the bullhorn, Percy immediately made to get out. Moss caught him by his overall straps. The convict shimmied backwards to clear more space at the front. "Sam," Moss said. "Last train down to Vicksburg."

Tucker's tired face clenched. He took a limping step forward, reaching out for the oar as though it might break his fall. The man tried to laugh but wound up coughing instead. "Ship of fools, more like," he said.

The canoe kissed the water, turned about and took flight. Moss was at the back, on his knees, his nose flattened against Percy Hart's bumpy spine and all four of them drenched in the space of a second. Tucker hauled the oar head-height or it would have been torn loose or snapped off, and it looked for all the world as though he were waving goodbye to the men on the shore. Last train down to Vicksburg, ship of fools or whatever, they went out to the river as a stone leaves a sling.

The roar of the water drowned out Piper's bullhorn. The red-nosed levee captain raised his revolver and fired, but his aim was all wrong and the bullet went high. If he'd kept his eyes closed he might have had better luck. Both vessels—the rowboat and the barge—were the property of the river now and it dragged them and swung them depending on its mood. And Moss had been wrong, because it was clear that they were moving not down-river but up, and he realized too late that what the barge had been fighting was the funnel of water leading through the crevasse, and this was why its engines had been going full-steam in reverse.

Spray slapped his ears. He clamped a hand to his face to hold his glasses in place, because if he were going to heaven he thought he would at least like to see it. Upfront, Sam Tucker was praying aloud, probably not even conscious he was doing so. "And he lets me lay down in green pastures," he said. "He leadeth me beside quiet waters, shit, hold on, he leadeth me."

Nothing to be done; they were the river's property. The current scooped them and turned them and sighted them at the breach. Then it drove the boat forward among the pinwheeling scraps of wire mesh and wooden posts as Tucker waved his oar for balance. The flow thickened and rose until it became as hard and smooth as glass and it poured them through the gap, through a hard block of shadow and out into daylight again. God's four holy fools: the cropper, the child, the convict and the boy who made music. They rode through the crevasse and came out the other side.

Mrs Elizabeth May Piper was in her favorite chair, admiring her hanging baskets, when she heard a noise from the north, like the morning sky ripped in two. A tremor ran through the ground and the birds left the trees. The baskets shook on their chains; a shingle on the roof was dislodged.

Instinctively, she half-rose and stood for a moment—bent at the waist, her head cocked—until the force of gravity returned her to her seat. "Goodness," she said.

From the town at her back came the sound of church bells—and this, too, was untoward, because it was Thursday, not Sunday, and a full week after Easter. On and on went the bells, turning and turning as though in dispute. And what jumped to mind, of all the foolish things to be thinking, was a story she'd heard about the Virgil slave revolt. This was a tale from long ago, passed on by her mother, although it predated her, too. It told of the hundreds of slaves who had risen up, bent on murder, and advanced in a long line through the field like an army, and how the white wives had rung bells to summon the guns and how in this way the uprising was crushed: the killers cut down, every one, as they crossed the lawn to the house. The way her mother told it, the story had a happy ending. But hearing it as a child had scared her half to death. She was unable to shake the image of all of those men spread out through the field, pulling closer and closer with every running step.

The tremor had run under her feet for a breath, but it left her unsettled; the morning felt out of joint. She thought she'd go and check on Anna, who had a habit of lying in late but who must now be awake. Then she noticed the trashcan in the yard was over on its side. She stepped from the veranda to set it right-side up

It was a handsome house, the Piper residence, and stood apart from its neighbors in that flat open country. The ruby-red gate opened onto the red dirt road and beyond that lay the cotton field and beyond that lay the woods. Elizabeth always said that, were a visitor to drive up from Greenville, the sight of the dust plume on the road gave her just enough time to change her dress, comb her hair and put a pot of coffee on the stove. Sometimes George came home with the boys who he called his deputy's deputies and then instead of coffee she'd put out rye. And then on other occasions he'd drive up on his own like he was in a great hurry and he'd swing his legs from the cab and say, "Upstairs, Missy, quick, I got to put Mr Johnson in you." Elizabeth didn't care for rude talk, especially when Anna might overhear. Nor was she partial to silly schoolboy names. Still, it was nice that a man could hurry home to his wife, aching like a schoolboy even after fifteen years of marriage.

She eased through the gate and stepped into the road. And it came to her then, the other thing that was wrong. She'd been so distracted by the bells that it took her a moment to realize that this was all she was hearing. Normally the air around the house was full of birdsong and buzzing flies. Since that initial loud noise, though, the animals had all fallen silent.

"Goodness," she said.

Elizabeth Piper gazed across the cotton field to the woods. And presently it seemed that something was moving, far away through the trees. It bent the branches like a gale. It popped and crackled like a forest fire.

"Goodness."

The thing came out of the woods and crossed into the cotton, six-feet-high and the color of leather. Too fast to outrun, too broad to outflank. It stretched from one end of the field to the other.

Virgil, she thought. The Virgil plantation slave revolt.

By the time the woman's paralysis broke, the floodline had moved halfway through the bushes. The noise was immense. On the veranda, flanked by the hanging baskets, Anna had her hand to her mouth and was staring owl-eyed, struck dumb.

Elizabeth pulled the gate closed, much good that would do, and ascended the steps on bloodless legs. She said, "Onto the roof, Anna. The quicker the better, my sweet."

The girl stared past her left shoulder. "Is it the levee, Ma?"

They were both speaking so softly, leaning into one another, that they might have been sharing entertaining town gossip. She said, "It's the funniest thing, because at first it made me think of something else from long ago. But yes, it's the levee, it's the Landing, it's caved. Quick as you can, onto the roof, my sweet."

In the course of their journey from one side to the next, Moss Evans had got twisted up, turned about. He righted himself in the tapered rear of the dug-out and hooked his glasses back behind his ears. "Where's Perce?" he asked. All he could see was the convict's wet back.

"Ain't he with you?"

They found him dog-paddling wildly. Waves ran over his head. Moss reached out a hand and was able to haul him on-board. "Am I dead?" asked the boy and Sam Tucker coughed and replied that no, he was not.

The other side. The flooded fields. The current shoved the boat inland but the crests were less violent than they had been at the crevasse. For a minute they saw fences, bushes and small trees. Then the floodwater rose further and these landmarks disappeared. At their backs they were aware of the roar of the river as it shouldered its way through the breach. But the further east they were thrown, even that began to fade.

Tucker risked dropping the oar so as to give his arms a rest. He had the convict reach forward in order to help keep it steady. Moss was aware of the two men talking back-and-forth; taking the measure of each other; establishing whether they might become friends.

Tucker said, "What did you do to get put inside anyhow?"

"Killed my pa and ate him."

"Yeah?" Tucker said, "That's what you did?"

"No," said the convict. "But it would have gone better if I had."

When Noah was away on the Ark with his wife and the kids and the animals bleating and growling on the lower decks, he'd come up with the idea of sending his dove to ascertain how things stood. And eventually this dove had flown back with an olive branch in its beak to prove that land was near. But the fugitives in the boat had no dove to send out. They had the wet clothes on their backs—and that was very nearly it.

Tucker sneezed and turned his head. His scalp was bloodied and his lip had been split. He said, "Please Jesus, a hillside. A roof, a tree, anything."

"How about a chophouse?" the convict said. "How about a hotel?"

"Hello now, room service? Please bring me my supper on a nice silver tray."

"Stop laughing," said Percy. "It ain't funny one bit."

Adjusting his position, meaning to stretch out his legs if he could, Moss felt the strap tighten at his collarbone and was gratified to discover that against the natural run of events, and in spite of the spinning and plunging and turning end over end, he had managed to retain more than the clothes on his back. He swung the case round and set it on his lap.

Still chuckling, relaxing into the experience now, the convict said, "I'll tell you, gentlemen. If we can't find that chophouse, I'm going to have to eat Perce."

Parked at the back, rocked by the waves, Moss paused to allow the merriment to subside. It was replaced by a silence that was almost companionable. He hated to break it but he could not hold his tongue. Some subjects still mattered, even when most of the others did not. So he steadied himself and cleared his throat. He said, "One good thing, though. I still got my guitar."

The river moved through the breach and fanned out through the Delta. Unhurriedly, it flooded the canebrakes, the fields and the woods where red wolves made their dens. It smashed the corn cribs and the planing sheds and gouged out the sawmill foundations so that the supporting walls buckled. It gathered the livestock and stirred them together. It gathered the people and stirred them in, too.

Drawn onto their porches or struck dumb on the street, the citizens heard the coming tide as a rustle through the land, a breeze in the branches. When the sound grew louder they realized what it meant and carried their most valued possessions upstairs, or crawled onto rooftops to lash themselves to their chimneys. Those who were smart opened windows and doors to allow the brown waves the chance to wash through the house. Those who were foolish closed the shutters and sat tight. The floodwater arrived in a leisurely manner. But it struck the buildings broadside with an oil tanker's blunt force.

Downtown, the fire whistle was screaming while every church-bell kept turning. Now the residents stood six deep on the platform, fighting to board the final train going east. Men and women pursued it along the track, pleading with it to stop, clawing at the door handles. The train thundered out of Greenville, kicking sparks, belching steam, and passed through the Delta on its way to higher ground

On either side of the railroad, the cotton and cornfields extended for mile after mile. The passengers sat at the window and anxiously watched them go by. The alluvial plain. The Almighty's tilled soil. The ground here was dark and fine-grained and so rich with nutrients that it was all you could do not to eat it like molasses. It was said that a man could stand in the Delta with a dollar in one hand and a plug of earth in the other and feel safe in the knowledge that the dirt was worth more. The dirt raised the crop and the crop brought the dollar and the dollar in turn built everything else. It built the Greenville Opera House and the Knights of Columbus Hall. It put up collonaded palaces, stocked the stables with thoroughbreds and sent Mississippi's best children to Princeton, Harvard and Brown. A golden southern society; intricate and well-ordered, successful and content, and all of it grown from that black Delta soil.

The river arrived at Greenville that night. The brick buildings were breakwaters and the waves collided at the crossroads. Store-fronts underwater; schoolhouses and restaurants submerged. Nelson Street a torrent. Oil tanks and felled trees. The old world torn down and replaced with the new: a churning brown ocean that rode east for fifty miles.

14

THE FINEST HOUSES are built from love, she said, and pressed his hand for emphasis. You might build a house with bricks or lumber. You might build it with mud and top the roof with thatch. All of these, though, are merely secondary materials, because without love there's no footing, no purpose, and the building will buckle. Comfort Hall, she explained, was a house that was built out of love.

It was also built by a giant, by the renowned Jackson Bird, and perhaps it is true that giants possess a greater capacity for love than the average man—love for country and family; love for God himself. In any case, it was to these hills that Jackson came in the early 1800s, after distinguishing himself in the Indian Wars, and it was here that he resolved to stake his claim. He took a wife at that time, Agnes Powell, and the pair had a habit of strolling the woods and planning their future together. They were going to clear the ground and put up fences. The schoolhouse would sit here and the church would stand there. It was as if they were creating the country every time they walked through.

Upon arriving at a certain unnamed stream, Jackson waded across with the girl in his arms. He would later describe this as his happiest moment. But the steam was deeper than he realized, with the water still chill from the springtime melt. Aggie caught pneumonia and within five days she was dead. To make matters worse, she had passed away without issue.

A tragedy of this magnitude can impact a man in any number of ways. Some men collapse and some go to ground. In the case of Jackson Bird, his wife's demise lit a flame and spurred him to still greater heights. Love does not perish, it simply finds a fresh focus, and for Jackson this focus was the creation of Comfort Hall. He named it Comfort because this is what she provided, during the brief span of months God had allowed them to share. He made it beautiful, like her, with fluted columns and open balconies, double-folding French doors and black-and-white diamond tiling. He made it strong, with solid oak flooring and its walls two-foot thick. Jackson always did say that Aggie had been strong—and no doubt this was true until the day that she went into the stream.

Naturally, in private, the man was bereft. If giants possess a greater capacity for love, it must therefore follow that they feel greater pain. Jackson commissioned a bronze statue to be put up in the grounds. He laid flowers at her grave beneath the chinaberry tree. But all through this mourning, Comfort Hall gave him hope—and as it rose from the land, so his spirits rose, too. Within a year he had taken a second wife, Amy, only fourteen years old on the day of their nuptials, and nine months after that a son and heir was produced. Jackson and Amy went on to have ten children together. All grew to great heights within the walls of Comfort Hall.

Coughlin was presented with the house's full history as he lay on his back in an upstairs chamber, his forehead bandaged, a patch over one eye, while Mrs Gwendolyn Bird sat at his bedside with her knitting and a small silver bell she would periodically shake to fetch the servants. He figured she must have been talking for several hours before he had fully regained consciousness because he woke from a dream of Confederate soldiers who brought him bouquets of flowers and declared undying love.

He wished he could see her more clearly: she was like a vision herself. The swell and dip of her voice made him think of warm thermals. But his head pulsed and his eye was sore and his right hand was swollen and would neither open nor close. In almost any other circumstances, he would have thought himself blessed to have Gwen Bird by his bed.

She said, "So much has changed, Mr Coughlin. Storms and dark forces. The country is in turmoil. Civilization is under threat. But the greater the changes in the world at large, the more we cleave to the old traditions. The chinaberry still stands where Jackson Bird planted it. The statue he built still catches the sunlight. And our five children still play where his ten used to play. All of this is so reassuring to me."

He stared at her through his good eye. "Five? You have five children?"

"You sound surprised."

"I am a little."

She smiled. "That's not so many. It isn't ten."

"No," he said. "But five, good God."

The fight at the trailers raised a commotion. The dogs had been barking. The drunken lovers had fled. Then the Grady boys had run in to prevent further damage. The Grady boys, she explained, were about the sweetest and funniest trio of brothers in the county. Ordinarily they wouldn't so much as hurt a fly. But each knew to stand tall when they witnessed an injustice, which is what they had done, and rather more besides. She understood that the principal culprit, the youth with the duster, had since been diagnosed with a broken back.

"Jesus."

Gwen shook her head. She said, "It is terribly sad. But well, one reaps what one sows."

He had dozed for a spell and sat up with a start. "I had a van in the lot—a panel delivery. My recording equipment. There were some cases in the back."

"Hush. They are safe. The vehicle is now parked outside the Hall."

Relieved, he settled back and mentally willed her to stay. He liked the click of her needles and the climb and dive of her voice.

"We have many people who are most eager to meet you," she said. "Colonel Bird, first and foremost. But also the children. And we have my brother here, too." She dropped a stitch and retrieved it. "This very morning, after breakfast, all three Grady boys called to ask how you were. They lined up at the door with their little hats in their hands and not a mark on their faces, as pink and clean as newborns, and they said, 'Please, Miss Gwendolyn, is the northern gentleman well?'. And I said, 'Certainly he's well. But he is concussed and he's bruised. Come back when he's recovered and is able to thank you in person'."

Fuzzily, drifting off again, he promised that he would. Finally, more fuzzily, he said he ought to thank her as well. His savior, his nurse. The companion at his bedside.

"Bless you," she said. "You ought to thank Colonel Bird."

He had heard that most of the plantation homes had gone to rack and ruin, but Comfort Hall—framed by live oaks, surrounded by farmland—remained in decent working order. Its diamond tile flooring was soaped and swabbed every morning. The doors were opened and closed in rotation to allow the April air through the rooms. Released from his sickbed, he picked his way downstairs, past the somber gaze of the elderly houseboy, Nicholas. The Bird offspring—identically dressed in white sailor suits—bid him a sing-song good morning before continuing with their games. One boy, the smallest, liked to ride on the banister, brandishing the maid's broom as a lance. Another—so far as he could tell, the only girl of the five—banged a piano inexpertly behind the music room door.

At the head of the stairs stood a portrait of a handsome, head-strong-looking gentleman on horseback. But although Coughlin saw his guns and his boots and the mounted remains of the animals he'd shot, the Colonel was conspicuous by his absence that day. He had set out before dawn to go riding with friends. Sometimes he broke the night at a hunting lodge in the hills. Sometimes he broke two. The men of that country were perpetually wanting to saddle up and set forth. No house, however large and well-appointed, could contain them for long.

He assumed that Gwen's brother, Comfort Hall's other guest,

must be out riding too, but she said he was not. "He is convalescing, like you."

"Nothing serious, I hope."

The woman smiled but she looked downcast. "My brother is a clever, successful young man. If he has a weakness it is that he over-taxes himself and suffers—well, I suppose you would call it a nervous collapse."

It was some comfort, Coughlin decided, to have another invalid in the house. Another idiot who had over-reached. Another arrogant chancer who'd been crushed and humiliated. But Gwen was having none of it. She regarded Mr Coughlin's misfortune as a temporary setback, all part and parcel of an adventurous life. They would have him back on his feet in no time and after that he could continue with the job he'd come to do, recording the region's hill country musicians. The eye patch, she joked, would be a fitting adornment. It gave him the air of a story-book buccaneer.

"It's funny," she confessed. "When they first brought you up and checked your paperwork, we worried you might be a recruiter from the north."

"Ah," he said. "No."

"You may laugh, Mr Coughlin, but this has become a quite serious problem. Recruiters from the north, wanting to round up our negroes. They lure folk off the land with false promises of a better life and then, sure enough, they set them to work in foundries and factories where they never see the light of day."

Coughlin shook his head. "I'm not that kind of catcher."

"Of course not," she said. "You are a catcher of songs."

At the polished bathroom mirror, he lifted the patch to inspect the damage. The eye was half-closed and the yolk remained red. His brow had scabbed over. Probably he'd be left with a scar. He had started his journey as an unremarkable man. He'd finish it as a gargoyle, forever dented and strange.

He had assumed he'd wake early, but had lain in bed until nine.

The Bird children were playing tic-tac-toe on the diamond tiles in the hall. Were it not for their noise he might have slept even later.

The children bowed at the waist when he descended the stairs. Coughlin had an idea that they were play-acting the formality, pretending that they were the footmen and he was the king.

Feeling foolish, he attempted a bow in return. "Good morning," he said. "What day is it today?"

"Friday," said the middle boy. "April 22."

"Friday." He whistled. "As late as all that?"

The small library smelled of cigar smoke and parchment. He studied the shelves until he found what he wanted: a Rand McNally road atlas to show him the way back home. On a blotter he mapped out the route, circling up through the Smoky Mountains this time. Huntsville, Crossville, Middlesboro, Hazard.

The library door opened and the eldest boy sauntered in. He was dressed like his siblings, in dark blue knickers and a sailor blouse, with oversized tassels that leapt with each step. The child was too old to be put in costume, Coughlin thought, although he seemed unembarrassed by the get-up and carried himself with a princely air. In a comical basso-profundo voice, he said, "Please call me Joshua. We haven't yet had the chance to converse man-to-man."

Coughlin stifled a sigh. He set aside the road atlas. "Joshua, I'd like to shake hands," he said. "But I had to knock down a bad man at the fair. And see, my paw is still a little swollen."

Joshua appeared to weigh this information. He frowned for a moment and then his face cleared again. "Mama informs us that you are a song-catcher. She says that you made the Spider Joe song, or were responsible for it in some way."

"Yes, that's true. A scary song for stormy nights."

"We liked it, I'll confess. Everybody enjoyed it around here."

He had hoped the boy might leave him in peace after that. But it transpired that Joshua had a surfeit of time on his hands. He plopped himself onto the armchair opposite and thumbed at the catch of a silver case on the desk. Coughlin decided to risk returning to his book.

"How about a cigar?"

"No," he said shortly. "No thank you, Joshua."

"You don't mind if I do."

Coughlin looked up. "I don't," he said carefully. "But I worry that your parents would."

"My parents."

"Well, your mother, certainly. But maybe Colonel Bird, too."

Joshua blinked. The fetching frown had returned. He said, "Mr Coughlin, you are confused. I dare say that it's an effect of concussion."

In Mott Haven one summer there had been a troupe of small clowns who performed cartwheels and pratfalls. Coughlin, not yet ten, had been transfixed by the clowns and shouted, "Da, look at the midgets" and his father had hushed him and said they were not midgets but dwarfs. "You got to get smarter," his old man had said. "Think for a second before you open your mouth."

Colonel Bird of Alabama was, strictly speaking, neither a midget nor a dwarf. Nonetheless he was five-feet tall and built along the lines of a boy nearing puberty, with slender wrists, smooth skin and pink ears. The grand oil portrait did him no justice at all. Coughlin felt his heart lurch. Were it not for the relative gloom of the room, he might have known sooner and been able to cover his tracks. Up close, the man had crow's feet and appeared to be graying at the temples. Colonel Bird, he now saw, was older than his wife by some considerable margin.

The Colonel clipped the end of his cigar. "We had the small trunks from your motor brought into the house. Am I correct in surmising that they are some form of oral recording equipment?"

"A recording lathe. Very expensive. It was almost my first thought when I woke up." He was struggling to regroup. His mouth had gone dry. He said, "Never mind, it's safe. Thanks for bringing it in."

"We are musical people in these parts, it's true. Not me, I confess,

I am an outdoorsman. But Mama. My brother-in-law." His features registered a momentary distaste. "Also, you will have heard Bonnie practicing on the grand piano. I dare say she is not up to your standard quite yet. But what she lacks in expertise, she makes up for in . . ."

"Vigor?"

"The real feather in our cap, so far as I'm concerned, are the Grady boys. These are the brothers who saved your skin at the fair."

He nodded. "I'd like to thank them if I can."

"The Grady boys sing in blood harmony." He fixed Coughlin with a look of queer intensity. "You understand what I mean by blood harmony?"

"I was wanting to ask what became of the pair who jumped me. The brother and sister. Morton Haines is his name."

Colonel Bird relaxed. "Morton Haines is not his name. Believe me, that boy is well known to us here."

"Your wife, Gwen. She said that he ended up badly hurt."

The Colonel sucked the cigar and blew smoke through his nose. The smoke was only one shade darker than his white sailor blouse. "Broke his back," he said. "The Grady boys."

He had a horse, Cadmus, that would tolerate no one else on its back. He'd walk to the stables in the half-light of dawn and the animal would recognize the weight and span of his stride and start kicking at the stall in its eagerness to be out. They would ride through the fields, the Colonel bouncing on the saddle, his knees locked about Cadmus's flanks until they became almost indivisible, like one of the centaurs that were reputed to have scared the Iroquois. As a boy he'd learned the art of good horsemanship to the point where he could mold himself to the animal's rhythm, let the reins drop and bring around a rifle in both hands. Cadmus would feel the shift of his weight and slow the pace just a hair, which was all he required to sight the barrel and shoot. "That's the Colonel out shooting again," the county mothers would tell their children. "You know how you can tell it's the Colonel? Because there was only one shot. The other hunters need two."

He was descended, they said, from the horse-lords of Alabama and could never abide being indoors for too long. Never happier or more alive than when he was riding the country with a gun in his hand, blasting bears, deer and bobcats, whatever crossed his path. All being well, he would prefer not to add the Kennards' dog to the list, but was resigned to the possibility that one day he just might. The Kennards, a family of colored tenant farmers, worked the southern strip of his land. They weren't the worst tenants he had, but they owned a large, ugly hound—predominantly Irish setter—that had once barked at Bonnie and made her cry out from fear. So, what with riding up to the Thorburns' farm, where the grandfather was dying, or down to the Kennards' farm to scold them about the dog, it seemed to him that he spent most of his days in the saddle. Back and forth, up and down, the stony ground running through his system like a woodpecker's tattoo. And despite his youthful bearing, he was no longer a young man. He joked that he rode home with aches in places he didn't even know he had.

In the evening, then, the Colonel had a routine. First, he'd have Nicholas run a hot bath and add rosemary sprigs. After that he'd order the foldaway table to be opened on the upstairs landing so that Butterscotch—the youngest and prettiest of the Hall's housemaids—could give him an athlete's massage. The Colonel liked the upstairs landing because the window was large and it took the late light, and because it meant that the children, passing by on their gallop from one game to the next, would occasionally gather at the table to talk. Only after a rub-down did he feel ready for dinner. He could not relax into the night with his muscles bunched-up.

Arranging the towel on the table, Gwen said, "This is a course of treatment that I would also commend to you, Mr Coughlin. My husband says Butterscotch is a miracle worker."

"Thank you," he said. "No."

Gwen caught his discomfort and was amused by it. "There is no need to be bashful. It is an athlete's massage."

The window gave out on Comfort Slope, which rose from the creek that Jackson and Aggie once crossed. Family legend had it that, after completing the house, Jackson went in search of another grand project and had eventually alighted on the business of air travel. For years he worked at a variety of flying machines that would be run or pushed on Comfort Slope. The early models all failed—but then, at a relatively advanced age, Jackson Bird finally put himself aloft in a conveyance that he operated by rotating a horizontal bar with his feet. The spinning bar turned the wings and in this way he was able to fly for three minutes at a stretch. When the definitive history of aviation was written, Colonel Bird expected his ancestor's exploits to merit a standalone chapter.

Pink from his bath, a towel around his middle, he arranged himself on his front and turned his head to one side. Butterscotch stole in from an adjacent room. The girl had her hair pinned and her smock-sleeves rolled. She said, "Good evening, Mr Colonel" and, receiving no reply, bent to run her fingernails up the length of his legs.

The charge of the connection inexplicably jumped from the Colonel to Coughlin and made the catcher's scalp prickle. The man on the table remained as still as marble. "Horses," he said. "Airplanes. And yes, I'll admit, we produce fine music also."

The children thundered by, brandishing mops and brooms. The girl paid them no mind. Having completed her work on the Colonel's legs, she switched her attention to his back, using the heel of her hands in a circular motion. So far as Coughlin could tell, the housemaid's massage did not involve any great exertion. Nonetheless, he could see that her chest was heaving and the nape of her neck was glossy with sweat, which suggested the process must be more arduous than it looked. He was about to make his escape when the man spoke again.

"Butterscotch doesn't sing—not that we've ever heard. But

Nicholas, he sings. Plantation songs. Colored songs. What was the song we had Nicholas sing for Mama's birthday last year?"

On a breath, almost moaning, she said, "I can't recall, Mr Colonel."

"Something about chickens. Something about sleeping. Say, you may want to record Nicholas on that recording machine, too."

Coughlin cleared his throat. "I'm more in the market for hill-country music. Old-time pieces. My employers in New York, they don't go in for race music."

"Race music?"

"Plantation songs." He risked a glance at the girl. "Colored songs."

"I understand," said the Colonel. "We shall limit ourselves to the Grady boys."

Where Butterscotch dragged her nails, the Colonel's flushed skin came up white. She drew lines on his legs and his arms and his neck. She tousled his hair and inserted her thumbs in his ears. Passing by, her skirts swinging, Gwen Bird laughed in delight at the sight. She said, "Bless your heart, Butterscotch, what a treasure you are."

"Tell the hens and tell the gander," the Colonel said. "Me like to sleep beneath the master's veranda."

Gwen raised an eyebrow. She looked to Coughlin for assistance.

The Colonel said, "Nicholas's party piece. The plantation song."

"Why yes, of course. My birthday party."

The trouble with these people, Coughlin thought, was they got so knotted up about race. The Colonel was an outright bigot. His tragedy was that he didn't even know it. But maybe every white man in the south took a similar view. He thought of Stubb, the hotel manager, who had refused to allow the Copeland singers inside to audition. Or Bucky Garner, friendly and charming with everyone else, who had a habit of clicking his fingers to shoo black pedestrians from his path. Probably even Gwen disdained black folk on the sly. Coughlin wasn't sure if that was her tragedy, exactly, but it was certainly his. During his time at the house he'd grown to like her a great deal.

Athlete's massage or whatever, the business on the table was nearing its crescendo. Butterscotch spread her hands on the Colonel's back. Her forearms tensed; a moan escaped her lips. Descending the stairs, speaking over her shoulder, Gwen said, "There, you see, Mr Coughlin. What man could refuse such expert treatment?"

"Do my undercarriage next," the Colonel said indistinctly. "The saddle has rubbed it all black and blue."

So as to avoid the sight of the Colonel's undercarriage, Coughlin whipped his head to face the glass. Outside lay the slope where Jackson Bird had launched—or tried to launch—his flying machines. Most, it was said, had belly-flopped the instant they were rolled off the ramp and it was not until the construction of Aggie XII that Jackson could claim to have made his breakthrough. The rotating bar. The dihedral planes. He rose over the heads of the men and women who'd gathered—and reportedly over the roof of Comfort Hall itself—before landing unscathed in an easterly meadow. This same meadow, incidentally, would later play host to the Herbie Lax carnival.

Coughlin was skeptical. "When did this happen? Aggie XII and the powered flight?"

"A long time ago. The 1840s, I believe."

He turned back from the window and saw that the danger had passed: Butterscotch was now rubbing away at her master's feet. "But those dates can't be right. You're saying you had a working airplane here in the 1840s?"

"He was an exceptional man, my great-grandfather. His achievements, you might say, simply beggar belief."

Coughlin laughed. "I would say that, yes."

Butterscotch drove in her thumbs and grunted from the strain. But still the Colonel remained motionless. His head was turned to the side and his pink face was creased. He said, "What have you been taught in your northern schools, Mr Coughlin? It is all fiction, all lies. These are the true facts that you're hearing today. The real southern history. The Birds of Alabama."

15

H E WAS IN the library when he heard the sound: crude chords played on a good guitar. The structure was shot and the melody skipped. The arrangement was strange, it didn't remotely add up. He opened the French doors and stepped outside, drawn by the music and yet suspicious of it, too, as though he recognized it even then as a work in translation—the shadow of the thing as opposed to the object itself.

The veranda was dark. Brown moths brushed the glass. There was a young man in the rocker, a Gibson guitar on his lap. He had stopped picking the instant the song-catcher walked out. This made Coughlin wish that he had kept himself hidden.

"Miss Gwen's brother. I'm guessing that's you."

The musician smiled at his hands. Even in the gloom Coughlin thought it a poor excuse for a smile.

"Mr Coughlin," he said. "Mr Coughlin, the catcher."

He had previously worked as an engineer out of state and one day would again, assuming there was a job to go back to. Assuming there was a state to go back to. For the time being he was content to sit on the veranda and follow the news from afar. Hundreds of square miles underwater. The Red Cross boating in, the evacuees boating out. Terrible situation. A thousand drowned and lost souls. The man laughed and apologized and twisted his pretty mouth in a smile. There was nothing funny about it all, he admitted.

Coughlin hesitated. "This is recent? This is happening now?"

"Yesterday. This morning." But it had been coming for years and no one, it seemed, had paid any mind. Not the men at the River Commission. Not the men on the levee board. Not the National

Guard or the state legislature, absolutely no one except him, much good it had done, shouting his pitiful little warnings as the river rose day-by-day.

A wicker chair stood by the door. Coughlin pulled it over. He said, "That piece you were playing . . ."

"On the wireless they are saying the Delta is flooded. All of it. The entirety."

"Yeah, it sounds bad, a disaster." He attempted a joke. "That piece sounds bad, too. Even so, it's got something. It's interesting, it's unusual."

"All of it, Mr Coughlin. The place won't ever be the same again."

"No doubt. That's terrible." One of the brown moths tapped his ear.

There had been a boy on the levee—a negro hooch-boy by the name of Moss Evans. It had been this boy, Blind Moss, who had taught the songs to Gwen's brother. It was Gwen's brother who had then carried them with him when he left Mississippi. Not physically, he added, that would be too much to ask. What he meant was that he had transported them in his head and his heart. They were his souvenirs from the Delta; possibly the only things that got out.

He looked up at Coughlin, still laboring to maintain his sad smile. He said, "How much would you pay for Delta songs such as these?"

"I'm not even sure that they're songs," Coughlin said. "I don't know what they are. Maybe a song's distant cousin."

"I like that," Miles Craven said. "That's pleasingly poetic. A song's distant cousin."

They sat on the veranda, the two convalescents. Craven picked out several more pieces, mumbling the words because he explained that this hooch-boy, Blind Moss, mostly sang scat anyway. He said that the bulk of the songs were incomplete, or unfinished, and were possibly never intended to be finished, because Moss changed them each time he played them, so that the pieces never truly settled and firmed up. Then he laughed and said that they were at least settled now. The river had stepped in and finished Moss's songs for good.

Coughlin nodded. "So he's dead then, this picker?"

"Oh, quite likely, I'm afraid. If he was on the levee, quite likely."

Coughlin had hoped that Gwen might eventually join them outside, but it seemed that she was busy supervising the children's bedtime, which left just them and the moths and the faraway bark of a dog. The way Gwen had described Comfort Hall, sitting at his bedside, he had pictured the house as a medieval castle, perhaps even surrounded by stone walls and a moat. She had made the place sound ancient, heavy and ironclad, which didn't seem to be the case at all. So far as Coughlin could tell, Comfort Hall was a standard southern plantation house, made elegant to disguise its flyweight nature. He could feel the boards of the veranda shift under his weight. The French doors conversed every time the wind blew. He liked Comfort Hall, but it was no different from every other country joint that he'd passed; perched on the landscape, scratched into the soil. Never mind a giant flood, he doubted the place would survive a single night of heavy gales.

Craven gripped the fingerboard and worked his way through another of the pieces the hooch boy had taught him. Coughlin shut his eyes and listened hard. The phrasing was wild; the changes were shocks. The melody jinxed left when he thought it was about to turn right. "Jesus," he laughed. "Everything about it is wrong."

"Interesting, though. And as you said, unusual."

"Interesting, sure. But that doesn't mean that it's good."

Huntsville, Crossville and Middlesboro. Then upwards and onwards, into the coal-mining country around Hazard. He'd be working blind, but he might strike lucky; plenty of miners played music on the side. Crucially, too, it meant that he was heading in the right direction. He would be traveling north. He would be on his way home.

"Interesting," he said. "It's got that at least."

Tomorrow, ideally, he'd make his excuses and leave. Would his hosts regard it as rude if he absconded so soon? Or would it somehow be ruder if he stayed another few days? The finer details of southern manners. It seemed that whatever he did, he caught the locals by surprise. Given the choice, he'd leave tomorrow. That said, he was conscious of the fact that Gwen and the Colonel had been generous hosts and might even have saved his life. He had no wish to behave in a way that might cause offense.

Also, he remembered, he had half-made a promise. "I can't leave for another day or two. I said I'd record the Grady boys."

"The Grady boys." Craven missed his stroke. "The Grady boys are savages."

If he were reassembling the lathe for the Grady boys, he figured he might as well record Gwen's brother as well. The young man would love that, he could tell; the hope clung to him like a stink. And if this were the cost of bed, board and medical treatment, so be it. Four sides of bad music. Coughlin might not even have to pay for them, because the very act of recording would be seen as a payment in itself. But if he had to part with another $120, he decided that Humpty could take the hit. A few sides of bad music: it was part and parcel of every catcher's haul.

Record Gwen's brother, then, what the hell? Because it was true what he'd said, the pieces were interesting. With a little fine-tuning they might become more than that. So what if they were Craven's misinterpretations of songs he'd been taught elsewhere? So what if they were all learned, not instinctual. So what if this man, nice as he was, clearly had no feel for music? Back in Manhattan, the Humpty house band made copies of original, better work. The musicians listened to Did You Ever Dream a Dream and repeated it back as Did You Ever Dream of Jean. Here in Alabama, he decided, Mr Miles Craven was doing something similar.

"You are lost in thought, Mr Coughlin."

"I am," he said. "There's a lot to consider."

Out in the darkness, the farm dog was still barking. On and on it went, like a barn door in the wind. Craven said that this was likely the ugly mongrel at the Kennards' shack, the hound that often got loose and had once spooked his niece. He didn't much care for dogs, but had grown quite partial to this one, due to the fact that it so annoyed Colonel Bird. Every time the hound barked, it made the Colonel jump and turn red and this was funny to witness, a welcome distraction. Probably one day it would all be too much. The Colonel would seize his shotgun, tear away down the track, blasting away at every breath of wind in the trees. That's just how he was built. He was a silly, hot-tempered fellow.

"The first time I saw him . . ." Coughlin caught himself. "Never mind, it doesn't matter."

"You thought he was one of the children."

"I did, yeah."

Craven chuckled. "It's a common mistake."

If the situation were different, he might even have added a few more days to his trip. If he were less spent, less beat-up. If the land wasn't flooded. If the kid wasn't dead.

"Pick me out another of those things," he said, because if everything had been different, it might have been worth the gamble. Forget the impostor. Forget the Grady boys. Leave the recording lathe in its packing cases upstairs. And after that, what? Drive west, fetch the kid. Record him back at Comfort Hall.

He glanced up. "How long would it take me to get there and back, do you think?"

"There? There is no there, Mr Coughlin. The entire Delta, it's flooded out."

"Yeah, I get that, I know. I'm only thinking aloud."

If catchers had a failing, Honest Jim used to say, it was that the good ones—the great ones—never knew when to quit. They were never settled, never satisfied. They were always off chasing the next big fish. Yonder, they called it, as though that were a place. Yonder mountain, yonder stars.

Craven brushed at a moth that had landed on his sleeve. "You might record me tomorrow," he said. "And then the Gradys on Sunday afternoon, after church."

"Yeah." Coughlin nodded. "That makes sense, yeah." But his

thoughts were elsewhere. Looking back on it now, it seemed that this, his first trip to the Corners, had begun not in Lower Manhattan or on the Hoboken ferry, but at the Bide-a-Wee outside Harpers Ferry, beneath the antler chandeliers in the trophy room. "Bad weather a-coming," the innkeeper had said. Torrential rain, snowstorms, flooded rivers, upturned cars.

There had been three of them in the room that first night, he told Craven. Two song-catchers and him, who was not really a catcher at all. An Italian, a Jew, and an Irishman, like a trio of fools at the start of a joke. Coughlin had stared at the fire and listened as the two men talked shop, minded to memorize everything that they said; studying their body language, the stylish cut of their suits. These men were his instructors. They were the best catchers in the land. But they weren't on the same page and went about life differently. Rinaldi, the Italian, was cautious, superstitious. He carried lucky stones in his pockets and refused to catch on Monday. He checked the ground before driving, wore his St Christopher on the road. Whereas Jim Cope, Honest Jim, was cool and unruffled; he was in control at all times. Coughlin liked Rinaldi. He even admired Rinaldi. But Honest Jim was a legend and existed on a different plane altogether. In his wildest dreams, then, Coughlin wanted to be like Honest Jim, pushing south through the Corners in search of treasure. Probably in search of danger, too, because without the danger, what's the point?

"The biggest dragons," Craven murmured. "The richest treasure."

"The thing is, he never got as far south as this, Honest Jim. He never got to Alabama. He barely got to Tennessee."

Craven was picking idly at the strings. "He will be impressed with you, then, I dare say. When you return to New York."

"No, he won't, that's the thing. The man died on the road."

Craven stopped picking. "He died?"

"He's dead." And there was something about this blunt back-and-forth that struck him as funny. He's dead? Who's dead? He died? He's dead. What was it about death that made men want to laugh?

Was it because they saw death as simply too vast to deal with? The greatest danger, the biggest dragon. Do men laugh because they're powerless? Or do we laugh out of joy because the deaths of others means that, for the time being, the rest of us are still alive?

"He's dead," Coughlin said. "His car went off the road. So after that, it was me and Rinaldi left."

His adventure had begun at the Bide-a-Wee beside the river. From there he had traveled down the spine of Appalachia, in and out of the mountain towns, searching for something; he couldn't even say what it was. And at every fork in the road he had asked himself the same question, "What would Jim Cope do?" and each time he knew the answer. He'd go yonder, he'd look harder, because that's what great catchers did. And so that's what he'd done, or tried to do, because he was largely learning the trade as he went along. But the more a man learns, the more he comes to trust his own judgment. The more he then starts to question everything he's been taught.

It had turned cold on the veranda. He might soon step inside.

"Stay awhile," said Miles Craven. "I am enjoying our conversation."

Well, here it was, Coughlin thought, another fork in the road. Comfort Hall, Alabama. Turn left or turn right? The music was strange, it might even be great. But enough, he decided. Enough now, it is done. He had learned some important life lessons these past few days.

"The thing is," he said. "The thing is, he was wrong and that's why he's dead. It came to me just now, sitting here, thinking."

"What came to you?"

"It's the opposite of what he said," Coughlin said. "The good catcher isn't the one who keeps going. It's the one who knows when it's time to quit." He smiled in the darkness; his mind was made up. Tomorrow, after breakfast, he would turn the van to the north. Tomorrow or the next day or the day after that.

16

TO GUARANTEE A warm welcome, carry a prop in your hands. Something practical and cumbersome. The heavier the better, in fact, because the empty-handed man is a loiterer or worse, whereas a man with full hands has authority and purpose. He's come to help out, so open up, let him in.

Back in Mott Haven, before he cleaned up his act, he had once robbed the payroll at the Fiesel factory, armed with nothing more than the stepladder he'd seen propped against the side of the janitor's hut. The ladder had been his magic key. The freckled Irish guard bid him a merry good morning. The employees obligingly held open the doors. He walked it into accounts, took the money and left. Outside, pockets full, he had propped the stepladder right back where he'd found it.

He parked in the lot, on the last patch of dry ground and joined the line of tired men passing sacks of grain to be loaded. After a few minutes of this back-and-forth, he tottered down to the duckboard jetty with a sack clasped to his chest. In the boat, two darkened figures sat amid the bags and boxes. The nearest—a Red Cross volunteer—shimmied across to give him room.

The other figure—the boatman—bled the engine and got it turning. He registered Coughlin's presence with barely a glance. "I thought the rest of you fellows were staying put."

"I did, too," Coughlin said. "It's fucking chaos back there." And it was as simple as that. He had passed; he was in.

The sea-sled left the jetty and turned west out of town, past the scaffold of electric lights and the upper stories of gingerbread homes. He looked over his shoulder, checking whether he could still see his van and the line of relief workers on the waterline, but it seemed that the night had already swallowed them all.

He realized the sack of grain was still in his lap. "How long until Greenville?"

"Several hours," the boatman said. "Relax, my friend, enjoy the view."

They left the drowned road and nosed out to the Delta. The darkness now was almost total but the faint light that remained played tricks on sore eyes. Here and there he made out black shapes—the square sides of a barn, the softer lines of a tree—and these made him think the flood was not especially deep. But such was the sense of space all around that it was hard to judge distance or to tell how fast the boat was traveling.

Also, the buildings moved, the Red Cross worker told him. The cabins and cotton houses. They wandered about.

Coughlin nodded. "It does look that way"

"It is that way," said the Red Cross worker, whose name was Oxley. "No joke, it's true. The buildings move. Not all, but some."

The day before this man, Oxley, had spotted a family camped out on their roof. Father and mother. Three small 'uns and a dog. He'd drawn alongside to let the family get in. But no sooner had the children dropped into the boat than the house itself began to list on one side and rise up on the other. It was only the combined weight of the family that had been holding it in one place.

"Barn-sides and roofs. Railroad ties, fences. Round and round in the water, like a lazy tornado."

"Bodies, too," the boatman said.

"Sure, bodies too. Except that bodies ain't going to capsize us. Bodies ain't going to knock us into splinters."

The boatman was doubtful. "Hog's body might. Horse's body might."

"Lonnie Hargrave," said Oxley and Coughlin took this to be a joke because the men's prolonged silent laughter rocked the boat from side to side.

Oxley and the boatman: they were black shapes themselves. He knew them by their voices and by the movements they made. Oxley was a scratcher, a fidgeter, whereas the boatman kept steady. Come to that, what was he to them? Just another dark figure with a sack of grain in its lap.

"Like a mixing bowl," the boatman said. "You say tornado, I say bowl."

"If it's a mixing bowl, who's mixing?"

"Well, God, who else? The big man with his spoon."

"Ain't God with the spoon. It's the other fella's got the spoon."

All day, all night, the boatman made his trip across the flooded Delta, ferrying supplies into Greenville, ferrying survivors out. Until last week he'd been a bootlegger, moving barrels on the Mississippi. Now he assisted the relief effort, working alongside the Guardsmen and the Red Cross volunteers. The bootleggers, he explained, ran the quickest boats on the river, discounting the pirates and you couldn't recruit pirates. Their boats were like lightning but they were not men to be trusted. That, he reckoned, was what made them pirates to begin with.

Oxley chuckled. "Even in a national emergency, you got to keep some standards."

"Maybe more so. Otherwise what's the point?'

This was his third day with the relief effort. His fourth, come to that, given that it was now past midnight. The first day was like showing up at the tail-end of a drunken party. Everyone waving shotguns and screaming from their rooftops. The second day was different. The dogs had stopped barking and the rooftops were mostly empty. Maybe that was good and maybe it was bad, it was probably too early to say, but there was no doubt it made these back-and-forth trips more efficient. Easier to do the job if you're not zigging and zagging to pick up castaways.

"What a mess," Oxley said.

"No argument there."

"I heard that they put every colored man on the levee. It's like a prison out there."

"Prison, hell. They're all fed and watered. They're on dry land, they're fine."

The Red Cross worker plucked at his jockeys and resettled himself on the bench. "One thing I will say, Hoover's the man charged with cleaning up this mess. And if he does it, I'll bet, he's our next president."

"Who's doing it, though?"

"I just said. Hoover."

"So you don't know his name."

"Hoover. Herbert Hoover."

"Oh," said the boatman. "I thought you said 'whoever'."

"You thought what?"

"Whoever's in charge. Whoever's doing it." Their silent laughter rocked the boat again.

Halfway to Greenville, whatever that meant. Halfway along his fool's errand, discounting the fact that he then had to get out. When Miles Craven said flood, Coughlin had pictured boggy roads, submerged fields and cheerful men passing buckets. He'd not pictured this: floating houses, dead bodies. He'd not pictured this: mile after mile of black ocean. And what awaited on the other side? A hooch-boy musician who was in all likelihood drowned.

He dozed for a spell, upright on the bench, and on waking was told that they had another hour still to go. He guessed the boat must be on the right course but there was no way to be certain, he had to take it on trust. On the open water, the boatman navigated by the telephone poles. He followed the line across the Delta and back.

Coughlin squinted. "I can't see any poles."

"He's got city eyes," said the boatman, addressing Oxley. Except that now, peering hard, Coughlin believed he could half-make them out. Threads of black on a field of black. The poles traced the line of the road between the city of Greenford and the city of Greenville and this therefore must mean that the sea-sled did, too. It was riding west on the same route that had been used by cars, trucks and buggies in the reassuring old world of three days before.

"Unless all of them have come loose as well," Oxley said.

"Oh sure," said the boatman. "You've got to accept that possibility."

"All of the poles pulled up by their roots and left to float where they want. Then what are we following? Where are they taking us?"

"Round and round the mixing bowl," said the boatman, although on this occasion neither man chose to laugh.

One time, half awake, Coughlin saw a large shape break the surface and roll. This was likely the carcass of a horse or a cow, although its unhurried movement had seemed sentient and even sensual, as if what he had witnessed was some exotic sea mammal swimming up from the depths so as to sip the night air. The thought turned his stomach. He crossed his arms to stay warm. He said, "You know what this feels like? It feels like the end of the world."

17

WHEN THE RIVER came dragging through the fields outside town, it had carried a jon-boat right up to her porch. Knock-knock, said the jon-boat, rubbing itself sidelong against the wooden steps like a cat, until she consented to step in and be saved. The engine turned over and the brown current swelled. And just like that, as they say, she was free, she had risen.

In the weeks, months and years leading up to that moment, Mrs Darryl Benton of Washington County had not been free, nor anything remotely resembling it. She had been trapped and submerged; she had been a woman laid low. Weighed down by sacks of meal and pails of water and by the baskets of laundry from the white folks in town. Weighed down by Darryl, Lord bless him, laid on her like a wardrobe with its hard little key sticking out. Day after day, chore after chore, no rest for the wicked, the sharecropper's wife. Then the river arrived to change everything at a stroke. The entire country transformed. All of its people as well. She said, "If you came here last Thursday, you'd have met a nice washer woman named Mrs Darryl Benton."

"And who are you now?"

"They call me the Troller. I'm out fishing all day."

He shielded his eyes with the flat of his hand. "The what?"

"The Troller," she said. "You want me to spell it?"

Specifically what she fished were the corpses of those who had drowned in the flood. Her rod, she explained, was the hooked stick which had previously been used to open the upper windows in the schoolhouse. If the body was light (a slim woman; a child) she would reach over the side and haul it aboard. If it were heavy, she tied it and tugged it and rode back into town with a train of tethered floaters. Mother Goose and her goslings. She brought them all safely home.

"Home?" Coughlin said.

"Upper floor of the lumber mill. Set them in rows. Salt and ice every one." She caught his reaction and grinned. "Why, you got to salt and ice them cos they all filled up with river water, they all on the turn. Salt and ice takes them back to their normal size."

He said he would have to take her word for this.

"Yes sir." She grinned crookedly. "Little pinch of salt brings everybody down to size."

Greenville had become a kind of Venice, it was said: a city of canals, with raised wooden sidewalks and sunlight bouncing off the greasy water. Wherever he turned, he heard the thump of gumboots on duckboards and the squeak of wet ropes against posts. Men clambered in and out of windows like thieves. Sandbags got under his feet at street corners. A new town had been scaffolded over the lines of the old.

For several hours he stationed himself at the Red Cross hub, standing in line, passing cornbread and milk. The scene stirred a memory of Spider Joe's hunting ground by the El: the same huddle of beat-down, hungry men shuffling their feet to keep warm; the same sense of surging traffic all around, except that the traffic in Greenville was the floodwater itself. It roared downtown and crosstown and collided at the intersections in whisked whites of foam.

He had cooked up a story and tinkered with it on the boat. In this tale he was a Red Cross worker from the camp across the water. Spirits were low at the tent city back east. The evacuees were in terrible shape. Countless bereavements; children in tears. It might therefore be nice to lay on some musical entertainment. He'd heard of a hooch boy on the levee who was said to be good with a guitar and had been sent to Greenville to bring him back. A negro kid called Moses Evans. Did anyone know where he might be keeping himself?

A fellow at the hub, lean as a whippet, drew him aside. Only when the man spoke did Coughlin recognize him as Oxley. "If they want a musician, we'll dig one up someplace. But quit harping on about this colored boy. Remember where you are, pal."

Coughlin gestured at the drowned road. "And where the hell's that?"

"You're in Mississippi, Red Cross. Underneath all the water, it's still Mississippi."

In any case, there were no colored pickers allowed in Greenville. No coloreds of any stripe, come to that, because this was an emergency situation. If the boy had been on the levee, he was most likely drowned. And if he were still alive, he'd be back on the levee, or what was left of the levee. All coloreds and livestock were to be moved to Mounds Landing and then kept on Mounds Landing. That was just the way it was.

Coughlin shook his head. "All coloreds, all livestock."

"Sure," Oxley said. "They got to keep order here."

Order. What order? The place was a mess, it was every man for himself. Boats jockeyed for position; their churning wakes shook the boardwalks. The damage to downtown was comparatively minor. A person might conceivably step into the sunken street and wade. All the same, the strength of the current put the catcher on edge. There was an elastic snap to the water which made it stretch and contract between the buildings. It slapped the sides with such force that the spray reached the shingles. The Red Cross ran the hub, but it couldn't control the water and could barely keep a grip on the town itself. In the days since the breach, Greenville had become a battleground of overlapping jurisdictions. If Coughlin had the time, he could pull up a chair and watch the various bodies duke it out. The levee board versus the River Commission. The flood relief committee versus the public health service. A representative of Mississippi Power and Light had arrived by sea sled that morning, come to plant his flag where he could. And then tramping through with the loudest boots and the biggest voices came the National Guard to set everything back the right-side up. The soldiers carried themselves with the performative swagger of hoodlums and brought an eddy of violence wherever they went. The sheriff and his deputies might like to think they ran the town. But if it came to a fight, Coughlin would put his money on the guardsmen.

The levee board's office had been lost to the waves, but he'd heard that the boats at the post office ran supplies to Mounds Landing. So he sat for an hour on the stone steps with his hat in his hands and the thin sunlight on his face and it was here that the Troller took pity on him. Afterwards he had an idea that she'd been observing him for several minutes, hanging back in the shadows of the columns, wondering whether to abandon him to his fate.

Most negroes spoke softly when addressing a white man. The Troller, though, abided by her own set of rules. She said, "Mister likes sitting on the post office steps. Only place in town that ain't rolling and rocking."

Coughlin looked up, squinting into the sun. "I guess that's true."

"Only place in town that ain't moving with the tide."

She was a square-built young woman but she was dressed as a man, in boots, bib overalls and a brakeman's cap. An Enfield army rifle had been looped across her left shoulder; a metal canteen across her right. Even at arm's length, she reeked of the river—of mulch and oil and diesel fumes—and her hands were crusted with the grains of salt that she threw. She had a habit, he saw, of licking the seams of her palms when she thought nobody was looking, not that she much minded being caught in the act. In a queer way it seemed to amuse her, being caught. Or maybe she was easily and conspicuously amused. Her smile was so fierce that it shut her eyes and creased her face.

"Mister's looking for the hooch boy. I can take you where he's at."

"Moss Evans, yes. I'm told he might be on the levee."

"White folks told you that. You got five dollars?"

"Maybe."

"You got ten?"

Coughlin shook his head a fraction too late. She saw his hesitation

138

and pounced. "If you give me ten dollars, I'll ride you there and back," she said.

It had been a rich, handsome city, the Queen of the Delta. One day, God willing, it would be so again. The jon-boat bobbed and scraped through the downtown district, past the department stores and hotels. Several of the large houses still appeared occupied. A woman on her veranda looked over and waved, although Coughlin had the impression that she was waving at him, not his guide.

The Troller licked at her hands like a bird pecking worms. She said, "They don't like what I do, but they like me to do it. Poor Mrs Calhoun sits outside like it's an everyday April morning and here I come tugging my floaters right up past her house. 'Why Mrs Calhoun, you'll never guess who I just found. It's Mr Jameson Keane, all puffed up and oily, so you be sure to let Mrs Keane know'. No," she said solemnly, "they don't care for it one bit."

"Shouldn't that be what you're doing now?"

"Couple hours won't matter," she said. And then as an afterthought, "Floaters ain't paying me ten dollars a ride."

They moved out of downtown into what had been the black neighborhood. This, she said, was called the bottomlands, low-down country. Beneath the hull the water deepened. The houses were sunk to their rooftops and the boat bumped through a flotsam of fence posts, chicken-wire, and school after school of dead fish.

It was funny, the Troller said, because you'd imagine that fish would be fine in a flood and yet here they were, killed by the thousand. The bigger beasts at least tried to put up a fight. Over the past few days she'd seen all sorts—dogs climbing trees, bears grabbing driftwood—and that was mainly why she had the rifle, so she could put the animals out of their misery. It was cruel to leave them clinging on. All the same, she admired their courage, the bears, mutts and mules. Mammals, she decided, were that much braver than fish.

She said, "Like you, Mr Coughlin. I seen you on those steps, all bashed up from a fight, with your black eye, cuts and bruises and

I thinks, 'This Red Cross man is a fighter and that's good enough for me. That speaks well to his character'. You got to fight in this world or you'll end up like the fish."

Coughlin shrugged. "Maybe you should have put me out of my misery."

"No sir," she said quickly. "I ain't never shot a person, no."

The worst thing about the bottomlands, no doubt, was the stink. The Troller pointed left and right. She said that those shacks contained bodies and there was no easy way to reach them. For every corpse that the Troller was able to hook in open water there were probably five or ten others inside, pressed up against ceilings and windows, full of bilge, full of rot. Once the floodwater drained off, she reckoned that even the buzzards would think twice about picking them over.

She cried, "Pinch your nose, Red Cross. Pinch your nose or you'll lose your lunch."

As for those who'd survived, why, they'd be on Mounds Landing now. That was where the camp was pitched. This was where they had all been put. Thousands of folk on a narrow strip of land, the river lapping at their skinny ankles. Every colored in the county— round them up and send them to the levee that wasn't really a levee no more, to the relief camp that wasn't a camp, more a prison in disguise. Guns in their faces and rations in a cup. The Troller had managed to make herself useful, hauling bodies, so they hadn't ordered her onto the Landing just yet. The hooch boy had lit out and was believed to have drowned, and so they hadn't been able to put him there either.

Coughlin turned his head. "So where are we going if it's not the levee? They told me it's the only dry land around here."

"White folks told you that. It just goes to show."

Beyond the bottomlands loomed the tops of tall trees, their boughs caked in mud. The pair had left the city by this point and were heading north across the flooded farmland and through a cobwebby mist which never quite became fog. Whatever fight had once been in the livestock had long since run its course, because now they turned in the current with their bellies swollen and their legs gone stiff. Two cows lay at starboard; the Troller swung the tiller to swerve them. Somewhere near here was General Clarke's land, where she and Darryl used to farm, although their acres were still a mile or so yonder and Darryl never made enough money to so much as look at a cow. She licked at her hand and said that if she had to guess, she'd say that these were probably Mr Ferrero's cows. Or maybe they belonged to the General himself and that what they were seeing was the end of his reign and all that was left, a few dead cows in the drink. This was her point. The Delta had gone upside-down, cattywampus. Nothing was the same as it had been before.

"Terrible," she said. Her voice cracked with emotion. "Poor General Clarke."

The sky was yellow and the light was dull. He saw clumps of trees in the distance, a line of telegraph poles, nothing else.

"So where's the other patch of dry land? If it's not the levee."

"No sir," she said, perhaps mishearing him on purpose. "It ain't the levee, sir, no."

The first time she rode out in her stolen boat with a stolen rifle slung across her back, the people she hooked had been as light and floppy as seaweed and she was able to recognize faces she'd known all her life. Soon after that, though, they had begun to stiffen and darken, while the faces had lost their original shapes. It was getting so that nobody but her would set foot in the mill because they said that the stench was too bad and that the place had drawn rats. But the Troller didn't care. The rats weren't interested in her anyhow and she was used to the smell and had grown to like it a little. She said that even the sourest fellow turned sweeter in death, as if they needed to be dead for their inner goodness to drain out. She lined the corpses up end-to-end on the floor with their necks inflated like inner tubes and their feet pointing up, and they smelled of wet molasses and fruit that had stood for too long in the sun. When you thought of it that way, it really wasn't so bad. There are worse smells in the world than soft fruit and molasses.

They were traveling north, he decided. This far from town, the Delta was a sea. He saw whitecaps and whirlpools and curds of tan froth. The surface, though, retained the elastic consistency he had noticed in Greenville. It seemed to bunch up around the boat, lifting it on the waves so that it felt like the highest point for miles around.

She said, "What a terrible thing, I still can't believe it. This time last week I was Mrs Darryl Benton."

"He might still be alive. Your husband, I mean."

The Troller licked at her fingers. "Bless you, sir, no. The river came and ate him up."

When she had first set to work salting and icing the bodies, the pastor walked to the lumber mill in person to thank her for her service, and also to check that she was treating the deceased with the respect they deserved. By which he meant that she was ensuring that members of the same family were laid out together and that the races didn't mix. Had the pastor seen fit to inspect the lines at that moment he would have been reassured this was so. Would he feel the same if he did so today? The Troller feared that no, he might not. Because on the second day she had started heaping the carcasses near the doorway, intending to arrange them in lines as soon as she'd had some rest. By the next morning, however, the scene in the mill had changed. Every corpse on the floor was exactly where she had left it. But at some point overnight they had all swelled and changed color so that each one was now indistinguishable from its neighbor. Not even the pastor could have said which sheep belonged to which flock.

Shouting to be heard above the noise of the motor, she said, "Mr Coughlin, I swear that was the worst sight of them all, the most terrible sight I ever seen in my life. All those respectable white folk turning into dead niggers."

Such was the emotion in her voice that he thought the Troller might be crying. But when he turned to check it seemed the woman had already recovered. She was smiling so broadly that her eyes had screwed shut.

18

T HE RIVER MOVED through the land and the people did too. Sometimes they moved of their own accord and sometimes they were moved by outside forces, fighting the currents, pinwheeling downstream. The Delta is a riotous and unstable country. The river twists and meanders for more than two thousand miles. It corkscrews in places, slows and widens at others. Little remains fixed in one place very long.

Before the cane forests were cleared to build the city of Greenville—before they put up the gins and planted the cotton in rows—these lowlands were home to a race of people who loved the river and knew enough to fear it as well. Later these people would be called Choctaws and Chickasaws by some, and savages by others, although what they had called themselves is unknown and it may be that they called themselves nothing at all. They pulled catfish from the water and hunted deer through the cane. They lived among panthers and bears, alligators and snakes and therefore felt no need to call themselves anything other than people.

Like everything else in the Delta, these men and women were passing through, living off the land so long as time and circumstances allowed. These days they are mostly gone. They forded the river and went into the west, undone by the Treaty of Dancing Rabbit Creek and swept out to make space for the railroads, lumber mills and plantations. But at some unspecified date before their departure these people or their forebears had dug up the black soil to raise a number of earthworks that stood taller than the trees. In times of flood these hills became islands, flat at the summit, with their steep sides clotted with wild grape and muscadine. Locals had named them the Indian mounds. They were older than the levee and stronger than it, too.

The jon-boat nosed north through the darkening day and it seemed to Coughlin that he smelt the islands before he saw them and caught the clues of their presence before they materialized, because suddenly the water was littered with branches and bushes. Ahead, two enormous billboards had been arranged side-by-side, each angled so as to half-face the other in the manner of a double-gate propped ajar. The words COCA-COLA were printed ten feet high on the left billboard. The UNEEDA BISCUIT logo was arranged in blue and white on the right.

"Where the hell are we now?" he asked, but his voice was lost beneath the motor's grumble.

The Troller hung left and navigated the gap and just as he had sensed the islands before they appeared, now he heard the boy before he saw him, caught the sound of a guitar and recognized the melody as a variation of one he'd heard three nights before. The picking was purposely soft so as to not be overheard. Too late, he thought, and he felt his blood jump. But it seemed that no sooner had Coughlin waved for the Troller to cut the motor than the playing stopped and he was left in an undignified half-crouch in the bowels of the boat, the treasure whipped from his grasp as he reached out to claim it.

The Troller hooted at his back. "You heard him and he heard us. The boy don't know if we're friends or foe." Lifting her voice, she cried, "Friends! Friends! You ought to know the sound of this old engine by now."

Several of the mounds barely broke the waterline. The Troller made for the largest, where the music had come from, and probed for a spot to pull in and tie up. The first time she made the trip there had been five men hiding here. Now she reckoned there was double that—all of them black, all runaways, all preferring this place to the prison camp on the levee. She brought them cornbread and clean water and they promised they would pay her back later. Were it not for her visits, the men would be starving by now. Even as it was, they were hungry, cold and scared. Having taken the first step towards freedom, they now found themselves with absolutely nowhere to go.

The mound had no natural harbor, which meant that a visitor was forced to wade ashore, planting his feet in the mud, fighting the pull and suck of the current. The Troller went first and laughed when she saw Coughlin hesitate. She joked that the boy's playing had made the man change his mind. "Now you heard him, you don't want him."

"No," he said. "It's not that at all."

She had gripped the bough of a buckeye tree, her bib overalls already soaked to the waist. On a ragged breath, she said, "Come on, Mr Coughlin, don't be turning back now."

There were no trails on the mound; one had to claw and clamber through the vines. The Troller explained that she'd left her flashlight in the boat. She said that sound was a problem but that light was the worst. It bounced off the water and left a silvery trail. Swing a light on the mounds and it could be seen from the levee, maybe from the middle of Greenville itself. Next thing you know you'd have Deputy Piper dropping by for a visit.

Halfway to the summit he became aware of the presence of a number of men and instinctively hung back, allowing the Troller to step forward and give the reason for her visit. She spoke with the men for several minutes and although Coughlin was unable to hear most of what was said, it was clear that an argument was taking place. The runaways were angry with the Troller for bringing a white man to the island. They were jumpy because they figured this was bound to lead to their recapture. On previous visits the woman had brought them fresh water and food. This time, shit, she might as well have brought poison, or a length of rope to put around all their necks.

"Poison," she hooted. "Poison, oh mercy." But Coughlin thought that, despite all her prattle, the woman was clever and knew what she was doing. She treated the accusation as a joke as a means of

146

drawing its sting. The Troller assumed that her laughter was infectious. Coughlin hoped for his sake she was right.

"You hear that? You're poison, Red Cross. I mean that's right, the man ain't washed in days. You wouldn't want to eat him, but poison? Oh my."

The king of the island was a small man in prison stripes who went by the name of Mousey Thomas. It was said that, in his time, Mousey Thomas had been the most notorious thief east of the Mississippi river. He could lift purses and wallets as easily as scratching a spot on his ear. He stole in broad daylight and in full view of his victims, because he was so shy and retiring as to be all but invisible. He said that most white folk don't care to look at niggers anyway. What he provided, you could say, was a service, a favor. He helped them not to look and in doing so helped himself.

Mousey Thomas detached himself from the shadows and picked his way down the slope. Coughlin held out his hand but the man would not shake.

Without preamble, with his gaze directed over Coughlin's shoulder, he said, "Gentleman wants a guitar picker to play at the relief camp. Gentleman says not the colored camp, the white folks' camp. Now, we ask ourselves, why does he say that?"

His voice was so low that Coughlin had to lean in to hear it. The other runaways, he noted, had drawn a step closer too.

"Now why does he say that?" He was still looking past Coughlin.

"It's for the relief effort," he said, uncertainly. "I was sent to fetch him."

"Moss ain't white. Why does the gentleman want Moss?"

"I was told he was good."

"And who told him that?"

Coughlin hesitated. "A fellow named Miles Craven," he admitted and was relieved to discover this was the right thing to have said, because even if Mousey Thomas did not know Miles Craven, several of the other men did. The air of tension lifted; the runaways laughed among themselves. Miles Craven was cracked, they said, and therefore not the best judge of music. Come to that, Miles Craven wasn't the best judge of anything. He'd lost his mind on the levee, some of them had seen it happen. And now back came the Troller, speaking across the runaways' talk and seeking to maintain the mood of jollity. She told of how she had seen Coughlin's face drop as soon as he heard the boy playing and how she had explained that it was too late to turn back, not after she'd brought him all this way. Mostly, she felt sorry for the white folk in the relief camp who would soon have to listen to Moss Evans pick his songs. She said, "Land sake, poor people, ain't they suffered enough?"

The thief had been at his right side and now stood at his left. Mousey Thomas waited in silence until the Troller's prattle had finished before picking up where he'd left off.

"The gentleman boats the boy across to the Red Cross camp. And then what happens, he boats him back?"

"No," Coughlin conceded. "Probably not back here."

"Not back here, he says, not back here." The thief cupped his hand to his mouth as though he were about to cough. "Boy costs twenty bucks," he said in a murmur.

The catcher winced. "This is for the relief effort."

The relief effort, though, left Mousey Thomas unmoved. What was the relief effort to him? What relief did it bring to the men on the mound? The thief slid back to the catcher's right side, smiling vaguely at the bushes as though his thoughts were elsewhere. Instinctively, Coughlin clapped a hand to his pocket, checking the billfold was in place. The man was circling him with those delicate, gliding steps. His face was inclined and his black eyes gleamed. Twenty bucks, Coughlin decided, was probably getting off lightly.

"I need to hear the kid first, though," he said. "I'm not paying a cent until I hear the kid play."

"Gentleman wants to taste the fruit before buying."

"I do. That's it exactly."

They brought the boy through with the minimum of fuss, as though rolling a man out of bed, or dumping a sack on the wharf.

Moss Evans, he saw, was an undernourished youth with a clenched, anxious face. He wore a pair of Harold Lloyd horn-rims and brandished his guitar case like a shield. Coughlin waved for him to play, but there was an older man with him—a sick man, Sam Tucker—who said they ought to be careful, the sound carried at night. They had trouble enough with the boy as it was, Tucker said, because he was always wanting to play and they were always having to hush him. It was only safe when the wind was blowing in the right direction—and even then, why risk it?

"One song," Coughlin said. He looked about for the thief. "One song or no deal."

One song, short and sweet. The kid hunkered down on his heels in the mud. His fellow runaways gathered about him in a loose semi-circle. He played a spiritual piece—Satan, Your Kingdom Must Come Down—touching the strings softly and murmuring the words so that they ran together and became music too. It was a strange, savage song in a strange, savage place. It made Coughlin dizzy. He coughed and turned away.

"You want him?" said the thief.

"Yeah," Coughlin said. "I'll take him, what the hell."

Several of the men had stepped up to the summit. The catcher went with them, meaning to get some air and clear his head, although it turned out that the top of the mound was just as close and damp-smelling as everywhere else around Greenville.

From this vantage he could make out the glow of the lanterns on the levee; a syrupy smear through the lacework of dark mist. It was at Mounds Landing, said the thief, that the break had occurred. The break and the flood. Everything that came with it. Four sorry fools inside their dugout canoe. They had each thought they were dead. But sure enough, here they were.

Mousey Thomas smiled. For the first time that evening, he met Coughlin's gaze. "The kid can't play worth a spit, but that's your business, Red Cross. Ain't no refunds here."

The catcher said nothing. He had no wish for a refund. Still, he felt a certain sympathy for this man, Mousey Thomas, who now had $20 and nowhere to spend it and who had escaped from one prison only to wash up in another. There were no refunds for him either, most likely. He might have been better off staying put. The county's negroes, Oxley said, had all been ordered to the levee, which meant that the men on the island were law-breakers, vagrants. No doubt the police or the guardsmen would eventually pick them up. But Mousey Thomas was a fugitive, which meant the authorities would be looking for him even now. More than likely the mound would be the thief's last stand. The cops would happily corral all the vagrants, but they'd already have orders to shoot Mousey Thomas on sight.

The thief had now turned and was peering at the lights. He wouldn't meet the catcher's eyes again. "Red Cross takes care of the people, they say. Sees that God's children don't come to no harm. Don't matter if you're black, white or yellow. Red Cross sees that you don't come to no harm."

Coughlin nodded.

"Is that true? Red Cross helps the people."

"Sure," he said.

"Do right by the kid," Mousey Thomas told him. "Do right by the kid. Get him north if you can."

It was an elaborate business, returning to the boat. They floundered on shoals of gluey sludge. The kid had his guitar which he was using for balance; Coughlin pinwheeled his arms and almost went down several times. All the while the Troller was talking fit to burst—something about gas cans and dead fish—and gesticulating at the slope as if to bid goodbye to the men. Except that when Coughlin turned in that direction he saw that the runaways had already vanished, which meant that the Troller had been waving at nothing all along.

Kneeling to clear space in the boat, his head bumped the guitar case and Moss jerked and recoiled. They referred to him as a boy, Coughlin thought, but he wasn't much younger than he was himself—jug-eared and skinny with some kind of allergic reaction across his long neck and bare arms. Moss Evans, the firefly. A scared negro runt with big ears and pimples.

He cleared his throat and adopted a rueful air. He said, "You've already cost me a small fortune, kid. I pray you're as good as you're cracked up to be."

The weight of their bodies made the boat list and squelch.

"Miles Craven, you know, he speaks highly of you. He reckons you once played a chord that made a dead pig explode. I'm guessing that was a joke, though, right?"

Moss Evans had taken the middle bench. He scowled at his hands and did not reply.

The Troller chipped in. "Man asked you a question, Moss."

In a mutter he said, "I don't know, sir."

"What do you mean you don't know? Either it happened or it didn't."

"Yes, sir, it happened," the kid said with apparent effort. "But I can't say it was my guitar that made it happen."

They swung out from the mounds, threading between the wooden billboards. COCA-COLA and UNEEDA BISCUIT. On receipt of a further $10 the Troller had agreed to ferry them across to the place he'd left his van, or as close as she could put them without inviting trouble. Any vessel pulling into Ford was liable to attract attention. Also it was better to avoid the quickest route along the telephone poles because it was bound to be busy and the other boats would flag them down. Safer to angle the prow a little to the north and correct the course after an hour or so. She said that the moon was the opposite of the sun and therefore rose in the west and set in the east. That was how folk knew which way they were going each night.

"What?" he said. "What?" He felt reasonably sure she was wrong.

"You just keep your eyes on the road, Mr C. We ain't going no-place if we hit a big bump."

He was perched on the front bench, with the Troller in the back and scared, silent Moss Evans slotted in between. Waves slapped the hull. Shapes moved in the darkness. Metal drums, half-stripped bushes. Livestock rolled in slow circles to show off their stiff legs. Coughlin pointed left and right and in this way the boat managed to avoid a collision. They were heading north-east, or at least he hoped so, across the submerged, ruined land. The floodwater, he decided, was neither river nor sea but something else altogether: a vast, restless graveyard, with all of its corpses in motion.

Over his shoulder, the Troller laughed. "Red Cross man. I don't believe you're a Red Cross man at all."

"Who says that I'm not?"

"It don't matter to me. You be who you like." She gave another laugh. "This time last week I was Mrs Darryl Benton."

Sure, he thought. Why not? This time last week he'd been John Coughlin, the rookie, plying his trade in the shadow of Rinaldi and Jim Cope. This time last week he'd been riding dusty mountain roads, about to turn back for home. He hadn't boated across the flooded Delta and climbed the slopes of a secret island and stood in the darkness listening to a boy pick guitar. This time last week he'd been a catcher of minnows. He did not believe he was that man any more.

19

SHORTLY BEFORE DAWN, plowing through the unquiet water, the Troller became agitated and said she needed to confess what she'd done. Yesterday she had told Mr John Coughlin a lie and this had been eating away at her ever since. She was ashamed of the lie and still more ashamed of the deed that lay behind it. Every carcass they passed served as a taunting reminder. If she didn't 'fess up she'd never be right with her maker.

"Not to say I'm certain I believe in my maker. But I like to think that he believes in me."

"Confess what?" Moss asked. Coughlin had an idea that the boy had been dozing.

"I told Mr Coughlin that I ain't never shot a person. And then I said to myself, 'Why, as a matter of fact that's the truth'."

Coughlin glanced over his shoulder. "So what's the problem?"

"I shot two persons. One after the other."

"Oh." He cleared his throat. "Then yeah, that's a problem."

The incident had happened not two days before and already felt like a dream, or like a story she'd heard. In her previous life as Mrs Benton, she'd never have dared raise her hand to anyone; she'd always been taught to turn the other cheek. Sometimes, when he was tired and scratchy or had come by some hooch, Darryl had been known to smack her face or grab her throat, but that was no hardship and even good men hit their wives. Then that afternoon she had just ferried provisions to the runaways on the mound and on turning for home had heard cries from one of the smaller islands. Two white men were washed up there. They looked dirty and desperate, a pair of real-life Robinson Crusoes. The older fellow said that he was a preacher and that he had broken his ankle and could not walk a step. But that man was a liar, just as she was herself.

She licked her fingers. "Just as you are, Mr C. Red Cross worker, ain't that so?"

"What of it?"

"I'm just saying, that's all."

"Go on with your story. We're listening here."

The Troller had called back to the castaways, saying that of course she would help. She tied up and clambered into the muscadine, whereupon the pair had set on her with a vicious intent. The younger fellow, ginger-bristled as a pig, put a penknife to her ear and said that they were going to take it in turns, pass her back and forth and maybe get her with child, half-black and half-white. The preacher made a big fuss that he wanted to go first, saying that he was about to go off and that he'd be done in no time. But she had an idea that he couldn't get his thing to stand upright and while he was cursing his bad luck and fussing at himself with one hand, she was able to slip loose and throw herself at the water. The blade cut her ear and scored the side of her foot. That aside, she was fine.

Moss spoke up. "We heard the shots. It was right close by."

"That was me shooting them."

"Yes," he said. "I reckon it was."

If she'd become tangled in the vines it would never have happened. They would have caught her, dragged her back and done their business. If they hadn't waded out in pursuit it wouldn't have happened either. She'd have started the motor, unhooked the boat and been gone. As it was, she never even had time to climb aboard. Instead she reached over the side for the Enfield, meaning to scare them off, nothing more, except that when she spun back the ginger man was closing fast with his knife, and she brought up the barrel and got him dead center, mid-stride. The report sent the second man, the preacher, turning on his heels, waddling for dry land with his britches still undone and his arms flapping for balance. The very sight of him, though, made her angrier than ever. So she reloaded at speed and shot off the top of his head.

Moss fidgeted on the middle bench. Presently he said, "If they catch you they'll hang you."

"I know it. Mostly that's what I'm scared of."

Coughlin frowned. "Both of these men, they went down in the water?"

"Yes sir, Mr C." She considered this. "The preacher-man's brains maybe went in the leaves."

"Lots of bodies in the water, though. I don't suppose you'll be caught."

He would have preferred that to be the end of their conversation, because he did not wish to dwell on the details any more than he had to. But he thought that he owed her a proper response. He said. "I don't know about your maker though. Those castaways on the island. Would you say they were good men? Christian men?"

"No, sir."

"Well then, me neither. I figure you're most likely OK."

The boat bumped and listed. She put both hands on the tiller. Sitting astride his bench now, Coughlin tried in vain to read her face. He'd hoped to reassure her, but it seemed that she was still preoccupied. Try as she might, she could not shake off the image. How the big ginger man suddenly folded in on himself. Or the way the preacher man's brains jumped out of his hair like a frog. A horrible sight. Two horrible sights. She said no decent woman should ever have to see such a thing.

He heard her voice catch and she wouldn't meet his gaze. She said, "The other thing that troubles me. What happens if I get a taste for it?"

Daybreak revealed a low line of hills: the end of the Delta and the start of dry land. And when the sun lifted, the Troller's spirits did too. No more was said about the incident on the mound. Instead, it was as though she had turned the clock back and was meeting John Coughlin for the very first time. This, he thought, was the nature of the woman; she regarded each day as a new beginning. So she explained that they called her the Troller but that not long ago she had been Mrs Darryl Benton and had lived in a tar-paper shack on General Clarke's land. Now it was all flooded out—the mule, the shack, the rows of coddled bushes. Everything shaken up and turned about and if he were to come back next week, who knew what she'd be? She said that most people couldn't abide the smell of wet bodies whereas she didn't especially care. When you broke it down, it showed that every human being—be they white or colored—was made out of softness and sweetness. It had now reached the point where she almost missed it, the smell. She'd neglected the warehouse for too long as it was. She needed to get back in a hurry and sling some more salt and ice.

Reflexively she licked her fingers. "The ice supply is running horrible low, the pastor says. But salt is still plentiful. I reckon we'll always have salt."

Coughlin sat back and allowed her to talk herself dry. She spotted a corpse and pointed it out, but reckoned she'd have to let this fellow go; didn't want to make the whole trip back to town dragging a floater behind. Unless they were happy to reach over and haul the poor fellow aboard. He could sit right between them, how about that? Or maybe Mr C could put the dead man on his lap. The mental image made her rock with laughter. She said, "How about that, Mr C? Just sit him on your lap. Hold his hand. Hold your nose."

Coughlin was squinting at the darkened bluffs up ahead, looking for lights that might herald a town or a house. Finally he said, "I'm not seeing any sign of Greenford here."

"May see it, may not. May have to walk a mile or two when I set you down."

"Ain't no trouble to walk," Moss said.

"Well, there you go. Colored boy don't mind to walk. It's always the white man who says, 'Where's my carriage? Where's my chauffeur?'."

In the warm months that followed the breach at Mounds

Landing—when the flood-water receded and left the land ruined—many of the state's workers decided to pack up and leave. Some boarded steamers and some took the train. Some took their chances and simply set out on foot. The old society had been gutted, which was perhaps not such a great loss, and its workers fled north in the clothes they were wearing. They poured onto factory floors and learned a new way of business, a new way of being, to the point where they could barely recall the people they had been before. Eighteen year old Moss Evans was among the first to make the move. Tens of thousands followed after and the Delta changed for good.

Beneath the hull the land was rising; the ground raked so gently that it registered first on the surface of the water, which broke into lacy frills and small islands of bubbles. Next came the bushes and barns and a stand of slash pine. They passed a woodie wagon, submerged to its windows, and a clapboard Baptist church, very nearly unmarked. And now there were birds overhead, wheeling and complaining. Still the dark line of dry land didn't appear any nearer.

At his back, the Troller said, "Minute or two more and it's the end of the road. Propeller keeps snagging on branches already."

He started. "You want us to get out and swim?"

"Ain't having my bottom torn out by a rock. Who's going to round up all the floaters then?"

She found a fence-line and followed it for a further one hundred yards or so before coming to rest in the muddy shallows beside a set of dog-run shacks. A red-painted mailbox stood half-out of the water. How tall was a mailbox post anyway? Two feet? Three? Or did it depend on the height of its owner?

"It's been nice getting to know you, Mr C," said the Troller. "Moss Evans, you be careful now."

The boy shouldered his guitar, but he looked perturbed, Coughlin thought. Poor bastard; everybody kept shoo-ing him on. With faint hope he said, "You ought to come with us."

"God bless you, boy, no. I got myself a job. I'm going to top up the tank and get back to work."

She reached for one of the cans at her feet, sloshed its contents to gauge the weight and unscrewed the top, which had rusted shut. The chords in her forearms pulled tight; the top turned and came loose. The Troller splashed diesel on her wrist and put it under her nose, as if she were a customer standing at a perfume counter. Coughlin caught himself wondering if she sometimes dabbed it behind her ears.

He got to his feet and stared at the brown water. Rarely had he felt such a son of the city, timid and fastidious. The water, he thought, would almost certainly contain snakes.

"Goodbye, Mr C. You're my twenty dollar man."

"How deep is it here? I can't see the bottom."

"Only one way to find out."

But he did not want to step out and risk drowning. He wished she would continue for another few hundred yards.

The Troller left off rubbing petrol on her wrists. She studied the catcher from beneath the brim of her brakeman's cap. "It ain't so bad," she told him. "And might even be good. It's like that thing that they say when the water is over your head. They was right about that, God bless them, they were."

He slapped at a fly. "What thing?"

"You know the saying. Moss knows the saying."

"I don't," said the boy.

She was beaming broadly again, but this time her eyes remained open. She said, "It's a test of character, Mr C, think of it like that. If you ain't in over your head, how are you going to know how tall you are?"

20

THE SHALLOWS WERE muddy because the earth was a soup. It sucked at their feet and they proceeded in silence, each man focused on maintaining his balance. The air that morning was full of small biting flies. Whatever rash that the kid had lately thrown off would be back with a vengeance by the time the sun sank again.

Presently they arrived at a gravel road, raised from the ground but dipping in and out of the water. Coughlin turned right, which he guessed was south, although for all he knew the town might be a day's march away. For all he knew it might be a full fifty miles in the opposite direction.

Moss's guitar case slapped at his hip with each stride. His bare feet slid and splashed. Coughlin said, "For Christ sake, what happened to you?"

"Lost my shoes in the mud, sir."

"You should have laced them up tighter."

"Ain't got no laces, sir." His tone was polite, but the look he gave Coughlin was one of frank mistrust.

So here we are, he thought. The catcher and his catch. Bedraggled ramblers, miles and miles from home. When Coughlin pressed on, he became aware of the boy holding back. He turned on the road to beckon him on. "Come on, kid. The relief camp's this way."

Moss fidgeted. "Is that where we're going?"

"Sure. Where else?"

"Troller was saying that you ain't Red Cross at all."

"Oh." Coughlin waved a hand at the flies. It was a mistake, he had learned, to remain in one place for too long.

"OK. Well, she was right about that." Honesty, most likely,

was the best policy here. "I'm on the lookout for good music, good songs. I have a recording machine at a house in Alabama. If you come with me there, I can record you and pay you. Lots of money in cash. A hundred dollars or more. That's the business I'm in. I'm a song-catcher, you see."

Moss stared at his bare feet. "We got to walk to Alabama?"

"Of course we haven't got to walk to Alabama. Christ sake. We walk to the camp. My auto's parked there."

The flies were a bother. Coughlin got moving again. And there was a moment—longer than he would have liked—when he feared that the boy had turned off in the other direction. He willed himself not to look and eventually heard the slap of bare feet on the wet road behind.

They walked in this way, single file, for nearly an hour, past submerged pastures and small stands of trees. He saw wading birds, carrion and several dark shapes in the ditch that he chose not to study too closely. He figured that they were on the Delta's margins now. No man's land. What few houses he saw were washed out and abandoned. But with a little attention they might be made habitable again.

Moss piped up. His voice was strained. "How long are we fixing to be on this road?"

"How should I know? I've never been here before."

"Car might want to come along this road."

"Maybe." But he didn't see it happening: the track would be waterlogged for a few more days yet.

"Sheriff's car might want to come along this road."

Reluctantly, Coughlin turned to face him. "No one's going to pick us up. Use your eyes, clean your specs. The sheriff's got other things on his plate."

Moss shrugged.

"Oh," said Coughlin, trying to control his temper. "You think I'm wrong?"

The kid, he noted, would rather not meet his gaze. Moss heaved a breath. "The police drive by, we're bound to get stopped. The flood don't make a difference. More chance of getting picked up if there is a flood, come to that."

"How so?"

"Well, sir, I can't say." Another pause. "Show the Sheriff a flood and the man don't know what to do. Show him a colored boy on the road and right away he feels better. He thinks, 'I know about this. I can do something about this'."

"Right," Coughlin said. "So that's how it is."

"Yes, sir."

"But we're out walking together. He's not going to pick you up if you're walking with me."

Moss's bare feet slapped through the puddles. He said, "Yes, sir, if you say so." But all at once he sounded cold and mistrustful again.

On they went, the catcher and his catch. He had paid Mousey Thomas ten bucks for the boy. He had paid a further twenty for safe passage through the flood. So he was already in a hole before he'd even bought the songs. For good measure, he seemed to have broken several of Rinaldi's great commandments. Look at me, Coughlin thought. Look at me, I'm a joke.

Judging from the position of the sun behind the clouds, it must be nearing midday. The temperature rose and the biting flies ran them down. Mud had spotted the boy's glasses and caked Coughlin's pant-legs. By this point the Troller would be safely back in Greenville, maybe dragging a train of bodies, all set to line them up in the mill and start slinging her salt. Cool and dry and happy as a clam. He mentioned this to Moss and the boy made a face and said that yes, maybe, but that the woman would come to a bad end all the same. They'd either pick her up for what she'd done to those men or for something else that she'd do in the next couple of days. The Troller was trouble, that was plain to see. One way or another, they'd round her up soon enough.

"That's your opinion," said Coughlin. "I reckon she'll be fine."

Mostly what he thought of, that long walk up the road, was the music that the boy had played last night on the mound. It was the music that mattered. The music, not the boy. The first thing he'd do on reaching the van was have Moss sit on the running board and pick him out some more pieces. Until then they would walk, barely speaking, as though they simply happened to be going the same way. His legs felt OK. He was confident he could manage another hour of travel at least.

Blessed shade was provided by an avenue of great trees, the trunks thick with green, the boughs hung with Spanish moss. Emerging from the far end, he saw a bedraggled plantation house, marooned and alone at the edge of the flood. The house had columns and green shutters. It looked like Comfort Hall's impoverished country cousin.

Beside the gateway, half-cloaked by the mist rising off the land, was propped a fabulous scarecrow. The scarecrow wore a tricorn hat and an oriental robe studded with reflective paste jewels—and it was only on drawing near that Coughlin caught the whiff of tobacco from the corncob pipe and realized his error. The man stood stock-still, his gaze on the road but his expression entirely blank, as though he believed that the travelers might yet pass him by, and it wasn't until Coughlin and Moss drew abreast that his face cracked into a bright false smile. Speaking louder than was necessary, he said, "Now, would you feast your eyes on these two mud puppies. Good gracious, my friends, you must have walked all the way from Memphis."

Under the robe, Coughlin saw, lay still more finery. The tall negro wore a shirt of satin, or maybe silk. He combined a brown bootlace tie with a lightweight gold chain. His name was fine too: he called himself Scipio.

The camp, said the man, lay some seven miles to the south. Moreover, he understood that a section of road in that direction had crumbled. He spoke to Moss and not Coughlin, but he swung his big smile back and forth between them.

"The house," Coughlin said, pointing. "Is there anywhere we could sit and rest our legs for a spell? Maybe get a drink, too."

Still addressing Moss, he said, "There is a pump round back of Upsala. The water is . . ." he paused. "Passably fine."

"Where's Upsala?" If the man were to tell him that Upsala were a town several miles down the road, he thought that he might sink to his knees in despair.

Here, finally, Scipio turned to study him. He labored to maintain his grin but the effort seemed to pain him. "Why, sir, this is Upsala. This house right here." He pivoted back. "You may want to wash those filthy britches, boy."

"Who owns it?" said Coughlin. The mist off the ground made the house look quite ghosty.

Scipio brought the corncob pipe to his mouth only to find that the coal had gone out. This appeared to dampen his spirits still further. Still looking at Moss, he said, "Why, I own it, white mister. I own it, it's mine."

21

I F A HOUSE is abandoned and might remain so indefinitely, it falls to the bank to determine its owner. Until then it belongs to everyone and could be used by anyone. Deeds and titles are only scraps of paper and what you claim today, the river claims tomorrow. Here one minute, gone the next. A man can no more say that he owns a house as that he owns a plow, a mule or another man.

This at least was the philosophy shared by the occupants of Upsala, the flood-damaged house seven miles from town. And if Scipio owned it, it followed that others did, too, much as the respectable Fettes family had owned it before them. Where the Fettes had gone, nobody could say. But they'd left their clothes, food and wine as a housewarming gift.

Six people claimed ownership of Upsala now: five men and a girl, every one of them black. Coughlin had the sense that they were runaways, vagrants, and that they'd adopted false names and fine costumes to disguise who they were. The house was communal, but each occupant had a role. Octavian was the leader by dint of the way he commanded a room. The sentinel at the gate, Scipio, saw himself as the enforcer, which left the most outlandish of the three, Lucius, playing the role of court jester.

Probably not even Lucius's family would recognize him today. From Mrs Fettes's walk-in wardrobe he had purloined a taffeta dress and a knitted toque adorned with egret feathers. In her jewelry chest he'd found bangles and a pair of clip-on earrings. Sat at the cosmetics table, he'd applied rouge and lipstick. It was Lucius who led them on a boisterous tour of the rooms.

"Prettiest house in the county. Built by our ancestors. Lived in by us. Prettier than a barn. Prettier than a shack. Hand-turned windows. And muntins—look, see—with a nice flower theme. Ain't nothing more pretty than a flower theme." He was as drunk as a sailor, but then they all were. For better or worse, Upsala was a house full of drunks.

On picking his way across the flooded fields, from wherever it was that he'd started his journey, Lucius had happened upon a bootlegger's cabin. He knew it was a bootlegger's cabin because the owner had buried his barrels across the front yard. Ordinarily even then, he would have remained none the wiser. But the rainfall had softened the ground to such an extent that, at the very moment he leaned on the gate to catch his breath, three of the barrels had ridden up from the mud. It was as if they'd been lying low, eagerly awaiting his arrival.

Here, of course, Lucius faced a quandary. The barrels were altogether too heavy for one man to carry—and contained a good deal more whiskey than he could consume on his own. His first thought had been to jimmy the door and hole up in the cabin. Then he spied Upsala in the distance with its imposing white columns. He rolled the first barrel to the house with his feet and returned later with help to retrieve its companions.

He hooted with delight on hearing that they had a real-life hooch boy as their guest. "Why, then you're the expert. You taste that moonshine and tell me it's not up to scratch."

But Moss, though amused, would not take a glass. He said that while he could pour it out fine, he'd promised the Duke he'd avoid it. He'd seen its effects at first hand—on the deputies and the prison guards, if not on the actual cons themselves.

"Boy, your old Duke ain't about, you're in Upsala now."

"I guess that's true." More out of politeness than interest, he put the glass to his lips.

Coughlin's gaze flicked between the two. He said, "That's enough. The kid needs a clear head, he's gotta play me some music."

Lucius put a finger to his painted lips, even though Coughlin had not spoken loudly. "The boy gotta do whatever the boy likes. But there is no special hurry now, is there, Mister Man?"

In the months before the flood, the leader, Octavian, had worked as a lawyer—one of only a handful of negroes admitted to the Mississippi bar. He explained that he kept a small practice in the nearby town of Grenada, mainly dealing in cotton disputes and land battles—who put what fence where and what have you—and spoke with such cool conviction that Coughlin was inclined to believe him. He wore a claret-colored bow tie and a double-breasted waistcoat that was too small for his frame. He looked the very ideal of a lawyer, Coughlin thought, albeit one that had stepped fully-formed from the pages of a Charles Dickens novel.

Octavian was also high—but the man preferred red wine from the cellar and its effect was less obvious. He took the armchair by the shutters and said, "What's your story, Mr Coughlin? What path brings you here?" And so, trying to ignore the afterburn of the moonshine, Coughlin had told him about the Indian mound and the music and the panel delivery van at the camp.

The lawyer listened with a show of grave concentration. His forefingers steepled. "And were I to take Moss aside and ask him, he'd verify your account?"

"As much as he's able. I've known the kid for less than a day."

"And your job is to catch. You're a catcher, you caught him."

Coughlin wondered if he were being cross-examined. "I catch songs, not people. The people go free."

"I'm not intending to insult you, sir. Your line of work is interesting. You catch the songs but pay the people. And so far as the boy is concerned, you saved him too. He was stranded on an island. And now observe, he is here."

Coughlin shrugged.

"You catch the songs and save the people. That is a fair assessment, yes?"

"Maybe I saved him, I don't know. When all's said and done, it's a business arrangement." But he was left with the sense that he had passed an obscure entrance exam, because all at once Octavian appeared to relax. He lowered his hands and reached for his goblet. When the watchful air had left the lawyer's face, Coughlin could see that he was relatively young, certainly not more than thirty. He said, "Please feel free to spend the night if you wish. We are more than happy to have you here."

An external staircase stood at the rear of the house and the upper story was home to Upsala's other residents: Clarence, Epps and Dandelion. Clarence was the oldest: white-haired and mostly bedridden. He had expended the last of his strength wading up to the house. Coughlin had no dealings with the remaining two either, although the timid Epps had taken a moment to sidle crab-like down the stairs so as to introduce himself. Dandelion, Epps explained, was his surviving daughter, the only one out of four who had not been swept away by the flood. Furthermore, he continued in a low, tragic tone, the girl was touched in the head, a danger to herself and perhaps to others as well.

What the hell, Coughlin thought. All of this may be true. His attention had wandered; the whiskey was strong.

Scrooched, they called it, back in New York City. Featured. Stewed. Occasionally Owled. Whatever flavor of drunk, the citizens had a specific name for it there.

The flood had marked the downstairs walls and weakened the steps leading to the veranda. Inside, the house smelled of the river. Footprints on rugs instantly filled with water. Billiard balls in the games room left faint trails on the baize. It made Coughlin think of the way in which certain small mammals, out before dawn, left the marks of their passing on the dewy grass.

"It's up to you, Moss. Hole up or press on?"

Moss pursed his lips. "Proper bed might be good." They had each raided the wardrobe for clean clothes and new shoes. Coughlin had been relieved to discover that, in addition to its fancy-dress section, Upsala stocked more sedate and simple attire.

He leaned across the table, lining up his next pot. "I guess what

I'm asking is whether you feel safe. Or at least, safer than you did when we were walking on the road."

The boy considered this. He said, "Yeah, I reckon I'm safe. Likely that ain't the issue."

The rains had washed out the road, which ensured that Upsala was secure, as much an island in its way as the Indian mound north of Greenville. But before very long—maybe this week, maybe next—the road would be repaired and the idyll would be over. The sheriff's car crawling up the muddy track to the house. The stowaways scattering across the sodden fields. Life was sweet for a spell and then the world spun about. Ask the Choctaw and Chickasaw. Ask the engineers who built the levees.

"A toast to the flood," Octavian said. "Blessed act of God. It has liberated us, see?"

"Mother Nature," said Scipio, raising his glass. He called her Mother Nature out of respect, he added, although she likely wasn't a mother most folk would want. Smash the houses and drown the farms and murder the children as they slept in their beds. Murder Nature. That's what they ought to call her.

"Murder Nature." The lawyer smiled a little at that. "Well even so, she's our friend. She has not murdered us."

Coughlin wanted the kid to sit down and play right away—but Octavian, the bastard, decreed he should wait. He said they would all like to hear the hooch boy's music and that good house guests shared what they had brought or caught; they didn't hog it for themselves. Just as Lucius had come with barrels, so the new arrivals had come with music, and although there was no disputing the logic of the lawyer's argument, it left Coughlin feeling that he'd been outmanoeuvred.

In the event it was not until late afternoon that Scipio checked that the shutters facing the road were all latched so that the candles and oil lamps could be lit. Then Lucius changed into an evening gown and the chairs were arranged before the fireplace. The occasion was deemed to be of such significance that even ancient Clarence had been coaxed down from his bed. He sat swaddled in a blanket, not saying a word. Coughlin wondered if Epps and his daughter might also join the party, but the only evidence of their presence was the infrequent scurry of footsteps overhead. Octavian said that Epps was reluctant to bring the girl out in public because she sometimes misbehaved. But he was also wary of leaving her upstairs unattended, in case she came to some harm,

Lucius, not quite dancing, swinging his dress side-to-side, said, "Old Mr Epps has his hands full with that one, it's true. Screaming and carrying on half the night."

Scipio frowned. "It ain't our concern."

"I call him old but he ain't that old. Must have been an itty-bitty boy when he fathered that child."

"Lucius," said Scipio. "It ain't our concern."

Finally, Moss was permitted to play. He performed six songs in all—each unfamiliar to Coughlin, each of his own devising. He sang each piece loudly and struck the strings with full force.

Coughlin listened. His hands were balled into fists. The music on the veranda had been just a shadow. The music on the mound had been like glimpsing a shape through the trees. Now here it was, the beast itself, and he was determined to track its every twist and turn.

Scipio caught his expression and laughed aloud. "Look-it his face. The man's in love."

"Shut up," Coughlin told him. "I'm listening, shut up."

You'll know it when you hear it, Rinaldi had said, and to an extent this was true, except that beyond that—the knowing—Coughlin found himself mystified. The music rode out in strange directions and took still stranger routes back to center. Each song was haunted by the ghost of other songs and he could hear these ghost songs break cover and run under and across the main melody, like the stream in the woods outside Sutton, Tennessee. You'll know it when you hear it, Rinaldi had said—and sure enough, here it was. But maybe the reason you knew it was because you didn't know it at all.

Maybe this—the not knowing—was the evidence of real value. Some fireflies burned so brightly that they melted the jar. Some fish were so big they tipped the boat underwater. The angler cries, "Oh shit, what's this?" and in the space of a bar is dragged right down to the depths.

Moss played lead, rhythm and bass simultaneously. His dexterity was impressive, but he went at the strings in a way that bordered on violence. It felt inelegant and even unintentional. His closing piece was a half-formed scrap of something that probably ought to be expanded, and while he sang mostly scat, Coughlin caught the main drift. The song recounted the break at the levee and the miraculous journey of the dug-out canoe that traveled from daylight to darkness and back to daylight again.

Lucius put his hands together and nodded for his friends to do the same. He said that it was funny to think about what gets rescued from a flood; the people and things that survive a disaster. Maybe it was only the goodness that survived. That would be nice, wouldn't it, if the flood had killed off the wicked and spared all the righteous; if it drowned all the shit and raised up all the gold. Like the barrels of whiskey in the yard over yonder, or the fabulous songs of their house guest from Greenville. It was sweet to think that some precious goods from the Delta might yet escape and sail on and find themselves new homes out of state, where they might be more appreciated. How sweet to imagine people listening to Moss's music in Alabama or Tennessee, Baltimore or New York.

Scipio, reaching to refill his glass, lifted his voice to disagree. It would be nice to believe in fairy tales, but they were no longer little kids. This, sad to say, was the real world right here. Mississippi, Murder Nature. Wake up and smell the roses. Suddenly, disaster, and everyone's grabbing hold of what they can. Sometimes they're saving it and sometimes they're stealing it, and who cares, what's the difference? Maybe they stash it in an attic for safekeeping. Maybe they run it clean out of the state, and sell it on to some sucker in Baltimore or New York. This was the fact of the matter, he said.

The citizens of Baltimore and New York, well, they'd probably buy anything.

Lucius rolled his eyes. "Sure enough, Scipio hates the music."

"So I hate it, so what? The country-blues, it ain't for me."

"Is that what it is?"

"I don't know." The big man grimaced. "Can't say what it is. Country blues or some other name. Might as well call it Jim."

Lucius was amused. "Call it Jim, call it Maude. No, wait, call it Gertrude."

Octavian had settled into his armchair. "Some of the applause should be for Mr Coughlin as well. It was he who braved the flood and rescued the boy to begin with."

Lucius said, "That's right, he did," although this time when he clapped nobody joined in.

The light from the lamps jockeyed the light from the candles and painted spidery shadows across the ceiling and walls. Coughlin unclenched his fists and dropped his head. He heard the soft click of the clasps and Moss refastened his case.

Octavian had spoken again. He hadn't caught what was said.

"Forgive me, Mr Coughlin. I was questioning your priorities. There is a terrible flood, but you come here regardless. You come to catch music and the people who play it. This in your view is what's most important."

"Sure," he said. "The big fish."

"And that's what you call it. The big fish."

"Sure." He swallowed and pointed. "That's him, I suppose."

Now Lucius, on the couch, patted the cushion at his side. "Moss, honey, get over here. There's room for all types of fish in the sea, people say, but you're my favorite fish in this room tonight." Shadows sloshed at the ceiling rose. Scipio scratched himself and belched.

"That's the moonshine talking," Lucius said. And then to Moss, "You want to do a song about me turning up the barrels. They come out of the ground one after the other. It was like a blessing from heaven that came straight from hell."

He was a handsome fellow, this Lucius, and he knew it, too, because he tossed his mane like a pony and enjoyed showing off his white teeth. The more whiskey he drank, the livelier he became. Above the mantel hung a portrait of a fine-looking lady—presumably Mrs Fettes—and the jester made out that it was a picture of him, back in his youth when he had his coming-out ball. And then when Scipio laughed a little at that, Lucius feigned umbrage and added that he was much prettier now and that he had been sick with child when that portrait was painted. "I'm a monster," he said, pointing. "Cover me up, I'm a monster."

Scrooched, featured, stewed. Coughlin refilled his glass. He downed it quickly and refilled it again. He indicated Lucius. Scipio, finally Octavian. "You're Scrooched," he said. "You're Featured. And you, my friend, that must make you Stewed."

Scipio raised an eyebrow. "And yourself, white mister?"

"Me? I'm Owled."

Lucius whooped. "Let me be Owled. You be Scrooched and I'll be Owled."

"Don't shout so much," Octavian said. "Clarence is nearly asleep, you see."

They had almost forgotten that the old man was there. He sat wrapped in his blanket with his eyelids at half-mast and his whiskery chin on his chest. Octavian said that out of all of them at Upsala, it was Clarence who'd traveled the shortest distance, just the boggy quarter mile up the track from his cabin, and Clarence, come to that, who had the most compelling claim of ownership. If Upsala belonged to anyone it should by rights belong to Clarence. He'd been here planting corn since before the states' war.

"Reparations," said Scipio. "Ain't that so, Clarence?"

This reminded Octavian of a case he had worked on several years before. He'd represented a plaintiff who was very like Clarence—an elderly former slave by the name of Noah Jenkins. Now this gentleman had spent his life on land owned by a well-regarded white lady, Mrs Eleanor Winstanley, first as property, then as a hand and finally, perhaps, as a kind of helpmate. Mrs Eleanor Winstanley was deeply fond of Noah. They had grown old in each other's company and saw one another pretty much every day. So when Mrs Winstanley died she split her estate in five parts. Four of the pieces she bequeathed to her children. Most fortunate Noah, well, he got the fifth.

He brought the goblet to his lips and glanced across at Coughlin. "You can perhaps imagine how this happy ending played out."

When Noah heard the news he had to take to his bed for two days, such was the level of his astonishment. But the old man's shock was nothing compared to that experienced by the children. The mother, they said, had been confused and unwell during her final years and Noah, sly fox, had seen his chance to pounce. At any other time the Winstanley family lawyer would have been able to step in and protect her. But by this point the lawyer had himself become old and infirm.

Putting his mouth to Moss's ear, Lucius spoke in a stage whisper. "Those poor Winstanley children. That's who I feel sorry for."

Octavian, of course, had argued Noah's claim in the court. The judge, of course, had struck it down. The old man received nothing, not a cent, and this might have ended the matter. Except that by dragging the dispute through the county courthouse, Noah had sprung another cruel trick and humiliated the family. The case made the front page of the *Grenada Gazette*. The grandchildren were subjected to some vicious teasing at school. Therefore, three nights after the judge's decision, several persons unknown doused Noah's cabin and set it alight. Then they marched the man through the woods and set him alight too.

Coughlin saw Lucius tightly pressing the boy's hand. Lucius turned his head and caught the catcher's eye. He said, "That's a white happy ending. Different from a black happy ending."

"Moss," Coughlin called. "Are you doing OK over there?" But he figured that the kid looked comfortable enough. He was enjoying the attention; probably he was a little drunk, too.

Octavian coughed. "I hold myself partially responsible for what happened to Noah. But do you know who it is that I most hold to blame?"

"Sure. The old lady's children."

"Well, you are wrong, Mr Coughlin. Mrs Winstanley would have known very well where her decision would leave. She knew Grenada. She knew her children. She might as well have emptied the can and struck the match."

Shadows moved on the ceiling, some dark and some pale. When two came together it was as though they both took on water.

"Tell me once more how you came to catch brother Moss."

"I never said that I caught him."

"Boated into the Delta on a hunting trip. Came to catch a boy and sneak him out. Crook him of his wares. Make yourself a sweet pot of money."

"You have it your way. That doesn't make it true."

There was a sharpness to his tone which stirred Clarence from his slumber. The old man looked about the room with milky eyes. Octavian, speaking more generally to the group, said that the Upsala plantation had principally grown corn. Field after field and row after row, with the sun beating down like a hammer, and one of Clarence's tasks was to husk it every fall. Certain modern farmers employed a hand-cranked machine for this purpose, but Clarence did it the traditional way, with the metal cornshucker that his own father had used. He sat on the stump by the barn until dark, chopping the ends with an ax and then running each cob through the parallel blades. It was like an old joke, a tongue twister, a song. How many corn shucks does a cornshucker shuck?

"How many do you reckon, Clarence?"

"Plenty," said Clarence. "Sixty seasons. Sixty-three."

"But you liked it there. They treated you fair?"

"Oh yes," he said mildly. "Fine Christian people, the Fettes."

Lucius turned to Moss and took his hand again. He said, "Every time I go to bed I worry that little murderess will sneak in and stab me when I sleep."

174

"What murderess?"

"Why, the girl upstairs. Crazy Dandelion."

When it had been established that the boy was now too drunk to play music, it fell to Scipio to bring out the wind-up Victrola. He put on a record, Brahms' Die Manacht. Scipio said that this was real music, proper music. The music that Moss played—country blues, Jim, or whatever you wanted to call it—was too animal for his taste.

"Nobody caught me," the kid volunteered. "No one saved me either." His speech had slurred.

Octavian tipped his goblet at Coughlin. "So, you take brother Moss to your house in Alabama. You switch on your machine. You record his songs. What happens after that?"

"Nothing happens. What do you think would happen? I pay him in cash. He's free to go where he wants. He can head back home. He can come back here." Coughlin spread his hands. "I'm damned if I care, he can go to France if he likes."

"France." Inexplicably, this idea gave Moss the giggles. "France," he said. "What's France to me?"

"I don't know, kid. Go where you like. I could care less."

"Coon bagger," said Scipio suddenly. His shadow lurched on the wall.

"Forgive me," said Octavian. "What I meant was the song. What becomes of the songs he records on your machine?"

"Oh." Coughlin drew a breath. "We buy the songs. The song is our property."

"The song is your property."

"Our property. The company's property. Humpty Records. New York City."

"Coon bagger," said Scipio.

Coughlin frowned. "You're like a stuck record yourself, buddy."

But Octavian was now in lawyerly mode: it was as though he were making his closing argument. "My friend puts it crudely, but his message is plain. This, he is saying, is what you are. A coon bagger, a catcher, a snatcher, a thief. You come to this house with your talk of company property and business arrangements. When what you are, I'm afraid, is a simple conman. What you are, I'm afraid, is a trader in flesh."

Coughlin made to get up, then thought better of it. Scipio was close by and might intervene. "Moss," he pleaded. "Help me out here, OK?"

The kid dropped his gaze. "I don't know," he said to Octavian. "First he says he's Red Cross. Next he says he's a song-catcher. Tomorrow he'll say he's something else."

"Jesus Christ," Coughlin said. "Jesus, kid, thanks a lot."

On arriving at Upsala, the three men—Octavian, Scipio and Lucius—had clinked their glasses by the fire and arrived at an agreement. Fresh start, said Scipio. New world order, said Octavian. The house was theirs and they made a vow to defend it. Black runaways would be welcomed and cared for. But the reception for white folk would be rather different. These interlopers were to be brought inside and killed. Their bodies would then be buried in the grounds, deeper than the whiskey because who wants dead white folk crawling out of the soil? This was the pact made by the three kings of Upsala. And who was to say that it was even a joke? Who was to say it hadn't already been honored and that the surrounding land was not already planted with corpses, because what's another few killings when set against the river's mass murder? Come to that, who was to say that the house had been empty when these men first arrived? Upsala's occupants were slippery people. They joked to be serious and treated grave matters as a joke.

Drunk from the whiskey, Coughlin pictured the scene as a kind of choreographed slapstick, a Nickelodeon crowd-pleaser accompanied by a barrel-house piano. The three men falling through the doorway in their eagerness to gain access. Terrified Mrs Fettes with her hands in the air. Then perhaps an extended chase around the dining room table before she is tackled and brought down and has her head split with an ax. After that, the other residents. Grand Mr Fettes, set alight in his bed. The three angelic Fettes children, scalped one by one with the cornshucker. Now a quick title card—"Watch out! The flood!"—at which point the river breaks in to wash away all the blood. The dirt road collapses. The barrels break free. The house lights. The curtains. Lucius's black happy ending.

Octavian was observing him. "Our guest is amused. What amuses you, Mr Coughlin?"

"All of you." He hadn't realized he was smiling. "You're funny people. Sitting here with your costumes and your made-up names. Saying it's me who's the cheat and me who's the liar. For Christ's sake, look at yourselves. I'm about the one honest man in this house."

The lawyer looked to Scipio. "Our guest is excited because he has had too much to drink. I vote that we allow him to sleep it off while we remain here and decide the best course of action."

"I'm decided," said Scipio. "I decided the second I saw his silly ass on the road. But I'm easy with talking it out for a time."

Here, Coughlin thought, was his chance to make a move. Stand tall, face them down. If it came to a fight he'd give as good as he got. He'd absorbed enough whiskey, it would be like wearing armor. But he didn't think it would come to that. Probably he would take his licks until later. If they came for him it would be in the small hours, unannounced, not here in the big room with the lamps and candles all lit. So he remained in his seat as though he hadn't a care in the world, as though he were protected by his race and position—the white man lording it over the colored man—and wordlessly dared them to convince him otherwise.

The silence extended for a minute or more. To his great surprise it was Clarence who broke it.

"Stick him like a pig," the old man said. "Stick him under the ear. It's the only thing that makes sense."

22

ONLY THEN IT was morning and he was awake. The room smelled of river and liquor and sex. Time and again, dozing in and out, he'd confused Lucius's legs with his own. The dried scale of the man's seed on his bare belly and wrist. Or maybe his own seed? He couldn't recall the exact details of the night—who did what to who—and wished that he could. You wanted to remember the good things that happened, otherwise a man's life had no hills and no valleys and no rest stops on the way.

Sunlight slashed the shutters, but were they upstairs or down, the front of the house or the back? He disentangled himself from Lucius, fixing to crack the window and get some air, but this was a mistake because his brains were loose and his mouth full of bile and he'd barely opened the shutters before he had to stick his head out and puke. He was downstairs, thank the Lord. He sicked up in the bushes just as neat as you please.

Now swear to me, boy, that you won't touch a drop, Old Duke had said when he first took the job. Don't get high on your own supply. And he had promised this readily and kept his word the whole time. If anything, the job pouring hooch made it easier to keep his word. He didn't care for the stink of it. He didn't care for the effects of it. Every day on the line, seeing what it did to other men. The cons weren't the problem, they only got a taste now and then. But the superintendent, the guards, the officers who dropped by: they'd stand around drinking until they couldn't piss straight. You'd see them at the roadside with their pants unhooked and their water going down their legs and on their boots and they staggered back smelling awful and still wanting more. Who would want to be like those characters? Who would choose to be such a fall-down clown? Him, was the answer. This fall-down clown. He had broken his word. He had sicked up in the bushes. And he vowed there and then that he would not drink again.

Lucius wasn't fixing to be sick, but the exertions of the night had bent the man out of shape, or maybe bent him back into the shape he had been before, when his name wasn't Lucius and he wasn't wearing a dress. His voice lower, his speech less flowery, he asked whether it had started raining again and expressed his disappointment when Moss said it had not. The best they could hope for was another few days of wetness. Every day without rain was a day of drying out, like turning the hands back on a clock when they ought to be going forward. The more the country dried out, the more it resembled Mississippi again and the more likelihood of unwelcome guests dropping by. He wasn't so dumb as to stick around and risk that.

Lucius propped himself on an elbow and handed Moss his glasses. The fold of the coverlet had put a crease on his face. He said, "Colored-only exit door. This is white country again now."

"Upsala?"

"Mississippi. At least what's left of it."

Most people, he said, would be running north. St Louis, Chicago, maybe even New York. But Lucius had heard that these cities were cold and that the winter gales in Chicago had been known to kill certain people stone-dead. In any case, he wasn't the type to be sliding about in the snow, bundled up in galoshes, icicles on his nose—and therefore he had a different destination in mind. First east and then south. First to Miami Beach—and then on to Cuba. Lucius couldn't say for sure whether black folks were treated any better in Cuba as they were in Glendora. But what he could say was that Glendora didn't have beaches and palm trees and nice cocktail bars, and he reckoned that this probably swung it for Cuba. He could work as a barber, a waiter, or carrying suitcases from the car. Spend his money on cocktails and cool off in the sea.

"You fixing to be sick again?"

Moss shook his head.

"Havana," he said. "But don't tell a soul."

There was a book of maps on the shelf. Leather-bound; its pages crinkled. They opened it on the floor and found where they were. Mississippi, a world unto itself, was really only one world among many, all slotted together like jigsaw tiles. Chicago lay to the north and Cuba to the south. If you made a straight line there was no great difference either way. Except that one was cold and one was warm. One had palm trees, beaches, and bright blue sea all around.

Moss gave a snort. "Mr Coughlin said I should go to France."

"Octavian says he wants to go to Africa."

"Africa. Why?"

"Because he's stupid. He's smart but he's stupid."

They replaced the book and returned to the chaise-longue. When the fellow reached for his hand, Moss gently pulled it away.

"Is your name really Lucius?"

"What's it matter?"

"I don't know. I like to know who I've been with, that's all."

Lucius paused. "I love your music but we don't know the name for that either. So call it Jim, what's it matter? Call it Gertrude or Mary. Most likely it doesn't have a name. Most likely it doesn't matter if I love it."

Instinctively, Moss cast about for his guitar case. If it wasn't in this room it would be where he stowed it, beside the fireplace, but he preferred to have the Stella close at hand.

"You go to Chicago and your music fingers will freeze. Open your mouth and every time you'll be coughing. Trust me, honey, you won't be able to sing and play worth and damn."

"I ain't going to Chicago. I'm going to a house in Alabama."

"Your mind's made up?"

Moss said nothing.

"Not Chicago. Not Cuba. Only to Alabama, he says. Figures he's going to sell his songs and be rich."

On the shoreline, two nights before, when the Troller and Cough-lin were getting into the boat, Sam Tucker had drawn him aside and gripped his shoulder and wheezed in his ear. He said that when a man sees his chance to get away he has to take it, or he's a fool, and Moss had tried to make a joke and said that he couldn't see worth a damn, Blind Moss Evans. "Well then, keep your glasses on," Tucker had said grimly, not even pretending to be amused. "This is your chance, boy. Mousey's let you go. So get out, get away." And no doubt Sam meant for him to go further than some big house in Alabama, somewhere that was better. But still, nonetheless, Alabama was where he had promised the man he would go. He wasn't about to break his word two times in one day.

Lucius rose and slipped back into his dress. He scratched at his stubble and patted down his thick hair. "And you're going away with him through there? Thief in the night. The catcher, John Coughlin."

"Sure," Moss said. "That is if you fellows ain't killed him already."

The murderess came at dawn. Her warm breath was at the keyhole. Her fingernails raked the woodwork. He'd wedged a chair against the door in readiness and his sleep had been fitful, the slightest noise made him jump. But the creature who crept up was not Scipio or Octavian or even Clarence with his shucker. She said, "Mister, please help. I'm being held captive, please help."

He'd pictured Dandelion as a child but she was around Moss's age and had adopted the same habit of speaking low and fast while directing her gaze at the floor. He'd imagined her shrunken and plain, a smaller version of Mr Epps. And again he was wrong: she was not that way at all.

She slipped past his arm in a flash of white cotton, holding a lantern to light her way, so that his first impression—and the one that most lingered afterwards—was of the heat of the flame and the wild smell of her skin. It was as though he'd thrown open an oven door.

"Dandelion," he said. "You're Dandelion, right?"

She set the lantern before half-turning to face him, which meant she had a clearer view of the catcher than he had of her. He put his back to the door and heard it click shut. He wished he'd thought to fetch a weapon. He supposed his bare fists would have to do.

She said, "I don't know you but I must ask you for a favor. Please keep me at your side and take me with you when you leave. The sooner the better. This minute if you like. I am in great danger otherwise."

"Your father," he said—and she laughed brokenly.

"That thing upstairs. He is not my father."

He positioned his weight against the door, steeling himself for an attack. If only the light were not behind her. That way he might get a better measure of the girl. He fancied that her right hand might be maimed, because it turned inwards and appeared to be missing several fingers.

"We're walking south in the morning. Anybody can do that. You can walk where you like."

"I have to walk with you, sir," she said. And then, perhaps judging the extent and nature of his distress, her voice lost a little of its urgency. Forcing herself to hold his gaze, she said that in return she would do her best to give him what he needed—whatever that was and whenever it was required. "Now if you wish, so long as we are quiet. And then on the road when no one else is close by." She regarded him gravely. "You do take my meaning. I can see that you do."

"Stop," he said.

But she had read his thoughts now and they emboldened her further. She reached down and raised the hem of her nightdress. Again he was struck by the sensation of heat.

"Like this if you want. Or turn me around if that's better and have at me from behind. Like a dog, I don't mind. Look at me or don't look at me. I won't say a word."

"Stop," he said, and mercifully she let the hem of the nightdress drop. But she said she was desperate and therefore the offer still stood. This, you see, was what desperation did to a person. This is what it reduced one to. A shivering wreck, lying awake through the night, listening to the snores of the man beside her in the bed. Plucking up the courage to inch through the dark to the door. Well, now she had done it. Now she was here. Her first step towards freedom, maybe the most difficult of them all. She said the next step would be easier with a white man by her side.

"Wait," he said. "I got to think this over."

She left the window and drew closer as though she hadn't heard, and the loose roll of her walk worked on him like a spell. "You do understand, mister. They won't stop me leaving if they believe I'm with you. They won't like it, but they'll let us go."

"I'm in danger here, too," Coughlin said and as the girl slid into his space he caught the full humid scent of her and heard the whisper of cotton against her skin and saw the glint of the straight razor she'd kept concealed in her palm and against the underside of her wrist, and he seized at her forearm and ordered her to drop the blade and in his ear on an outbreath, she said, "It's protection, protection, not from you but from them." And absurdly even then he found himself in two minds—but by now she was twisting and pulling in an effort to free her arm and he bore down with enough force that the razor fell to the floor. "Oh bastard," she said. "You've killed me, I'm dead."

The door struck his back and when he skipped to one side to regain his balance it allowed time for the skinny man, Epps, to slip through sideways. His smile was stricken but he spoke in the murmurous tones of somebody soothing a horse. He said, "Sir, this is my fault. Please assure me you're unharmed." His gaze flicked from Coughlin to the girl to the weapon on the floor. He was, Coughlin saw, in a similar state of undress. He didn't smell like the girl. He smelled of spoiled meat and tobacco.

The catcher put his foot to the razor and swept it to the corner. Dandelion whipped her head to watch it go and he thought she might have pursued it if he hadn't still held her arm. "Dead," she said flatly, but he thought this was mostly to herself.

Now Frank dog-legged between them, still smiling. The man asked once more whether Coughlin was hurt and he shook his distractedly, forced to release his grip but still wary of letting the girl out of his sight. He said, "She doesn't want to be with you in this house."

"My daughter, sir, is extremely sick."

He stepped to his left and Epps went with him like a shadow.

"If she wants to leave, let her leave."

"One day she wants. The next she doesn't." His voice broke with emotion. "She is a vicious, lying child."

Coughlin braced for the girl to fly at them then. But it was apparent that the tussle at the door—followed so closely by the arrival of Epps—had taken the fight out of her. When the timid man called for her to follow she went with him listlessly, her face blank. Coughlin made a last effort to catch her eye, to force some fresh response or clue out of her, because while this affair was not his business, he was nagged by a suspicion that it perhaps ought to be. The two slid out to the darkened corridor. The man steered the girl with his hand on her back.

Coughlin said, "Wait, what is this? She had the razor because she's scared."

"She's scared of everything, sir," Epps said without looking around. "She's scared of the world. She's the cross I must bear."

Or maybe it wasn't just Dandelion, he thought later. Maybe the whole house had folded, capitulated. The storm that swelled in the drawing room had crested and collapsed with the brandishing of the razor and now it was over and all of the danger had passed, because when he and the kid were preparing to depart they found only Octavian out on the veranda and he looked faded and shrunken in the morning light. Coughlin decided that he probably wasn't such a young man after all.

The lawyer looked up, shielding his eyes with one hand. "Mr Coughlin. I can't say it's been a pleasure."

"We're going right now. Me and Moss. Right now."

Octavian nodded. "The hunter and his kill."

"You ought to go too. They'll run you down otherwise."

"Who will?"

"I don't know. The authorities."

"Men like you?"

"Not men like me. The owners. The police."

"Men like you." Octavian smiled and lowered his hand. In that instant he reminded Coughlin of the cripple he'd met back in Tennessee. The cripple had been transfixed by the saplings going up on his land. The lawyer was watching the floodwaters recede with the same fascination. Already there were hillocks and green patches that had not been visible the day before.

It was strange, he said. When he had first been called to the bar, he thought, "This is it, this changes everything," only to realise that it didn't matter a damn and in the eyes of everyone else he was still just a negro. In a strange kind of way it was the same deal with the flood. Now, he had thought. This time finally. This, finally, is what changes everything. Cities drowned, the harvest ruined, the brown water boiling; this is what does it. The worst thing to happen, which meant it was the best thing to happen. The greatest flood in the nation's history, a catastrophe beyond his wildest dreams, and yet still not great enough, nothing like great enough. A big mess but small beans, they'd have it cleaned away in six months. He laughed softly. "So I'm thinking that God's not my friend any more. He should have drowned the whole country. He should have flooded the world."

The whole time walking down from the house he had been haunted by the near-certainty that he would return to the jetty and find the panel delivery gone—either taken by thieves or swallowed by the waves—at which point he figured he would truly be lost. But his fears were unfounded, the van stood right where he'd left it. Coughlin suggested the boy sit beside him up-front but Moss reckoned it was safer if he hunkered down in the back where he wouldn't be seen from the road. Would be a waste, he said, to have fled the levee and dodged the flood only to get picked up by police on the drive out of town.

He clambered behind the seats, his guitar case bumping. Coughlin could feel the kid's warm breath on his ear. "How far are we going anyhow?"

"One day's drive, if the road is clear."

"Alabama," he said. "What's it like?"

The wheels stuck and then spun. They sloughed out across the lot to the track. "What do you mean, what's it like?"

"How it looks. How it smells. Like I say, what it's like."

The graveled road led through the relief camp, so that he drove against an incoming flow of supply trucks, several of which were angling to overtake and block his lane. He leaned on the horn to force them back into line.

"Looks like medieval England. Castles and thatched roofs. Brave knights and fair ladies."

The musician said nothing, only breathed in his ear.

"Alabama looks like Mississippi, for Christ sake. The one difference is that it's not underwater. So you ask me, it's better. Doesn't that make it better?"

"Yes, sir," said Moss, although he did not sound convinced.

The tent city ended at a bend in the road and was replaced by sodden pine forest studded with undressed dog-run shacks. The residents here would not have thought themselves blessed, but the flood in its wisdom had seen fit to spare them. They could sit on their porches deep into the night and sleep in the last line of dry beds between here and Arkansas.

The daylight was abrasive but his vision was good. He thought he could risk bearing down on the gas, pushing them towards the state line just as fast as he liked. Not too fast, said the kid, gripping the seat at his shoulder. The road was unstable. He might get them both killed.

Coughlin laughed but the kid was correct and so he eased his pace by a hair. "I know what I'm doing," he said. "Don't you trust me now, Moss?"

"Yes, sir." Moss shrugged. "Besides, who else have I got?"

23

A T THEIR BACKS, the flooded land. A million square miles of ground submerged. Thousands dead, countless others cut loose, and a hundred tent cities pegged along the shoreline. By day these relief camps were sodden and dismal affairs, but at night they took on a festive air. Workers and guardsmen dosed up on moonshine, demanding a little relief of their own. There were dances, boxing bouts and games of dice. Husbands roughed over and children chased off. Wives dragged from camp beds and laid out on the grass. An explosion of life on the edge of the ruins, the atmosphere so electric that from a distance it was hard to tell whether the people inside were laughing or screaming.

Jockeying the incoming traffic on the road out of town, Coughlin's van was briefly set upon by a trio of Chrysler Imperials, each painted in a combination of ruby-red and double-cream, each kicking up so much groundwater that it was as if the convoy traveled inside its own gauzy bubble. The Imperials blasted by in a flash and a splash, but had Coughlin turned his head in that instant he would have seen Herbert Clark Hoover, the secretary of commerce, enthroned on the rear seat of the middle car and staring ahead with a statesmanlike smile. However choppy the terrain, however bumpy the ride, Hoover had resolved to maintain a front of reassuring good cheer.

The week before he'd been up in DC, minding his own business. Now here he was in the sticks, operating out of a Memphis hotel, coordinating the flood response and answerable to no one but the president—assuming the president had a question, assuming he even knew what to ask. Old Calvin Coolidge, dozing off at the wheel. If Cal had only seen fit to pull on gumboots and walk some boardwalks, he would have all but guaranteed his re-election. As it was, he'd sidled off the stage and allowed Hoover to claim it. The Great Engineer. The Big Humanitarian. His handsome, fleshy face on the front page every morning. His Midwestern twang on the wireless every night. Recounting how he'd arranged this many tents and that many boats. Telling the tale of how his train had run off the tracks and into the bog but that this hadn't stopped him, no ma'am, not for a minute, not when there was the people's work to be done. Visiting one flyblown camp after another, he would hang his jacket on a nail head and pose for pictures that showed him with a dazzled child on his knee, or handing out soup with his white shirtsleeves rolled. He was an overnight hero, a movie star, a one-man cavalry come to save the land.

In what came to be regarded as his most celebrated broadcast, Hoover described a boat trip he'd taken across a drowned town, from the wealthy streets to the poor, from the Baptist church to the freight-yard, and how it had come to him, rocking on that brown tide, that God saw no difference between one side of town and the other and that so far as the Mississippi river was concerned, everything under the sun—humans and animals, white folks and coloreds—was of the exact same value. "The flood does not discriminate," he had said, slapping the desk for emphasis and no doubt this was true, so far as it went. But people discriminate. Systems discriminate. And water follows channels that have been carved out over time. Typically it targets the lower ground, society's social and economic troughs, so that in the city of Greenville it washed out the black homes in the bottomland while sparing the white homes on the slope. It smashed the sharecropper cabins and tore up the cotton fields, but it left the landowner's houses upright and unharmed. On the upper floor of the Troller's lumber mill, there were six black corpses for every white casualty.

And in the course of his back-and-forth escapades, Hoover himself was guilty of a selective partiality, guilty of following his own ingrained set of lines. Because while he frequently visited the relief camps at Vicksburg, Greenwood and Yazoo, he steered clear of the coloreds-only tent city on the levee at Mounds Landing. It was Mounds Landing, he'd been told, where they had put the laborers, farmhands and domestics; all the hardy foot-soldiers of the Mississippi economy. And they had put them there for a reason; held them there for the greater good. Because if the Delta stood any chance of getting back on its feet, it needed the people who turned its soil and kept its homes and loaded its freight and canned its fruit—and it therefore didn't want those people running north to find work. Hoover had heard that the negroes on Mounds Landing had grown frustrated and scared and he had some sympathy for that, it was a tense time all over. No doubt every individual in the county had a complaint they could lodge. It falls to the authorities, though—state officials, the federal government—to focus on the bigger picture. To protect society from the individual; to protect the individual from himself.

You want an example? he said. Well, here's one to consider. In the event of a thunderstorm, panicked horses are apt to jump the fence or roll themselves in barbed wire, such is their desperation to escape. This is why the responsible owner puts them in the stall, throws the bolt on the door and pays no mind to their kicks and their whinnies. That's not only good business; it's the kindest thing for the horse.

The work camp at Mounds Landing was long and narrow, snaking almost six miles along the earth-work's crown. Electric bulbs and lanterns burned from dusk until dawn since it was said that the levee never truly slept and that the inmates worked around the clock, offloading supplies from the barges and shoveling sand into bags. Steam whistles signaled the end of one shift and the start of the next. Guardsmen walked the line swinging rifles with fixed bayonets. The smoke from the kitchens made them cough like consumptives. The mud on their uniforms had hardened to a crust. Off-duty, the soldiers liked to gather at the water's edge and take aim at the dogs that foraged for food. They discovered that a bullet to the body drove a dog to the ground as surely as if a hand had reached out to grab it, whereas a bullet to the head made it leap into the air, splay-legged and comical.

One evening, shooting dogs, a soldier looked east and saw a light winking at the Indian mounds. Next day, Deputy Piper and three police marksmen picked their way up through the wild grape, swinging their rifles and breathing hard; so unnerved by the swipe of the leaves and the snap of the twigs that it was a wonder the men didn't shoot one another. On the largest island they found beaten paths and a several shelters made from woven sticks—and this led Piper to conclude that as many as six or seven runaways had been sleeping here, perhaps as recently as the night before. At some point in the early hours they had mysteriously melted away in search of the next patch of dry land, whether that was Greenwood or Memphis or some boggy ridge in between,

Thunderheads massed and the temperature dropped. The rain froze as it fell and was whipped by the wind. Hailstones roared in the upper boughs of the trees. They clattered on the tiles of rich homes and pounded the tin roofs of the shacks and split the canvas of the tents. Hail stirred the brown water in an ongoing drum roll. Red Cross supply boats spun about and upturned. A US Navy floatplane raked and ruined in mid-air. It was said that a hailstone could kill you as swiftly as a ball-bearing, and that anyone caught out of doors could be punched full of holes like so much Swiss cheese. Vagabonds, raise a roof. Fugitives, grab a trash-can lid. Only the most blessed children get out of the Delta alive.

Play a song, said John Coughlin. I've waited long enough. Now play me another, and another song after that. And so Moss balanced himself in the bed, one shoulder braced against the side and played Skillet Licker Blues, Come Over Here, Child and The Kowaliga Song, which he considered one of his best, bearing down on the strings until the metal siding rang so loudly that it hurt his ears.

It was good to play because it was always good to play. But it was especially good to play for a man who liked what he played and a white man, no less, shaming as it was. White men shouted at him to shut up when he played. The only white man who hadn't was Miles Craven—wonky, cock-eyed Miles Craven, supposedly waiting for him up in Alabama—and he probably didn't count. Whereas John Coughlin was an expert, a music scout from New York, and if even half of what he said was true, that put him two or three steps ahead of the rest. So that's how it was, a man couldn't help how he felt. It was like he'd just won a big prize, or gained the upper hand in a card game with all his money on the table.

He played The Beauty Queen of Arkansas, another one that he liked, and Coughlin pulled the van to a halt at the side of the road. Moss asked him what was the matter and the catcher told not to worry, it was just his leg cramping up from being at the pedal too long.

They got moving again. The sunlight came in bars through the trees, on and off, bright and dark, as though a kid was leaning on an electric switch. Coughlin said, "Where did you learn to play like that?"

"I don't know, sir," said Moss, although hadn't that been what Miles Craven had asked him that time in the tent? Like there was some school in the woods just for colored musicians, or typewritten lessons you could get by mail order. Where did you learn to play like that? No place. All over. Front porches, street corners. The church and the juke joints. And so that's what he told him: the church and the juke joints.

"Big difference between the church and the juke joint."

"Yes, sir," he said. And then, emboldened, "Maybe not so much different." Because it seemed to him that the songs they sang in church were about getting right with Jesus. They were about loving Jesus, getting Jesus close, feeling Jesus move inside you. Whereas the songs they played in the juke joints, well, they were mostly about getting right with a woman. And when you considered it that way, they weren't so different at all.

He said that when he started out, he didn't have a guitar and had to make one himself by stretching copper strings across an old cigar box. But then his aunt on his birthday had given him his $2 Stella, which sounded a good deal better and the songs came easier after that.

"Sure," Coughlin said. "But you play it like you hate it."

"No, sir. Two dollar Stella, I don't hate it, no sir."

"You go at it like you want to murder it. You've got to learn some finesse. It's like you take twenty years off that thing every time you play it."

Moss thought this over. "How old would that make it? Twenty years, every song?"

"Older than us," Coughlin said. "Old as the pyramids."

Moss covered a laugh and hoped the catcher had not heard. The idea was a good one. Old as the pyramids, his $2 guitar.

In any case, Coughlin said, the kid would soon have enough money to do better still. He could buy a $10 guitar, a 12-string Oscar Schmidt. As soon as they reached this big house, Comfort Hall, he planned to rig up the machine he'd brought down from New York. He had it in mind to record eight songs, maybe 10, although this would involve calling Humpty and having them wire down further funds. He said that this might take a day or two. "You don't mind waiting a day or two."

"Who's Humpty?"

"Humpty Records in New York. That's the company I catch for."

"Like Humpty Dumpty on the wall."

"Sure, kid," Coughlin said. "If that helps you out, sure."

Potholes rocked the van. He wished the man would slow up. Nobody's recording anything, he thought, if the motor shed a wheel or caught fire.

Where did you learn to play like that? An impossible question, an unanswerable one. Are all of these songs yours? Well, that was stupider still. All of these songs that I'm playing right now? Playing on my own guitar? Singing in my own voice? Are all of them mine?

Who else would they be? Except that Coughlin said that wasn't quite what he meant. Most songs were old—not as ancient as the pyramids, but pretty old nonetheless. These songs provided a basic structure, a frame, something to build a fresh song around. What he needed to know was whether the fresh build, the new stuff, was all Moss's doing, or if he was parroting—word for word, chord for chord—a recent piece he'd picked up. Humpty Records, you see, had to buy every song outright. That was how the business worked. It didn't want to get caught paying somebody else down the line. He was putting it as simply as he could; he hoped the kid understood.

"Yes sir," said Moss.

"Yes, you understand or yes sir, these songs are all my own work?"

"I don't know," he said. "Both." Because in his experience every song began as one thing and then became something else. Bit by bit and piece by piece, the more times he played it, the more it changed shape. Even an old, well-known song that he intended to play right: more often than not, it came out wrong. He used to play Midnight Special for the boys out of Parchman, on account of it being a prison piece, a working song, but each time he did so he mislaid some words and had to patch over the spaces until it got so the boys were complaining that it wasn't Midnight Special at all. Or just now in the van, when he was playing Come Over Here, Child and the road was so rough that he kept missing his stroke. Now those missed strokes were all mistakes, but a couple of them were good mistakes in that they had sounded good and carried the song to a different place. He'd have to remember them later; see if he couldn't work them into something fresh.

He said, "If you think of it that way, a lot of the big things—the best things—are accidents anyhow. Like America."

"Like what?"

"Sure," he said. "Boat goes to find China, finds America instead."

"It wasn't China," snapped Coughlin. "What are you talking about, China?"

Comfort Hall, said the catcher. That's what mattered right now.

Moss could hardly wait to be there and see the recording machine. But the road was long and the day was dragging and now his own legs had started cramping up, too. He rearranged himself on the bed with his back to the driver, found the fingerboard and began to tease out a melody. The voices were back in his head again: clamorous, persistent, telling him to do this and do that. Old as the pyramids: maybe he could make something of that. Boat goes to find China, finds America instead. That, he thought, had a sweet ring to it as well. Coughlin wanted him to play Beauty Queen of Arkansas again and he did so in a rush—happy to comply but just as happy to get it over with. Mostly what he worked on during those last hours of travel was the song about the levee break that he'd first roughed out at Upsala. Each time that he played it, it took on a fresh shape.

"Four-eight time," Coughlin said.

"Yessir," he said, to have something to say.

"Four-eight time. That's why it's sounding fast, see. Like a car speeding up. Or like the river, I guess."

Moss worked it over once more and it still wasn't quite there. But he had an idea that he could combine it with the spiritual piece he'd performed on the mound, the first song he played for the catcher, the one he'd to play quietly. If he could get the two songs intertwined he'd have a pair of dishes instead of just one and a pair of dishes made a balanced meal. Satan, Your Kingdom Must Come Down'. That was what they called the spiritual, although he didn't much care to have Satan's name on his song—partly because it wasn't Satan that he was talking about and didn't want people to assume that it was. Partly because it was safer not to put Satan's name on a song; it would only be inviting trouble. Don't let him in, don't put his name on your building. Satan might think that he owned it then.

The springs of the deep and the floodgates of the heavens. That's what it said in the Book of Genesis, when Noah had rescued the world's animals in his Ark and finally ran his boat aground on a mountain. He remembered, too, what Octavian had said in Upsala—about how he had thought that the flood was God's gift, or a blessing from Mother Nature, because it changed things around and at least sent some movement through the land. The break at the levee. The Delta submerged. The worst thing, the best thing. Your kingdom come down.

Bent over the wheel, tiring by this point, Coughlin said that he liked it, although he added that the changes still needed ironing out. "Satan, Your Kingdom Must Come Down," he said. "Only it's different, like it's not the same song. You may as well go the whole hog and call it something else."

"Yes sir," Moss said.

"The fresh build, you see? That's all your own work."

"The Floodgates of Heaven. Like out of the Bible."

"Fresh and original. Shiny new."

"The Floodgates of Heaven," Moss said. "Older than the pyramids." He found a riff and repeated it and in this way a song was built up from the ground.

24

SEVERAL MILLION BROWN moths hatch in Alabama each spring. By day these moths consume hickory, sweetgum and birch. By night they congregate around electric lights. Should a door or a window not be properly secured, the moths get inside and go everywhere, and a person is driven quite mad by the rustle and scrape of their wings on the walls. This, said Gwen Bird, was her one objection to the catcher's arrival in the dead of the night, long after the family had retired to bed. It meant Nicholas having to put on the lights and open the door and then, from the sounds of it, having to tramp from one room to another with his lepidopterist's net. All that being said, she was delighted to see him safely back from his travels. Her wayward New York pirate. Her proverbial bad penny.

They sat on the veranda, the morning sun in their eyes. The Bird children, already up and dressed, barreled in and out of the French doors, so that he was constantly aware of hurried movement at his back.

"Never mind," she said. "Of course, had I known you were going, I should have put my foot down. But then you surely knew this, which is why you slunk off like a thief, under cover of darkness. Reassure me, Mr Coughlin, that you have returned in one piece."

"I'm fine. Never better." And he thought this was true. His eye was mended; his hand had healed. The only thing that ached was his tailbone from an entire day on the road.

"Your tailbone," she said.

"Down here, lower back. But even that's not so bad."

She regarded him coolly, but her voice was amused. "Why Mr Coughlin," she said. "You are quite the John Scopes."

Spring was in flower across Alabama and still it had not lifted the spirits of Gwen's brother, Miles Craven, who had crawled back to his sickbed after that one night out of doors. Coughlin thought it was this, rather than the moths, which explained the woman's anxious air. Nor it seemed had the weather brought much respite for the Colonel, who was again on his rounds of the tenant farms. Much had occurred these past six days. Old Mr Thorburn had died to begin with, and his offspring were demanding he be buried in the front yard. Then there was the ongoing bother of the Kennards' Irish setter, which had slipped its chain and proceeded to run several laps of the grounds, yapping and snapping and doing its business. So the Colonel was tired, perhaps on the brink of exhaustion, and it was past noon by the time he was able to turn his horse and come home.

His smile was vexed. He nodded a curt greeting. "You are a man with a flair for the dramatic, Mr Coughlin. Sudden arrivals, sudden departures. I dare say that's how people conduct themselves in New York."

"It was rude of me. I apologize."

"Please." He waved his hand. "All we request is that you be mindful of the moths."

The recording lathe remained shut in a chamber upstairs, to be assembled and used as the song-catcher saw fit. Colonel Bird had rather been under the impression that he might want to record the Grady boys and had even gone so far as to mention this possibility to the boys themselves. He had been led to believe that his brother-in-law, Miles, might be recorded as well. But perhaps he'd been wrong; the catcher had other plans.

The Colonel crossed the library and climbed into his favorite armchair. The chill of the leather against his bare legs made him jump. "The Grady boys in particular have been hit hard by the news. It's a shame to let them down but then that's commerce, that's life."

"Of course." Coughlin cleared his throat. He had forgotten all about the Grady boys. "I mean, I should have liked to record them, of course I would."

"You owe the Grady boys your life, Mr Coughlin."

"I know," he said. "That's what I mean."

At intervals a small face would materialize at the window, peer in for a second and then disappear. The Bird children adored their father and liked to know his whereabouts at all times. Coughlin grew accustomed to the bump and squeak of their foreheads on the glass.

"Mama informs me that you are not our only house guest. That you have brought a companion—a colored runaway from out-of-state."

"That's right, Moss Evans. Your brother, Miles, can vouch for his character."

"And your intention is to record him in this house, my house, in addition to the Grady boys."

"Yes," Coughlin said. "If it's agreeable, yes."

"Agreeable," said the Colonel. It was as if the very word puzzled him.

They had put the boy up in the servants' quarters downstairs. He had a bed of his own; he said the room was nice enough. Insofar as Coughlin could tell, Moss seemed to have been folded in amid the domestic staff. The catcher padded into the kitchen to find him stationed at the counter, dicing onions for the sauce. Sweat drops were beaded on the nape of his neck. He moved the knife like he played, with a violent panache.

"They've put you straight to work, I see."

"Yes sir," Moss said without looking up.

"That's how it is at Comfort Hall."

"That's how it is all over," Moss said.

Coughlin had a sense he'd disturbed some ongoing conversation. Nicholas and Cook stood beside Moss at the counter, ostensibly engaged with their chores but clearly waiting for him to depart. Their masquerade was so inept as to be endearing.

"Hello," he said. "Hey. Are you taking good care of this kid?"

Nicholas glanced at Cook for assistance. "Oh yes, sir," he said mildly. "We do try our best."

"He's not here to fix dinner. He's here to play music."

"Mr Coughlin," Moss murmured. "It don't matter to me."

"I'm just saying. Let's not forget why we're here."

He had checked the cases and ascertained that the parts were all there. But he figured the recording could probably wait until tomorrow. Hadn't he been through enough these past few days? Greenville. The mound. The Troller. Upsala. It was a major undertaking, catching and recording the songs, and he wanted to know he was getting the best out of the kid.

Mid-afternoon the woodie wagon bounced up the rutted road to the house. Coughlin heard it long before he saw it, first because one of the riders had a handgun that he periodically discharged in the air and then a minute or so later because the three men in the wagon were singing as one. He stepped onto the veranda to find Colonel Bird there already, pink and damp from his bath. The approach of the wagon affected the little man like a tonic. Hours before he'd been weary; now he was practically skipping. He said, "You hear that, Mr Coughlin, that's a blood harmony. There are few things more pure than a blood harmony, but then you know this of course, it's your business to know."

The men in the wagon were nothing like the men at Upsala yet nonetheless were arranged in a similar loose hierarchy. It was said that Roscoe was the boss on account of his being two-minutes older than Virgil and that Sam was the baby by dint of coming down the chute last. It was also said that in Tuscaloosa every girl had her favorite and that the schoolmaster was forever having to break up their disputes, such was the girls' fierce loyalty to each man.

Try as he might, Coughlin couldn't tell them apart. The triplets wore matching uniforms of sky-blue overalls, red tam-o-shanters and black rubber goggles to keep the road-grit from their eyes. Their rapport was so tight that it became difficult to pinpoint which brother had laughed first or which had started the sentence that another had dived in to complete. Was it Roscoe, Virgil or Sam, Coughlin wondered, who had broken the boy's back at the fair? Or had they lined up, linked arms and then all jumped as one?

They spilled from the wagon and lolloped for the steps, smiling shyly at the ground and holding their hats in their big, buttery hands. Virgil blurted that they were right pleased to see the song-catcher back on his feet and Sam said that the man looked a sight better today than the last time they saw him and Roscoe sighed and said, "Oh, you said a mouthful there, yes sir, you did." The Colonel moved between them, ruffling each brother's blonde hair, rubbing each man on his belly. He said, "Now we're getting warm. Now we're getting warm," and such was the level of innocent delight on display that even Coughlin, an outsider, was momentarily won over.

They specialized in old-time pieces, the Grady boys, which didn't surprise him in the least. When the Church Bells Ring. The Little Log Cabin in the Lane. Roscoe played a Silvertone guitar and Virgil sawed a fiddle and Sam stood to one side and clapped his hands to set the tempo. Years of public performing had taught them the importance of putting on a good show, so that they grinned as they sang and sometimes pretended to squabble and at other times danced and feigned that they were about to fall down. The brothers were clowns. The music was fine. What the hell, Coughlin thought. Cut two sides, so what, if it gets the Colonel off my case. He figured he had $60 in an envelope upstairs he could spare.

The singing had made the brothers thirsty. Nicholas brought out a pitcher of water flavored with fruit cordial and the men rested in the shade, flapping their hands at the moths. Colonel Bird pointed out that there had been no moths in Alabama when his great-grandfather, Jackson, put up Comfort Hall. They had all arrived later, from out of state or overseas. He said that no doubt they'd be receiving still more unwelcome guests now the western lands were all flooded. Vermin, diseases, all manner of foulness—as if they didn't have enough troublesome types here already, whether it was the brown moth or the boll weevil or the Kennards' Irish setter, which had once barked at Bonnie. Somebody really ought to take that hound to task.

"We'll take it to task," Roscoe said. "You just say the word, Colonel."

"You? Why, you boys would drive down to the Kennards and bring it a bone. Drive down to the Kennards and throw a stick for it to chase."

Roscoe guffawed and agreed that he had said a mouthful there, yes sir, he had.

"All boys love dogs," the Colonel said blandly. "Are you a lover of dogs, Mr Coughlin?"

Coughlin thought of the stray dogs he encountered back home in Mott Haven; how he could never be certain whether they meant to lick him or bite him. "Sure," he said. "Sure. Who doesn't like dogs?"

The Bird children had briefly been assembled in order to hear the Grady boys sing. Now they poured out of the French doors again, breathless and flushed and clamoring for a ballgame. When they pressed up against the chairs the brothers play-acted the roles of frail old ladies and spilled themselves on the floor. The children were thrilled. They promptly jumped on their backs.

"To think," said the Colonel, raising his voice to be heard. "This was once a quiet, peaceful country."

Coughlin reached out to steady the pitcher of water. The children wrestled the men. The noise of the game was terrific.

"A battle for the ages," the Colonel declared. "The Birds of Alabama versus the sons of the Cyclops."

The table legs scraped. Coughlin cocked his head. "The what?" he said.

The Colonel tipped his glass in salute to the three men on the floor. He said, "The mighty trio right there. The Cyclops's sons."

He'd assumed a nervous collapse was precisely that, a collapse, like a landslide, an avalanche or a house falling down. But Miles Craven's was more leisurely and appeared to take many forms. Periodically he might surface to pick at his guitar and gaze at the sunset, after which he would pitch into another long, slow submersion, lying in bed for days on end so that it fell to Butterscotch to bring him his food and empty his pan and ensure that the shutters to his window were opened and closed. Gwen worried about him, her delicate younger brother, but was relieved to learn that he would at least be joining them for dinner. It wasn't healthy for a man to remain in his nightclothes all day. She'd heard about invalids who eventually grew into their beds, attached themselves to the mattress, or else gained so much weight they couldn't fit through a doorway.

"Lurid gossip. Old wives' tales."

She sighed. "You may be right, Mr Coughlin. And if anything he is losing weight."

The shadows of the oaks were lengthening on the lawn when the children dragged the Grady boys away to play ball. After a brief show of reluctance, Colonel Bird went to join them. The ball caught the sun as it traveled back and forth. The players collided and traded good-natured insults. Dressed like his children in a sailor blouse and blue knickers, the Colonel was distinguishable only by his voice. He ran with his head back, throwing his arms wide like a supplicant to greet the last turn of the ball as it dropped.

"He runs well, my husband. He is in exceptionally good health."

"He mentioned the Cyclops. I don't know what that means."

She brushed a moth from her arm. "The Exalted Cyclops. Ancient history. He served as the chief officer of this chapter, this province. The White Knights of Alabama, charged with upholding Christian values. But the man has been dead these past five years."

"Oh," he said. "Dead."

"He was clipping a bull when the beast rolled on him. Such an undignified end. The Grady boys were inconsolable." Her mouth twitched; she looked away. She said, "There was nothing amusing about his death at all."

"No. Of course not."

Gwen got her features back under control. "If you tell my husband I laughed, well, I should never speak to you again."

Nicholas, a grass stain on his white sleeve, collected the empty pitcher with his customary mournful air. The Grady boys shouted for him to bring them something stronger but they were only joking, Gwen said, and would have been horrified if he had. Dimly, Coughlin was aware that the focus of the game had shifted and the object was now the removal of the Grady boys' tam-o-shanters. Whichever child managed this became, in turn, the target of the next pursuit.

The breeze had got under Gwen's dress. She flattened it with freckled hands. "Do you have children, Mr Coughlin?"

"No wife. No children." No home, he almost added.

"No, as I thought. You would see them as a bother. An impediment to your life of restless adventure. But there is hope, I suppose. You are still a young man."

"Please, Mrs Bird. I'm only twenty-three."

"Oh." She blinked. "As young as that?"

They sat in the shade, watching the game on the lawn. The Grady boys, he conceded, possessed great physical grace. They could make themselves boneless and weightless at will, so that when the children ran into them they spun off-course or turned lazy somersaults. And more often than not, when one Grady went down it was the cue for his siblings to do the same, regardless of whether they had been tackled or not.

"Here we go," cried the Colonel. He held aloft one of the prized tam-o-shanters. "Here we go. Now we're cooking."

Coughlin had requested that Moss be allowed to join them for dinner. He had been braced for resistance and had his argument all prepared and was therefore wrong-footed when Gwen smiled and said yes, of course. Naturally they'd be delighted to have the colored boy at their table. It spoke well of Coughlin's character that considered this so important. Her one concern was that their enthusiasm might not be shared by the boy himself. From what she had gathered he had already made friends with Nicholas, Cook and the housemaids and may not relish the prospect of being dragged away from a table where he was comfortable to a table where he was not. She wondered if there might be a gentle way to ascertain his own preference—one that wouldn't make the boy feel that he was being put on the spot. They could have Nicholas do it and then report back.

"Fine," he said. "That's sensible." But he was left with the sense that he had been out-positioned.

"Last fall," she continued, "it was Butterscotch's birthday—her 16th, I believe—and I made her a gift of a favorite old dress. Empire waist, cornflower blue. She's worn it once and never since. It made her self-conscious and ill-at-ease, although she would never dream of saying so—not to me, certainly. You appreciate my mistake, Mr Coughlin."

He said nothing.

"I did it for me and not for her. It made me feel rather noble and it made Butterscotch feel wretched. And when you consider it in that light, it wasn't such a good deed after all."

By now the game had moved far enough afield that he was able to pick up the other evening sounds. Wind in the trees. The clatter of pans from the kitchen. He had fancied that Moss might be playing music in there and it was all he could do not to run in to check.

When Gwendolyn Bird had been young—before she was even Gwen Bird—she had sailed to St Malo and from there crossed to Paris. At the time she had entertained a romantic notion of having a European prince fall in love with her. She pictured herself in a fairytale chateau, or a pastel-colored villa on the Cote d'Azur. But when the summer was over she boarded the Mauretania and returned to the States. One adventure behind her; another about to begin.

She was looking for the pitcher, not realizing that Nicholas had already removed it. "I suppose the moral is that people believe they must travel vast distances in order to find their treasure, to find their gold. I found mine in Alabama. It had been under my nose the entire time. Perhaps one day, God willing, you will find yours in New York."

"I found it," he said. "Don't you worry about me."

"You mean that runaway boy. The negro musician."

"I do," he said. "He's . . ." He cleared his throat and looked at her. "He's incredible, Gwen. He's the best thing that I've found."

The sun in the west had turned red. The shadows lost their sharpness.

She said, "On the morning you left I was so angry with Miles. I accused him of sending you on a perilous errand. Chasing his fool's gold in a flood when you should have been in bed."

"Miles had nothing to do with it. It was my call. My decision."

"Good," she said flatly. "My brother, you see, is quite unsound. It made me worry that his treasure might turn out to be unsound as well."

25

SMOKED CHICKEN FOR dinner. Honey cake for dessert. Candles on the table and horse tack on the walls. Coughlin spotted a brown moth in his water glass and another on the candelabra. He wondered if these were survivors from the night before, or new arrivals that had managed to slip in at their backs.

Unsound or not, Miles Craven had been coaxed to the table, where he toyed with his napkin and picked dried wax off the cloth. The Colonel said that he had extended an open invitation for the Grady boys to join them later for coffee and that they had promised to do their level best to drop by. He very much hoped that they would. They always brightened an occasion, the Grady boys.

Craven, his mouth full, interrupted to say he was looking forward to sitting in on the recording sessions tomorrow. He said that it was he who had discovered the hooch boy, Moss Evans, and had once seen the kid burst a dead pig with one stroke.

The Colonel appeared to take this information on board. "Indeed," he said flatly. "And we shall be recording the Gradys, too, of course."

When he thought that the squeaking of the cutlery might drive him insane, Coughlin pitched in to distract them with his tale of the flood. He told how the supply boats had followed the telephone poles and described the way in which the brown water had seemed to expand and contract between the buildings downtown. The Colonel had read that much of the land was now ruined, which meant that cotton was finished, and possibly corn and lumber as well. Gwen said that she was more concerned about what now became of the people. Those who'd lost family members; those who'd been forced off their farms. A country is only as strong as its citizens and communities.

Take those away and even the most upstanding nation falls over.

The Colonel, his knife squeaking against the plate, said, "You rather upset Mama today. You didn't mean to, but you did."

Coughlin looked up. "I did? How?"

"Your silly joke about the tailbone. About it aching from the drive."

"Joshua," Gwen said. "You make too much of this."

"Because you don't have a tailbone, do you, Mr Coughlin? Horses have tailbones. Monkeys have tailbones." He smiled. "And you are not a horse or a monkey, Mr Coughlin."

They redirected their attention to the smoked chicken and greens. Gwen broke the silence to say that it would indeed be pleasant if the Grady boys swung by and her husband, speaking rather loudly, agreed that yes, indeed so, it would be. The moths in the drapes came to life and their impotent flutter seemed to rouse Craven, too.

"Where is Moss anyway?"

Gwen touched his hand. "I believe the boy preferred to eat supper with his friends in the kitchen. We can bring him in later if you'd like to say hello."

"Blind Moss Evans. I used to say I'd be his manager"

The Colonel had been making an effort to concentrate on his meal, but the mention of Moss seemed to irritate him still further. He said, "You see, this is what I fail to comprehend. The levee breaks and the Delta is flooded and our brave Mr Coughlin rides off to save the day. And what, pray, does he save? What does he bring back to us? Anyone care to take a guess?"

Coughlin held his gaze. "I rescued something good. He's the best thing I could find."

Seeking to change the subject, Gwen said that she imagined they'd build a bigger levee next time and Craven, more animated now, said this wasn't the answer, she was coming at it all wrong. He tapped his knife on the plate. The best course of action was to make room for the river by restoring the wetlands. Allow space for the river to periodically breathe and spread out. Not that they'd do it, the fools at the commission.

Gwen smiled. "Sacrifice a portion of land to save the rest of the Delta. Listen to him. My clever brother."

"Yes, but sacrifice is wrong. The wetlands can be beautiful. A man can still farm wetlands."

"Like a soup," said the Colonel. "Like a gumbo, yes I see. Everything stirred in together, water and earth mixed up."

"Wrong again."

Maintaining his air of amusement, the Colonel turned towards Coughlin. He said that his library contained a book so impressive he had read it twice over. It was a science text, a biology book, and its principal subject was hybridity, which is the result of a cross or a compound. Now this cross might be between soil and water, which makes mud. But it can also occur between plants, or animals, or races of people. Gentiles and Jews. White people and coloreds. In farming, he continued, hybridity can bring great benefits, whereas in almost every other instance the effect is negative. It leads to social collapse, the degeneration of the species and all of this has been scientifically proven. But it was a fascinating topic, hybridity. Most books he read once. That one he read twice.

"A cat may only lie with another cat. This stands to reason, it's how the world remains honest. Animals have an instinctive, intrinsic understanding of this, the natural order of life."

"Joshua, please. We're eating."

"I'm merely illustrating a point."

"Now I have fine food in my mouth and an image of cats in my head."

"For the hundredth time," Craven said. "That's not what this is about. Allowing space for the river, that's the natural order right there."

Coughlin could tell that the Colonel enjoyed these jousts with his wife's brother. He prided himself on his ability to win an argument. The world, he continued, depended on maintaining a balance and this balance required laws and divisions; certain lines which should not be crossed. The land and the river: a perfect example. And now look what happens. Fifty miles of chaos, neither river nor land.

"Which brings me to the other book that I have read more than once. A book that I have opened more times than I care to count. I'm assuming I don't need to tell you the name of this book."

Craven groaned. "Where's Moss?"

"Some will tell you that God is the great uniter. But this, too, is a falsehood. Factually incorrect. Because what is the first act he performs when creating the earth? He divides, you see. What he does is divide. He says, 'Let there be light' and separates light from darkness."

At some unknown point in the preceding few minutes, Coughlin's plate had been removed. In its place a wedge of honey cake had been set. Nicholas possessed a smooth sleight of hand that rivaled that of Mousey Thomas. He could have picked all of their pockets if he were that way inclined.

Sometimes, it was true, the question of hybridity came especially close to home. "And this is interesting, too. Lines can be crossed without anybody quite realizing, or out of a Christian desire to accommodate strangers in need." He nodded at Coughlin. "Your presence here is a case in point. An Irish-Catholic ruffian from the north welcomed into a Baptist home. Many people would have closed their doors."

Coughlin shrugged. He had no reason to doubt it.

"But oh no, not us. Quite the contrary. We say, 'Let him in, poor fellow' and we are happy to have you." He smiled thinly. "Others, perhaps, not so much."

How many moths had been in the room when they sat? In the intervening hour at least six more had arrived. Coughlin fished one from his sauce with the tines of his fork and set it gently aboard his napkin ring. Another had settled on the pomaded crest of the Colonel's hair.

Obviously it would be Moss. Moss was the issue; he was the line not to cross. You could say what you like, it never made any difference. People such as the Colonel would always hate people such as Moss.

Gwen hastened to clarify. Her chief worry was the vagrancy laws. "This very instant, Mr Coughlin, you have us harboring a fugitive. You must see how that places us in an awkward position."

"He's done nothing wrong, for Christ's sake."

"The Delta coloreds must remain in place. That is their civic duty, yes, but it's more besides. The Delta is their home. They are loved. They have purpose. It is not the same in New York, but that's how it is here."

She hesitated, picked up her fork and then set it down again. "Tell us, Mr Coughlin, about the colored situation in New York. I've heard that they're allowed to run wild and starve. Illuminate us, is it so much better there?"

"I guess," he said. "A little better, yes."

Miles banged the table. "Where's Moss?"

"Maybe washing our dishes," Coughlin said, conscious of the fact that he was speaking too loudly himself. "Maybe emptying your bedpan. Maybe at the washboard, scrubbing your shitty britches."

The Colonel's smile slipped; the moth took flight. He was a strong man, Colonel Bird, he could take a punch without flinching. Profanity, though, went through him as a knife goes through butter and he needed a moment to recover and regroup.

"Mr Coughlin," he said with great dignity. "It would be best if you were to leave this house at first light."

"First what?"

"Yes," he said. "First light. No later."

The catcher thought of the lathe upstairs; his painstaking plans for recording the kid. To do that properly—to truly do the kid justice—well, that would require a full day's work at least.

"We took you in because you were in need of help. But I dare say you have abused our hospitality long enough."

"Moss needs help too," Coughlin said, aware that he might be properly shouting now and it was here that the dining hall was overcome by a subaudible thunder which he felt through the table and in the small of his back. Water trembled in the glass, silver sang on the china, and this enchantment persisted for several seconds before he heard the noise of an approaching motor and even then his first stricken thought was that the police had been called. He pushed back his chair, noting that the Colonel was already on his feet and the moths were dive-bombing the overhead light, but the mood at the table was not fear but excitement. Miles gave a low moan that was almost a laugh while Gwen had her palms pressed together in a prayer of thanks. But it was the dapper Colonel who appeared most buoyed by the sound. He darted for the window and then swung mid-step to the door as though simply by staring he might make it open all the sooner. The fury had left him; he resembled a small child again. "To the rescue," he said. "The Grady boys."

Nicholas returned to the kitchen and set the tray by the sink. He said, "They going at it hammer and tongs through there. Hammer and tongs, going to be tears before bedtime."

"Yeah?" said Cook with mild interest. "Mr Colonel getting all het up again."

"Het and then some. That man's just as windy as a sack full of farts."

Moss sat on the stool, cleaning silverware with a paste. Nicholas held out Craven's half-finished plate. "You want this?"

"No, I'm fine."

He turned to Cook. "You want this?"

"Sure," said Cook. "I made it, I'll eat it."

Throughout the evening, while they worked, they had debated the subject of Nicholas's tattoo. Moss had an idea that maybe they had debated it on other evenings, too, and that the rest of the staff were already sick of the subject. In short, the houseboy had a tattoo on his right arm and now wanted a tattoo on his left. The existing tattoo was of a sailor's anchor and he'd had it inked years before, when he was still a young man and had barely given it a moment's thought after that. Only lately, of all the hair-brained notions, he's started to feel that he was unbalanced and that a second tattoo might steady him on his feet. So he had half a mind to head into town on his next day off and get a second tattoo to complement the first. Half a mind to make a whole body, he said.

"Now Butterscotch, her view is that I'm too long in the tooth for tattoos. Butterscotch, why, she about laughs fit to piss."

"It could be she's right," said Cook.

"Yeah, but what's old to 'Scotch ain't old to us. Look at this," he said. "This face is old but these arms ain't old."

The next issue was this: what tattoo should he have? Not another anchor, good gracious, he couldn't quite recall why he'd picked an anchor to begin with. Butterscotch said a rose and Cook suggested a seahorse although at first she'd said sea lion, which wasn't what she had meant. Nicholas favored a naked girl. He felt it might be the last chance, at his age, to be seen with a naked girl on his arm. "Only if she's inked there. That way she can't run away."

The kitchen door opened out onto the yard. Beyond the yard lay a meadow. Beyond the meadow, the woods. The houseboy had a joke—that was not completely a joke—of leaving the back door ajar so that the moths could get in. The moths drove Miss Gwen to distraction and they all hated Miss Gwen. They said that at least the Colonel was honest and didn't try to dress up his meanness.

"Ain't nothing to do with me if that door keeps creaking open. I'm on my chores, I ain't looking, I'm busy. What am I now, the door police?"

"Got to let some air in, too," Cook said.

He gave Moss a hard stare. "Somebody slips in, I ain't watching. Somebody slips out, well, I ain't watching either."

Moss shrugged. "Where would I go? They'd pick me up."

"Boy, you've been picked up," said Nicholas. "Don't you get it? You're picked up now."

He'd come to the house to play his music upstairs. He wanted to get his money and get gone. And if he couldn't do that, he wanted to at least play some music. So he took his guitar and picked some songs in the kitchen. He played Wayfaring Stranger, Cigar and Soda

Blues, and Midnight Special, the prison piece that kept shifting every time he walked through it. Nicholas said that the boy's music—all of it, not just Midnight Special—was about the worst racket he'd ever heard in his life, but he wouldn't hold that against him, the kid seemed straight enough. The real mystery, added Cook, was what a white man wanted with such music anyhow. It wasn't his music. It wasn't none of his business. "It's your music, child, don't be giving it to him."

"I ain't giving it to nobody. The man says he'll pay me $30 a song."

"Yeah, says he will. Maybe thinks he will. I'll believe it when I see it. Besides," she said, "whatever he gives you, you can bet he'll be getting more."

"Leave you broke and starving in a ditch," Nicholas had said with a gloomy relish. "That's what he'll do. Leave you starving in a ditch."

Now back he came through the swinging doors, a man of rigid decorum, carrying the remains of the cake, a stiff limp to his gait. He said that his mind was made up, he was putting a girl on his arm. Naked as the day, with her rear in the air and nipples like thumbs. If he were fixing to be foolish, may as well go the whole hog.

"You fixing to get it done down at Bomba's?"

"Where else? Bomba's the man." He held up Craven's plate. "You want this?"

"No," said Cook.

"You want this?"

Mos shook his head. He was working the paste out from under his fingernails.

"Well I guess it's down to me then, ain't it?"

"That's the one that I spit in," said Cook and the old man was still chuckling a little at this—holding his fork, about to tuck in—when the crockery in the cabinet started to vibrate, at which point he quit laughing and turned on his heel as though to busy himself at the sink. He said, "Now I got my back to you, boy, and I'm minding my own. This is your last chance, I reckon. Push at that door and then run."

26

IN THEY CAME, the Grady boys, Roscoe, Virgil and Sam, broadside in the doorway, talking across one another and jock-eying to get in. Too large and free-swinging to be invited to dinner. They'd upset the chairs and rub their mouths clean on the drapes. They were more suited to running about in open meadows, or standing waist-deep in water to hunt crayfish and beaver. Such was their haste to join the party that they still wore their goggles and tam-o-shanters, while their overalls were matted with a substance that might have been dirt or the rusty residue of whatever machine they had stripped. They had been shy when he first met them. They were not shy any more and even their shows of contrition seemed to bubble over with merriment. They apologized to the Colonel for not coming sooner and to Miss Gwen for crashing in and interrupting her evening and to Miles for making so much ruckus when they knew he was convalescing. They marveled at the number of brown moths in the room and said that the trick was to keep the doors and windows shut after dark. Roscoe, Virgil and Sam. They smelled of cut grass and fresh sweat and the sweet rust on their clothes. If Coughlin hadn't known better he'd have sworn they were drunk, such was the boisterous energy they brought to the room.

While they gawped at the moths, Gwen gawped at them. "Look at you, good gracious, you're head to toe in filth." And this prompted another tumbling rush of apology together with much pawing self-inspection because it was clear that the boys had been so caught up in their chores they hadn't had time to judge the extent of their dishevelment. They declared that they would step out to properly wipe themselves down but Gwen said that would be silly—that dinner was over and that, in any case, a little dirt never hurt anyone. Roscoe said if she passed across that pitcher of water they could scrub up right here. Just pour it over their heads and watch them shake themselves dry.

"Nonsense," she said. "The ideas that you have."

Roscoe had his handgun tucked into his belt. It joggled with each step, as shiny as a new penny. Its presence made Coughlin nervous.

"You'll never guess what we've been doing, Colonel."

"Up to mischief, I have no doubt."

"Guess!" they said. "Guess!"

Gwen ordered them to sit down but they were no sooner on their chairs than they were off them again, roaming and lunging at one another, much as they had when playing on the lawn. It didn't matter how many times she scolded them, nor how genuine was their desire to sit and be still. One brother's movement would trigger the others.

"Rolled your fool selves in some quicksand," said the Colonel.

"Wrong! Wrong!"

"Got stuck in a chimney and couldn't climb out."

"Wrong!"

What they had done was to drive to the Kennards and flush out the dog. The mean Irish setter; the hound that scared Bonnie. The Kennards had known what they wanted and had ran the dog out the back and there had followed a comical pursuit through the corn with the eldest Kennard boy dragging the animal by its collar and the brothers clod-hopping close behind with Roscoe shooting his gun in the air and the ground so dug-up and sun-baked that everyone had to lift their knees up to their chest with each step. They said that they could hardly run for laughing and had a notion the darkie had been laughing a little as well. And the whole way through the field the dog was dawdling so that the darkie was pulling it like a sack of potatoes so that by the time they caught up it had white foam on its muzzle and its eyes had rolled back and it was too tuckered to bite them when they took it to task.

The Colonel clapped his hands in horror. "And sweet heaven, you've tramped the mess of that beast across my nice dining hall."

It was a rare feat, catching the Colonel out, but the brothers had managed it and he was now in two minds. He upbraided the boys for their temerity in tackling a matter he believed he had in hand. All the same he couldn't help but applaud their gumption and gusto. He only wished that they had consulted him in advance.

He said, "Opened him up like a peach, how disgusting." And although his tone was severe, the boys seemed to have picked out a note of approval which had passed Coughlin by because they beamed at one another and toed the rug with their work-boots in bashful delight.

"Jesus Christ," Coughlin said. He looked to Miles for support, but the engineer had busied himself with folding his napkin.

Virgil—the middle sibling but marginally the largest—said, "We took him to task, Mr Colonel, just like you wanted."

"Well now," said the Colonel. "I'll admit that I did."

Gwen's chief concern, though, was for the Kennards themselves. They were fond of the dog and she was fond of them. It was difficult enough to find decent tenants to begin with and theirs was a relationship which had been built over years. In addition to this, she worried that the Kennard boy was impulsive and prone to panic. She did hope that the boy had not been caught up in the fray.

"No ma'am," Roscoe said, not quite meeting her eye. "I reckon he'll be right as rain soon enough."

Roscoe, Virgil and Sam. The Grady boys, the Cyclops's sons, who came into the world as one and in so doing managed to split their mother in two. God's miracle trio. Three boys of one voice, possessed of identical oral and nasal cavities whose singing was as snug as a line of synchronized fiddles. There was a magic, people said, to the boys' highest harmonies. They made bent men stand straight and burly farm-hands start sobbing and beautiful schoolgirls faint dead away on the floor. And all of this was true, said the Colonel. He had witnessed these miracles in person, first hand. Which made it all the more remarkable that this so-called catcher, John Coughlin, would choose to pass up the boys and chase runaway negroes instead. Had he not solemnly sworn he wasn't wanting race music? "Isn't that what you assured me of, sir? Upstairs on the landing, during my athlete's massage."

"Sure," Coughlin said. "So what? People change."

"Weak people," agreed the Colonel. "Men who have no conviction, yes."

The drama with the dog had mostly passed Miles Craven by, but one mention of music and the young man snapped to life. He said that if the catcher planned on recording Moss it was only fair that he, Craven, should receive a finder's fee and perhaps some royalties given that it was he, Craven, who had discovered the boy to begin with. Blind Moss Evans, he called him. One might say that this made him the boy's manager.

"Not a chance," Coughlin told him. "This is between me and Moss."

By this point it seemed that everyone was talking at once. The little colonel shouting about blood harmonies, Roscoe calling for the colored boy to come play his guitar and Virgil and Sam expressing further dismay about the number of moths on the wall. Sam said that the thing they ought to do was latch all of the shutters at night and Gwen said that she knew that, good heavens, she wasn't entirely stupid—and in the midst of all this the door was eased open and the boy was brought in.

"Blind Moss Evans," Craven exclaimed. "Moss!"

Coughlin had sat through the dinner with a mounting sense of unease. Now, with Moss's arrival, he became actively alarmed. "Moss," he said. "You don't have to do anything."

The kid stood by the table with his guitar in one hand, looking hard at the floor, refusing to respond to Miles's greeting, while equally unwilling to acknowledge the catcher. Roscoe wanted him to pick out a tune, but for once the brothers were not in harmony, because Virgil and Sam were occupied with the moths and had begun swatting the walls with their big open palms. Gwen implored them to stop but the boys were like children and the more they swatted the more they got a taste for it. Their eyes had glazed over; they were thinking of nothing but moths.

Coughlin tried again. "I mean it, Moss. You don't have to play for these people."

"Hush your mouth, Mr Tailbone."

"Please, boys, please. You're leaving marks."

Three moths perched on the picture rail. Sam jumped and slapped but the rail was too high.

Without looking around, he said, "Pass me over the nigger's guitar."

Coughlin rose from his chair, meaning to cut in front of the kid and prevent the guitar being seized, but then it was as if a black-out curtain was dropped, plunging him into darkness. When it came up again he found himself spreadeagled on his back, facing the opposite direction.

"Now then, enough," the Colonel was saying as if from a distance. "Remember, boys, that this is a Christian household."

The catcher rolled onto his knee and shook his head to clear it. Moss, he noted, had also ended up on the floor. The kid's upper lip had been split. His guitar lay in splinters. What a scene, Coughlin thought. Anyone walking into the room at that moment would have assumed it was he and Moss who'd been fighting while all of the others stood by.

Virgil, the nearest, gave him a worried smile. He said, "Are you alright, mister?" And then, to Gwen and the Colonel, "I reckon he's alright. He fell on his noggin, that's all."

When Virgil held out his hand, Coughlin batted it away. But the situation was ugly and he feared for their safety. The Gradys were more frightening than the men at Upsala—more frightening than Morton Haines, scarier than Mousey Thomas—because they appeared quite detached from the damage they caused. They'd glaze over and kill him, he had no doubt whatsoever. They'd kill him without knowing and feel sad afterwards. They'd regard the explosion of violence as somehow separate from themselves—part of some wider dispute that they'd witnessed and tried to step in to resolve.

"C'mon, mister," Virgil said. "No hard feelings now."

A pair of moths had settled in the Colonel's hair. In his shaken state, for a moment Coughlin mistook them for ribbons. It was a shame, Bird was saying, that the darkie's guitar had been smashed. It meant that they would all have to make do with the Gradys instead. Why, he said, warming to his theme, he had half a mind to record the boys this evening, this very minute, on the fancy recording machine upstairs. Why wait? Time was pressing. And their guest, as discussed, was leaving at first light.

"Nicholas," he called. "Nicholas. Will you be so good as to bring Mr Coughlin's packing crates down the stairs?"

Roscoe swung at a moth and missed. "Why blind?" he asked Craven.

"Why what?"

"Why Blind Mossy Evers? He ain't blind, he's got glasses."

"Blind Moss Evans. People like blind musicians. It makes him easier to sell."

Roscoe weighed this up. "Well then, in that case, he don't need his glasses."

Moss came out of his crouch and lunged for the door. Coughlin went with him, more alert this time, so that when Virgil drew close the catcher gripped his shoulders, brought his knee up hard and saw a look of deep consternation cross the man's placid face.

He had an idea that Moss, in the doorway, had managed to spin Sam and unbalance him—and this might have allowed the kid just enough time to make his escape were it not for Roscoe cutting in like a bully at a dance. And now, such was the squeeze and rub of bodies that the gun in Roscoe's belt went off and although the noise was muffled, it appeared that the bullet might have clipped the man's hand. He turned to one side and sucked on his thumb like a child.

"There, you see," Gwen declared, mainly addressing her husband. "This is why I won't allow firearms at the dinner table."

Virgil had caught Coughlin in a headlock. He now released his grip and turned worriedly towards his brother.

"Ain't nothing," Roscoe assured him. He inspected the wound; dark blood had gotten everywhere. "I took a little skin off, that's all."

The Colonel stepped forward. Some of the blood had spotted his shirt sleeves. He said that it wasn't Roscoe's fault, the gun going off, but it had been caused by the boy wriggling and grabbing like an animal. He said it was a wonder the damage wasn't worse. Roscoe might have been seriously hurt.

"That's right," Sam marveled, waving his hand at a moth. "Firing a bullet in your house. In Comfort Hall, of all the places."

"No Glasses, No Guitar, No Fingers Mossy Evans," Virgil said.

"Take him to task," said the Colonel. "Take him to task, dirty animal."

Third time lucky, Coughlin thought, darting for the door, but Virgil was ready and slapped him open-handed before he had taken a second step. He went onto the floor as though falling from a great height.

"Mr Coughlin," sighed Gwen. "You are your own worst enemy."

In the doorway, Roscoe and Sam had wrestled Moss to his knees. The catcher's senses were clouded. Events played out in a fog. He heard the two brothers' hard breaths, and the squeak of their shoes on the floor. He heard the distant scrape of the packing cases as Nicholas carried the Truetone lathe down the stairs.

Later, he would decide that it would have gone bad for Moss in that moment, were it not for Roscoe's revolver coming loose from his belt. The gun dropped to the rug and went off a second time, much louder than the first. The noise made the brothers let go of the kid and clutch one another. Jesus, thought Coughlin. But he was still in one piece.

Alone out of the party, the Colonel remained unperturbed. It was almost as though he were enjoying himself, as though the second shot had cleared his head. He explained that, yet again, the animal had caused the Gradys' gun to discharge which would only ensure that he received still stiffer punishment. He added that he was minded to have Nicholas bring in the recording lathe that instant. That way he could have Mr Tailbone set it up while the brothers took care of business with the darkie. Two birds with one stone, he said laughing. The Birds of Alabama.

Painstakingly, Coughlin got himself on his feet and surveyed the scene. At the sound of the gun, Gwen had put her hands to her ears. Her brother sat hunched at the table with a sickly grin on his face. Moss at least remained on his feet but his glasses were broken and his face was marked up. And what about me, wondered Coughlin. Do I look better or worse? Is my face bloody too?

He said, "I'm not recording those apes."

The catcher's voice was a croak, and the Colonel's ears were still ringing.

"I said I'm not recording those apes. So you can forget that idea."

"You will, though," the Colonel said blithely. "And we shall keep the recordings with us right here."

"You can go fuck yourself." With faint hope, Coughlin looked to Miles Craven for help. The young man remained at the table and appeared to be massaging his left hip, which made Coughlin wonder whether the second bullet had nicked him. The angle was awkward and the chances seemed slim but Miles Craven, poor bastard, had never been blessed with good fortune.

The Colonel had been talking. The catcher turned back to face him.

"Yes," said the Colonel. "We see you now. We know you now, Mr Coughlin. You are a weak man, bent on crookery and speaking the language of the sewer. My wife, I must say, made efforts to defend you. She tries to see the good in people, even when there is nothing good to see."

Coughlin pointed. "Your brother-in-law . . ."

"Miles cannot save you. He won't lift a finger. You will record every song that the Gradys wish to play. This may take you all night, so we had better begin right away. Only then, Mr Tailbone, might we agree to you leaving."

"No," Coughlin said, although he knew when he was beaten.

"Yes," said the Colonel. He sounded positively carefree. He reached for his water glass, almost curtsying as he did so. "Yes, Mr Tailbone, praise be, hallelujah. You will record the songs of the Grady boys and they will remain with us here at Comfort Hall."

With his gaze still on Coughlin, he lifted the glass to his lips. Gwen saw what was in it; the little colonel did not. She reached out to restrain him but the damage had already been done.

The Colonel's smile froze. The glass dropped from his hand. And now all at once the night's drama found itself a new focus. Roscoe bent the man at the waist and pounded on his back. The force of the pounding drove the Colonel to his knees. He moved his arms in the air and appeared to be trying to form words. His gaze, still on Coughlin, spilled over with tears.

"God save him," Gwen said. "He is choking to death."

Now Virgil and Sam pitched into the fray elbowing one another for space, they were that desperate to help. The sight of his distress was more than each brother could bear.

Gwen suggested fetching salt water to make the Colonel retch, while Roscoe favored removing the obstruction by hand. When he made to do so, however, the Colonel panicked and tried to fend him off.

"Tweezers," cried Gwen. "Nicholas! Tweezers!"

If the Colonel had been built along standard lines, he might have swallowed the moth without great difficulty. But his oral cavity was more compact than that of the average man and the medium-sized insect had stuck fast in his throat. Working in tandem with a crude, clumsy vigor, Virgil and Sam arranged him on his hands and knees on the table with his face angled towards the standing lamp. Coughlin saw that Roscoe had hooked his mangled thumb into the Colonel's mouth so that Gwen could reach in with her slender fingers. And already it seemed that he was drawing more air because he was whistling and kicking and whipping his head with an electric speed. The man was a fighter, Coughlin had to give him that at least. He decided that the Colonel would likely survive his ordeal.

Miles Craven had indeed been clipped. He was now on his feet, flexing his left leg to test it, steadying himself against the back of his chair. Coughlin could see rusty streaks on his pants-leg and beads of blood on his shoe. If Gwen hadn't been so preoccupied with her husband, she could have called out for someone to tend to her brother as well.

How much time had elapsed? An entire minute perhaps. It made no sense to waste another. He took Moss by the shoulder and spoke low in his ear. "Those packing cases outside. Help me get them in the van."

Moss nodded, without looking up. His nose had been bloodied and his lower lip had puffed up. The kid was so dazed from his beating, he needed to be physically steered through the door.

Coughlin feared that Virgil and Sam might intervene at this point. But outside in the corridor it was Nicholas who blocked their path.

"You're fixing to leave with this man?" he asked in a murmur.

"You bet I am. You're in our way."

"Sir," the houseboy said stiffly "I was not speaking to you."

Outside, the sky was thick with stars. Coughlin loaded the cases into the bed of the van, counting them twice, horrified by the prospect of leaving one behind. For a moment he thought he might have mislaid Moss as well—that the kid had passed out or wandered away in his daze—but he had barely begun to look for him when the gun exploded for a third and final time, so close to his ear that he initially feared it was his turn to be shot. What the hell, Coughlin thought. By this stage of the night, nothing would have surprised him.

On unsteady legs, his thoughts reeling, he retraced his steps and found Moss in the shadow of the Gradys' woodie wagon. And maybe the kid wasn't as punch-drunk as he looked, because amidst all the chaos with the moth and the Colonel he had been able to retrieve Roscoe's gun from the living room floor. The kid stank of gunsmoke. His eyes were alight. The situation was bad, but Coughlin supposed that it could have been worse. Moss might have decided to turn the small snub-nose revolver on the brothers. Instead he'd carried it outside and put a hole in the woodie wagon's front tire.

"Jesus Christ," Coughlin said. "You're going to get us all killed."

He ordered Moss to sit with him upfront and they might—and surely should—have peeled off there and then. Only then a thought struck him and he decided to risk one hurried last errand. He ran to the wagon and plucked the guitar case off the seat.

"Here," he said, out of breath. "I got you a present."

"I don't want it," said Moss indistinctly.

"Take it," said Coughlin. "You play it better than them anyhow."

The engine coughed. Headlamps raked the live oaks by the house. "We're off," he told Moss—and again, that should have been the end of it. But no sooner had Coughlin turned the wheel for the track than the two youngest Gradys sprang out from the house in pursuit. They loped alongside the van as it bumped up the gravel—Sam to one side, Virgil to the other—periodically dipping their big heads to peer at him through the glass. And this made little sense, Coughlin thought, because either one of the brothers could have reached for the handle or even used their great weight to bunt the van off the trail.

The chase continued in this manner for several hundred yards before the boys tired and dropped back—long enough for him to wonder whether it even counted as a chase at all. The Grady boys were savages. They were biologically geared towards violence. And yet here, in these final moments, it was as if Virgil and Sam were running for the pure pleasure of running, as if they regarded this pursuit as another fine game to be played, no different to the ones they had played on the lawn, when the Colonel had thrown them a ball to be caught and the Bird children had lifted their hats from their heads.

27

Moss HAD LOST his guitar. He'd lost his glasses. He couldn't say for certain his nose wasn't broken. He said, "You know what I'm thinking? I reckon I should have stayed at Upsala."

"Upsala." Coughlin laughed bitterly. "The fact is, Moss, I probably just saved your dumb life."

What a pair of fools, he thought. What a pair of fools; what an idiotic ordeal. It seemed that whatever could go wrong for him always did. Coughlin the accursed. The walking, talking accident. It was a wonder they had escaped Comfort Hall in one piece.

NORTH, said a sign at the fork in the road—and that's what he wanted, anywhere that was north. He figured by now he'd been in the South long enough.

"Saved my life, how?"

"For Christ sake, use your head. Those apes might have killed you. I got you out of that house."

Moss frowned at the glass. He said, "If it wasn't for you I'd never have been at the house," and Coughlin had to concede there was at least some truth to that.

He drove past midnight, into the small hours, aware of little beyond the pale dirt of the road and the drifting insects in the headlamps' beam. If anyone did choose to chase him, he wouldn't have a prayer. The engine, the lights. He might as well wave them down; he might as well hang out flags. No one drove after dark in this part of the country. Men went to bed early and rose again with the sun.

Not me, though, Coughlin thought. He was one of the night creatures now. At some point he'd crossed over and left the daylight world behind. Probably it had happened without him even noticing—during that long ride inside the Red Cross boat, say, or at the Indian mounds, or Upsala, that great rotting carcass by the road. He had stepped over the threshold and made a home in the shadows, inasmuch as anybody can lay claim to a home in the shadows. Men in the shadows had to be constantly on the move. They might survive and sometimes prosper, but it was a poor excuse for a life. Running and hiding, never getting anywhere but away.

What were they doing at this moment, all of the people he'd met? The Troller on her rounds, checking the dark water for bodies. Mousey Thomas's fugitives, shivering on their small island. The three kings of Upsala, drunk in feather beds. Moss had said that the Troller was doomed. No doubt he believed that the others were, too. But look at us, Coughlin thought, is our set-up better? Octavian, Lucius and Scipio would all be comfortably asleep, not riding hell-for-leather through the piney woods, scared out of their wits and nursing a fresh set of bruises. So he figured he'd have to give the Upsala lawyer his due. Octavian's home in the shadows was a good deal more cozy than his.

He pulled into a meadow, meaning to sleep for an hour, except that his nerves were too jangled and eventually he pressed on. Moss had half-turned in the seat and was resting his head on his arm. Coughlin had an idea that he wasn't quite sleeping either. The kid was nursing a grudge, wanting to avoid conversation. Given time he'd come around—and time was one thing they both possessed in abundance.

The men on the mound. The runaways at the house. They were all criminals, so called. Maybe Coughlin was, too. It struck him as funny to have come so far—to have dragged himself all the way to respectability, a good job, a little money, prestige—only to find himself right back where he started, living like a criminal in the dark. "This entire business is full of crooks," Oncins the bandleader liked to say, by which he meant everyone who he dealt with on a day-to-day basis. The house band musicians who blew their expenses on dope. The catchers, like wildcatters in the Texas desert, who were always out for themselves. Everyone except him, Oncins. Everyone except whoever he happened to be complaining to that minute. "Sure," Coughlin would say, pious and sympathetic, trying to stay on his good side. "Sure, that does sound bad, alright." But maybe he'd misread the business, come at it the wrong way. He'd been so desperate to make a good impression—softening his accent, putting on airs and graces—and thought he might have managed it, when Oncins and the bosses had seen through him all along. They knew what he was; that's why he was hired. If it weren't for the crooks there'd be no business at all.

Daybreak exposed a ridge of green hills: Appalachia again. They passed a forlorn crossroads post office propped up on gray bricks, and a shuttered fish stand which promised FAIR WEIGHTS & SQUARE DEALINGS. Moss was undeniably awake now, twisting and bending in a comical manner, as if he was searching for loose change on the floor. The kid wouldn't sit straight, even when Coughlin scolded him. It wasn't the Grady boys or the sheriff he was scared of this morning. It was everybody. It was the daylight world.

"Where are we going anyhow?"

"North for the time being. I'm figuring it out."

Bent into the footwell, he said, "I'm asking myself whether you're even a song-catcher at all."

He was better in the back, crouched between the packing cases, harder to see from the road. Yet still his mood remained sullen. Moss didn't like the guitar. He complained that it smelled of Virgil Grady's cologne and that the strings were sweet and thin like cotton candy. He'd had a good guitar and now he had a bad one. Only thing worse than having no guitar to play, he said, was having Virgil Grady's bad guitar.

"Quit it," Coughlin said, losing patience. "Firstly, it wasn't Virgil's, it was Roscoe's. He's the one who played guitar."

"Don't make no difference. They all looked the same."

"And secondly, you've got it all turned around. What you had yesterday was a $2 piece of matchwood. Today you've got a Silvertone. You've got his guitar and his gun. I'd say that puts you about three steps up on where you were yesterday."

That first day of travel was one of sunlight and blossom and barrel-chested young deer. They had passed out of Alabama and into Tennessee. The hairpin bends made their eardrums pop and the forests were thicker and cooler up here. Each bend in the road put them further from Comfort Hall, further from the Colonel and the murderous Grady boys, which had to be a good thing. Coughlin was starting to feel that his luck had turned. Finally, at long last, he had the wind at his back.

"Stay with us, don't leave," the hotel manager had said. And then, on the morning of his departure, on the steps, he'd said, "Please come and see us on your way back, Mr Coughlin." This probably was what most hotel managers said. They dressed up every check-out as a small tragedy. But he had been fond of old Stubb and believed that old Stubb liked him back. After the ugly events of the past week it might be nice to land somewhere he was guaranteed a warm welcome.

The city of Sutton remained a vast distance away, northeast through the mountains, almost into Virginia. He might arrive there tomorrow, more likely the day after. Sutton, he thought, would bring his adventure full circle. He thought of old Stubb. He thought of Bucky Garner. They would lag the walls and stoke the fire so as to keep the wax patties good and soft. A second spring session, upstairs at the Bedford. Just him and the kid. Maybe Bucky riding shotgun. A second spring session to put the first one in the shade. It would be a great thing to happen, he knew that without a doubt. And it was never going to happen, he knew that as well.

Stubb would be pleased to see him, that wasn't the issue. Stubb would be pleased, even delighted, right up until the moment he glanced over his shoulder and saw the boy standing there. That was just how it was—in the mountains and elsewhere. It was the lay of the land, it was the rules of the game. If the girls of the Copeland

Ladies' College weren't allowed at the Bedford, what hope did Moss have? They'd kick the kid out right away.

"New York then," he said. "It's the only thing we can do."

He pulled the van to the side and dug around for his wallet. He passed back a trio of $10 bills. This was a down payment, he explained, an advance on the money he'd pay once they'd arrived in Manhattan. It was proof of his honesty, a demonstration of good faith. "Fair weights," he said. "Fair weights and square dealings."

Moss studied the bills. Without his spectacles, the boy's face looked naked. "Thirty bucks only buys one song."

"Yeah, but we haven't been able to record even that. We haven't recorded shit. So that's money for nothing. I'm trusting you not to run off."

A farm truck clattered past. It raised a cloud of pink dust.

"How many songs are you fixing to record?"

"I reckon they'll agree to eight sides. I'm going to argue for ten."

"That's three hundred bucks."

"Yeah, but I don't have it now, you've cleaned me out. We've barely got enough to get ourselves back home."

"First he says the relief camp. Then he says a house in Alabama." He squinted at the banknotes. "Now the man says, 'Well OK then, New York'."

"Moss," he said. "Trust me. I haven't lied to you once."

There had been snow in these mountains barely two weeks before. Now spring had set in and the smell of sap was so strong he could taste it on his tongue. Wintergreen and sassafras. Yellow birch and sourwood. Look, he kept saying, each time the road turned and the forest dropped away to show off the valley, but Moss was determined to remain out of sight. Besides, the kid added, he couldn't see worth a damn without his horn-rims.

"We'll get you a new pair soon as we reach the city. Hell, you can have a new pair for every day of the week."

Moss coughed. "I believe it when I see it."

"You'll see it, don't worry. You'll see everything, that's my point."

He stopped to replenish the tank at a lonesome filling station. The place sold local produce; he bought biscuit, nuts and milk. Already the events of the past week felt otherworldly to him. The Biblical flood, too enormous to be real. The island, the house, the boat ride through the night. But that afternoon he stopped the van in order to relieve himself and watched a black bear cross the length of the forest clearing ahead. And this sight was so strange he hadn't even time to be scared, because the bear—a full-grown adult at least twice Coughlin's size—was walking painstakingly on its hind legs. It pawed the air for balance, keeping its muzzle raised and its gaze straight ahead, so that he could not honestly say whether the thing had seen him or not.

This spectacle lasted only a matter of seconds before the beast was swallowed again by the trees. But Coughlin was left with the idea that this might be how every bear walked when it fancied itself unobserved and that he had somehow conspired to slip backstage at the theater. Afterwards, on the road, the image of kept returning—those dainty dancer's steps, that dignified, solemn air—until he came to regard it one of the finest, most memorable moments of his mission to the South; a fabulous thing that he had carried out with him, although not quite so fabulous as the kid in the back with the stolen guitar.

28

T HERE WAS A tale that he had heard years before as a child. He remembered it now, riding through Tennessee. It was about a scorpion that wanted to cross the river and the small frog that agreed to carry the thing on its back. The frog wanted a promise that the scorpion wouldn't sting. "Of course I won't sting," the scorpion had replied. "Why would I sting? If I did we'd both drown."

So the two of them set off across the river. And sure enough, mid-stream, the scorpion broke its word. "You fool," cried the frog. "Now you've killed us both." Except that the scorpion couldn't help itself. "That's just my nature," it said.

The mounds, said Sam Tucker, his friend, and maybe the mounds were where he should have stayed. Havana, said Lucius. Palm trees and white sand. The kitchen door. The yard. The meadow, the woods. All those chances gone begging. He ought to have paid more attention.

New York, said the man—the song-catcher, John Coughlin. Trust me, he said. Everything is going to be fine. And so they drove north together. The scorpion and the frog.

It was getting on toward sundown when Moss took out the guitar. He did so feeling sheepish, as though this was another test he had failed. Except that nature was nature and a man couldn't help what he was. The voices had been clamoring in his ears all day. They were spinning their melodies and demanding he play them back.

"At long last," Coughlin said. "I've been waiting long enough."

"I ain't playing for you," Moss said. "It's only on account of having nothing else to do."

He'd arranged himself on a case, his hair brushing the van's tin ceiling. The Silvertone had a weight; it would take some getting used to. Roscoe Grady's guitar. That was especially hard to stomach.

"It's not the guitar's fault who owned it before."

"Yeah," he said. "I guess."

"I mean, fuck Roscoe Grady. He's history, he's done."

He twisted the knobs, tuning the thing to his liking, although however much he twisted it would never sound like the Stella; he would never play like he had back in Mississippi. And this of course was another thing he had to make his peace with. Moss had been all bent out of shape by everything that had happened. It therefore stood to reason that his music had too.

The panel delivery rocked and skidded on the road. It threw off his stroke and bumped his head on the sides. But he retrieved the loose melody that had been running around in his head and then set to work on building a bridge. And he had to admit it: the guitar sounded sweet.

Coughlin glanced over his shoulder. "That's a new one. You haven't played that before."

He'd roughed some words for the piece, but the Silvertone drowned them out. You had to hit the old Stella in order to get its attention. This one, when you hit it, hummed like a live wire.

He eased up on the strings, barely touching them now, and ran through his little melody until it tightened like a spring. The catcher at the wheel still couldn't make out the words.

"Two animals," Moss told him. "Two animals team up and cross a river together."

Coughlin was amused. "Just like you and me."

They parked in the woods between two giant poplars. Coughlin repositioned the cases so that they could both stretch out, and cracked the driver-side window to allow in the night air. He was asleep within seconds. Moss lay awake. He was thinking about Cuba. He was thinking of Lucius: his skin and his smell. Only half-a-mile down-road, right before they turned off, he had seen an unpainted shack with a colored man on its stoop. His thoughts turned to that: the old man on his stoop.

The woods outside were filled with noise. Appalachia's night creatures were out in force. Moss could hear, at a distance, the percussive thump-thump-thump as a goods train crossed the trestle. If there were a railroad up ahead, that might serve him well. Some trains would be shuttling back and forth through the woods. Others, though, would be roaming much further afield.

He turned onto the track, testing the ground with his toes, not daring to proceed at his normal walking pace in case he turned an ankle. He had Roscoe's gun in his hand, although he suspected that the thing was now out of bullets. He had the stolen guitar slung across his back. He had three $10 bills in his button-down pocket. His mind was made up, at least for the time being. He'd pay one of those bills to the fellow at the shack and spend the rest on his journey south. He'd take the train to Miami and then decide what to do.

Blind Moss Evans, Miles Craven had called him. Well, now it was true, he could barely see a thing. When the rutted track dog-legged, he scratched his arm on the brambles. He figured that he must be coming at the shack from the rear-side, not the road.

Keep walking, he told himself, and see where you end up. Rear-side or roadside or somewhere else altogether. He crept on through the darkness, holding the gun out for protection.

Alabama this way, said the song-catcher, John Coughlin. And now up through the mountains, all the way to New York. Full steam ahead and not a moment to lose, because one thing about white men, they always know where they're going. Even when they change their mind they make out like that's what they meant all along. And the reason, no doubt, is because they always get what they want. I want this, it's mine. I want to be there, let's go. White men, Moss thought, lived in a world of straight roads with all of the street-lamps lit up.

It was different for black folk; they never got what they wanted.

All their lives told what to do and where to work, who to wed, where to stand; they never expected anything. Whatever they gained came by accident or good fortune. Whatever they gained could be whipped away the next day. This was a poor state of affairs, no question about it, Given the choice, he'd prefer it to be different. But on certain rare occasions, the black life had its uses. Forbearance, they called it, the pastors and preachers. The life of the negro is an ongoing lesson in fortitude and forbearance. God grant me the serenity to accept that which I cannot change. And so on and so forth, hallelujah, amen.

When delivering barrels to the road crews out of Parchman, Old Duke used to point at the black prisoners and then compare them to the whites. Look at them, he'd say. See the difference right there. The coloreds mostly went about their business, pretty much the same as they had before they got collared. The white prisoners, though, fell apart and went crazy. The coloreds endured because they had all learned forbearance, Duke said, whereas the white folk broke down because they weren't cut out for hardship. They'd always got what they wanted and thought something had gone wrong with the world. Moss was a black man, raised in Washington County, Mississippi. He knew about forbearance and therefore didn't much mind walking on his own through these woods. Miles Craven, God help him, would have just about wet his pants.

Expectation is one thing. Trusting your luck is another. Stay hopeful, keep moving and see where the route takes you. Might not be where you're thinking. Might be better, might be worse. It was no different, Moss reasoned, to his escape from the levee in the dug-out canoe; all of them wedged in together, throwing themselves on the river's mercy. It had turned them around and shot them through the crevasse, from darkness to brightness, from danger to safety, in a way that had felt out of his hands, even preordained. No disputing the current. No arguing with fate. And so he wasn't altogether disheartened when, after inching his way through the trees for an hour, he saw the square roof of the van and realized that all of those dog-legs had circled him back. He put the whole thing from his mind, opened the door and climbed in.

His weight in the vehicle roused the catcher from his sleep. "What are you doing?"

"Nothing," he said. "Only taking some air."

Coughlin grunted and turned over. "Not running out on me then?"

"No sir," Moss said. "I reckon we're going to New York."

The gravel road straightened. He figured he could risk driving faster. The month of May took the form of dead flies and pink blossoms. When the covering got too thick, Coughlin had to stop and wipe the windows with his sleeve. But in the hour or so beforehand, Moss would amuse himself by naming the patterns of dots as if they were constellations of stars. Look, he'd say, pointing across the catcher's shoulder. That one is the widow. That's her hat and her stick. That there's the three cows. Look at them—one, two, three.

He took out the guitar, meaning to find a small song for each pattern, a collection of jokes to pass the time on the road. The Potato Peeler. The Scaredy Horse. The Lonesome Crow. The Land of Spain.

So far as Coughlin was concerned, the windscreen blots were just blots. But that was the measure of a musician: they could spin a piece out of nothing. He didn't want joke songs. Spider Joe was a joke song. But he suspected that some of these scraps might amount to more than just jokes.

The Drunken Road Crew. The Northbound Train. Moss said that this was the train that the black folk rode. It pointed the way out of Washington County. He'd fashioned a tune that combined finger-picking with slide. Open-D, top string, second string. The Northbound Train. Calling Celebration, Missouri. Calling Freedom, Illinois.

Coughlin laughed. "There are no such towns."

"Maybe not in your world. Maybe they're secret black folk towns."

The further they traveled, the more green were the trees. He saw barns and grain silos and fields combed in neat grooves. He saw a church in the valley, as snow-white as a bride. Behind one of these hills lay the house that belonged to the crippled saint, Brodie, who dreamed of making the land whole again. He looked out for the turn-off. Perhaps it had already grown over.

Ten sides, he'd told Moss, but which ones would he choose? The Floodgates of Heaven, although it would need to be shortened. His version of The Midnight Special. The Beauty Queen of Arkansas. The piece about the drowned town, Kowaliga. Except that now he'd grown partial to the little songs about the blots. The more the kid worked on them, the more they took shape and stood up. He played them through that long afternoon and tinkered with them deep into the night. Moss Evans's constellation series. In time they'd be seen as the kid's masterpiece.

Several times on the drive, Coughlin tried to describe New York, always with the sense that Moss wasn't getting it, that the city was hanging just out of his grasp. New York with its steam vents and baked stench and hard bars of sunlight. The electric letters galloping round and round Times Square. The sixteen different flavors of Italian ice in a cart. The guy spoons it out. Every scoop's a small planet.

"Yes sir," Moss said. He pointed at the glass. "The Headless Chicken," he said. "Its clawed feet and its tail."

Or how about movies?, the catcher persisted. There were about six or seven hundred picture shows in New York. You'd walk inside in broad daylight and step out when it's dark and in the meantime you've traveled around the world, pretty much. Except that Moss had seen movies and didn't much care for them. Everyone talked up a blue streak about movies, whereas he had never been able to see the point of the things.

The kid had watched a show, he recalled, not two months before. It was a comedy about a young bank-robber who'd given his captors the slip and was posing as a chef at a fancy-pants restaurant. So far, so good, except that things then take a turn. In come the gaolers, the policemen and the judge. In comes the fat manager of the big Main Street bank. The robber hides his face with his apron as he darts between the tables. He pours out drinks, he ladles soup, and then he slips on a spoon and is recognized by his enemies all at once. The screen goes black, the card says THE END and all you hear is men shouting and the smashing of plates.

Coughlin nodded. "Yeah, OK, so what?"

"Well, that's what I'm saying. So what happened next?"

"What's it matter?"

"But it was just getting interesting," Moss said. "You want to know if the robber gets away or gets caught. If he fights the cops and beats them down. They set it up pretty sweet. You want to know how it ends."

The catcher, though, was unpersuaded. He scratched at his forehead and stared at the smeared glass. He said, "You already know how it ends. It all ends badly."

Tennessee was behind them. Virginia filled the glass. And now the mountain towns sprung upon them—sudden bursts of activity, each lit up like a Christmas tree with their illuminated shoe stores and druggists and then just as quickly gone again, ducking back into the woods before the next one broke cover. They stopped for a spell to watch a hay-barn burn down. The blaze drew a crowd. Onlookers lined the road.

He had imagined himself to be anonymous, invisible, but there were men in that country who kept their ears to the ground. Because on the fifth night out from Comfort Hall, while eating dinner inside a noisy roadhouse, he became aware that he was being watched and was presently joined at the table by a man that he knew.

The visitor drew up a chair. He tapped it three times before sitting. He said, "By rights I should be dead tonight. Outside of Staunton some bastard tried to shoot me."

He had the salesman's habit, Rinaldi, of beginning each conversation as though it had already warmed up, as though they had already shaken hands and plowed through the small talk. The country, he said, was going straight to the dogs.

Coughlin set down his fork. "Who tried to shoot you?"

"How should I know? Some caveman in his yard. What, I'm going to stop and ask his name?"

Coughlin had ordered two portions and had the second bagged up. He thought that the catcher might remark on the bag, but Rinaldi did not; his thoughts were elsewhere.

"This country. I mean, what happened, right?"

He was on his way south, only a month behind schedule on account of the rain and the snow and the roads and his tarot. Virginia, he'd decided, was farmed out and stripped bare. "Are you doing Virginia? Don't bother, it's chaff. Grandmothers with washboards. Grandfathers with spoons. All nature's freaks and not one good tune between them." He snapped his fingers for service. "Kentucky," he said. "The next frontier, am I right? Virginia is dead, it's Kentucky for me."

Rinaldi, God bless him. Back from the dead, big as life. Coughlin had thought of the man often during his time on the road—and then again in the flood when it had seemed to him that he was chasing nothing but a hunch, trusting in magic and good fortune to somehow steer him right. He'd assumed that the man would find his way safely back to New York, but he hadn't banked on the possibility of running across him in the Corners. Evidently the world was smaller than he'd once believed.

The catcher's coffee arrived. He tapped his thumbnail on the mug. Riding around the fairgrounds, he said. Trapping fireflies in a jar. Except that next time the fair's just a little further afield. Next trip the bugs maybe aren't glowing quite as bright. Buffalo Bill hunted bison until there were none left on the plain. Prospectors dug the gold out of California in a year. Probably that was the logic of every wildcat business. A steady trade, yes, can sustain a man through a lifetime. But a hot one's on a stopwatch. The more a customer likes the product, the more of it he wants to buy. The more of it he buys, the quicker it runs out. Only so many songs in the mountain, he said, and only very few of them gold.

Coughlin by now was mopping up his gravy. "It's still a great business, though."

"Oh sure, it's the best. And when you catch a good one, you always know, am I right?"

In the corner by the door stood an upright piano. The fellow on the stool was playing Fur Elise.

"Music," said Rinaldi. "You explain that to me. A book can break your heart but it takes two hundred pages to do it. A motion picture works faster—maybe twenty minutes or so. But a song, holy shit, it can do it in a second, in the space of the first fucking bar. There's nothing else like it. You explain that one to me."

Coughlin could not. "But that's why we do it. That's what makes us go catching."

"Damn straight." He gulped his coffee, lit a cigarette. "By rights you should be dead as well. Humpty Records, God damn it, they've pretty much read you the last rites."

"I've been way out in the field. Tennessee and Alabama. Mississippi even."

"And now here you are, the Irish Rover. Fucking homecoming hero, heading back to collect his winnings."

"Heading home for a bath," he said. But Rinaldi had narrowed his gaze and quit his fidgeting. A smile, not entirely warm, played on the man's lips.

"Wait, you mean you ain't heard?" He looked around as if to address the other diners. "Would you ever believe it, the kid hasn't heard. I mean sure, of course, why would he have heard?"

"Heard what?"

"Your little animal song. It's just about saved Humpty's skin."

"My little animal song."

"Oh boy." Rinaldi whistled. "He hasn't even heard." Because the business moved at a terrific clip, that was just what he'd been saying, there's no time like the present. Tuesday morning's fresh catch is

Friday afternoon's rot. So put it out quickly, because what's the point otherwise? Press it and roll it. Electroplate the damn thing. The demand exists now. You run to meet it or die.

The Bedford sessions, so-called, had been brought to the city by train. Some country rube brought them in. From what Rinaldi had heard, the early reviews weren't so hot. Oncins, the bandleader, was unimpressed, verging on appalled, while the other Humpty musicians were lemmings; they took their lead from the boss. What the hell is this shit? Sounds like barnyard fucking. The Irish kid's laid an egg. But they were desperate, poor bastards, so what else could they do?

"Slow down," Coughlin pleaded. "My little animal song."

"Young Animals in Love," said Rinaldi. "It's selling all over. Big cities, small burgs."

He cast his mind back. "You mean . . . Peggy Prince?"

"What did you pay for that pup, thirty bucks? Hand on heart, Irish, it's going to shift half-a-million."

The fellow at the upright had moved on to Schubert. A muscular busboy brushed by with a tray. Coughlin shook his head to clear it. He felt like Rip Van Winkle, who woke to find the war ended and the world transformed.

"The moon so new, the morning dew, like something being born. And in the mountains, sure enough, young animals in love." Rinaldi laughed. "I mean, it ain't Shakespeare, but so what, people like it."

"My little animal song."

"My advice to you, demand a raise right away. I'd ask for eight and make them beat you down a little." He drew on his cigarette, all business now. "Because the danger is that they now get excited and put out all the other sides, too, and when the other sides flop, you've right away lost your shine. Today you're in credit. Tomorrow, who knows?"

He had left Moss in the van, in the lot. The roadhouse had a policy. By now the bag of food would have lost its warmth. He could see the grease already starting to pool at the bottom.

Rinaldi followed his gaze. "Who are you buying dinner for anyway?"

"Mississippi kid in the van. Plays guitar and sings too."

"Why's he in the van?"

Coughlin hesitated. There were several answers he could have given here.

He said, "Because he's too good for this joint. The truth is, Tommy, he's too good for most joints."

They walked out together and passed Moss his bag of food. They walked back inside. Coughlin had shown his treasure.

"Well now," said the Italian. "Give me a second, OK?"

Their table for two had already been cleared and reset, and so they parked themselves at the counter. Both men agreed that they could probably do with more coffee. Rinaldi said that, on balance, that might not be strong enough.

"Oh man," he said, again pantomiming as if he were addressing the gallery. "This is like a dream come true for me."

The roadhouse was done up in the style of a romantic French bistro with guttering candles and faux-Tiffany lamps and mirrors which were frosted with cherubs and nymphs. But it sat off the road amid towering conifers and catered to an unruly crew of itinerants: loggers and hunters and traveling salesmen in need of a bath. It refused to serve negroes. Perhaps it refused women, too.

The burly young busboy brought the coffee across.

"Well, so what?" Coughlin said. "Who cares what they think? It's like you were saying, they'll have to take what I give them."

"Ten sides of race music. Why not record twenty?"

"Maybe I will."

"I think that you should." It was noisier at the counter than it had been at the table. They had each raised their voices to be heard above the din.

What a thing, said Rinaldi. What a thing and what a day. After that hillbilly took a shot at him, he figured he had better pluck his lucky Homburg from his bag. Bad shit tended to happen when he went without his lucky Homburg. He had worn it, then, for the whole rest of the drive and like magic felt better than he had at lunch.

He turned on the stool and made to slap Coughlin's shoulder. "You threw out all the guidelines," he said. "Just ripped up the road map and went your own way. Bully for you, I'm impressed."

Coughlin looked at the window. "He should have finished his food by now. Let's step back outside. You hear him play."

"I don't need to hear him. I've seen him. He's perfect."

"Tommy. I'm right about this one. It's like you said, when you know, you know."

"Twenty sides," said Rinaldi. "My God, why not forty?"

He brought up the mug. Anxious, pugnacious Rinaldi. White stones in his pockets, paperclips on his tie. The piano had fallen silent now but several loggers had lined up by the door and were singing Liza Jane. Rinaldi said that if the mug contained something stronger, they could both toast their good fortune. If they were back at the Bide-a-Wee, with a decanter of whiskey on the table and a log fire in the grate. If Honest Jim were alive, he'd insist on a toast at this point. He'd lift up his cup and toast the song-catchers, every one. The winners and losers; maybe the losers most of all. Maybe they were all losers at heart. The tragedy was that they hadn't realized it yet.

"All good music's a risk," Coughlin said and the Italian slapped the counter and agreed that this was it exactly, he'd hit the nail on the head. Spoken like a true catcher. All good music's a risk.

The loggers had linked arms. The busboy cleared the tables. Coughlin was struggling to order his thoughts. "I wish those bastards would pipe down for a spell."

"So I'm in two minds," said Rinaldi. "I'm in two minds, I'm torn. There's a big part of me that wants to knock some sense into you."

The bare boards thundered beneath the loggers' boots.

"The other part of me," he said, lifting his voice to be heard. "The other part, Coughlin, I'm honestly sorry to miss it. I'd like to be there in the city when you bring the kid in."

29

L ET'S HEAR IT for the catchers, Honest Jim Cope used to say. The losers, the boozers, the heroes, the crooks. The men who went into the mountains and came back with the gold, or who died in the trying, or who came out empty-handed. Every trip is a gamble, every piece you buy is a risk, but what's life without risk, the world is dull enough as it is. And without the gamblers, the heroes—and yes, the losers, too—they'd never have made the trip south and unlocked Appalachia. No Deep Down Mountain Blues or Did You Ever Dream a Dream. No Rattlesnake Daddy, no Copperhead Mama. They'd all still be downtown, selling musty imports from Europe.

Good times never last. Every boom turns to bust. Either the product runs out or the public loses interest and so it would be with the song-catching trade. In another year or two, maybe less, there'd be no call for hill-country sides any more. The catchers, the pluggers, the fat boss at his desk. Everyone all at once would be kicked to the curb. Grab your coat, grab your hat, go find a new line of work. Business was good while it lasted. It never lasted very long.

It was funny, Cope said. Every time he assembled the lathe—every time he set the weight and repositioned the stool and turned the musician so he was playing into the horn—these hillbilly pickers always said the same thing. "Three minutes?" they'd say. "Three minutes is nothing." And they said this because they didn't understand time. That's what it came down to: they didn't understand time. People lived in the moment and couldn't see beyond that. Thirty bucks for a song? Well now, ain't that swell. Three minutes to record it? Well now, that ain't right. Not grasping the fact that those three-minutes of work bought a second life down the road. Not realizing it meant that their little piece had been saved. The business would fold but the songs would survive. They'd last for as long as there were turntables and needles and men and women who'd listen.

Camp Yarrow, mostly built, sat lakeside in the woods. It had been meant for hunters, anglers and vacationing families from Allentown and Philadelphia, but the investors had pulled out before the work was complete, forcing the opening festivities to be put back by a year. While the sign at the turn-off still looked freshly painted, it pointed the way to an overgrown track and an acre of raw ground. A semi-circle of cabins looked out on the water. Coughlin stepped from the van. He thought he'd seen a fish jump.

"Is that a river?" asked Moss, useless without his glasses.

"It's a lake."

"Looks like a river."

"It's a lake."

The cabins were shells, with canvas sheets for windows. The interiors, though, smelt pleasantly of pine. Each contained integrated wooden bed-frames plus a small water closet, as yet unplumbed. They would suffice for the night; they had bedded down in worse spots. Moss wondered if there might be a guard on the site, or whether some local fellow was employed to give eye to the place. "What local?" said Coughlin. "There's nobody lives here for several miles or more."

Invisible crickets sawed back and forth in the dusk. Moss built a bonfire so they could heat up some food. Two cans of sausage, one can of corn. The lake had changed color; it glowed as orange as the flames. As soon as he'd eaten, the kid brought out the Silvertone. He played for an hour. Coughlin hated for him to stop.

"There," he said finally. "You have to admit, I stole you a good guitar."

"I liked the old one. Older than the pyramids."

"So we said."

"Burst the dead hog. Made the bullfrogs explode."

Moss worked his way through the constellation songs one-by-one. The Widow and The Scaredy Horse. The Northbound Train and The Land of Spain. And it was strange, he said, because it was almost as if the songs had changed color, too. The first few times he'd played them, they'd been small sketches, light jokes. But each time he doubled back they came out sounding more serious, less funny, and he couldn't say whether that was him making it happen or the songs themselves somehow getting out from under him. Coughlin had noticed the change as well. He said this proved they needed to get the songs down on wax right away. Leave it another week and they'd be full-blown tragedies.

"You're fixing to buy the consolation songs too?"

"Constellation. You bet. I'll take all you got."

Moss picked out a riff. His face was unreadable. "That would mean a big heap of money."

"Sure," Coughlin said, although this was a problem he'd tackle as and when it arose. The first order of business was getting the kid in the studio, spiriting him in under the noses of Oncins and the boys. And if that proved impossible, then facing them down, forcing them back on their heels. Right now you've credit, Rinaldi had said, so don't blow the goodwill on something—somebody—they'll want no part of. But what good was credit if it only sat there doing nothing? You took your winnings, said a prayer and slapped them straight back on the table. Credit, he reckoned, would buy him a clear day of recording. Goodwill a second; finally pity a third. Three days ought to do it. The boy's best work etched on wax.

"I'm going to buy some new horn-rims. I'm going to get me some new clothes."

"You'll be able to do what you like. You'll be rich. A free agent."

"True enough," Moss said. "I can catch a boat across to France."

Camp Yarrow, the Poconos; forty miles from home. When the bonfire blew out, the sky above their heads was enormous and the spray of stars almost liquid, like paint on a palette just beginning to set. To think, Coughlin said, that the boy might still be on the mound in the flood, staring up at those same stars and hardly daring to play for fear of being caught. All those songs in his head would have stayed there and faded. All that music which would have lived inside him, died inside him and never seen the light of day. It almost made Coughlin think that he had done a fine thing, for maybe the first time in his life. He'd done it for himself, of course, he wasn't about to pretend otherwise. He'd done it for himself but also for the kid.

Moss had leaned across to stir the embers with a stick. "You came out for the songs," he said. "You didn't come for me."

"Yeah, but what's it matter? What's the difference?"

Moss said nothing.

"There is no difference," said Coughlin. "You can't separate it out. It's all the same thing."

From time to time on the road—and again tonight, by the fire—he'd recall the faces and voices of those he'd encountered on the trip, so vivid and specific it was as if he'd only just turned his back. Octavian in his armchair; the Troller in her boat. Bucky Garner waving his newsboy cap and soliciting donations. The holy cripple at the wall, leaning into his crutches and gazing at the golden west.

He thought of lanky Morton Haines, lolling by the coconut shy at the Herbie Lax carnival—except that Haines would be a cripple, too, these days, because hadn't the Grady boys broken his back that same night? He remembered Miles Craven, Gwen's pitiful younger brother, limping about the dining room with blood on his shoes and a faraway look in his eyes. Three cripples from the mountains, three young men in disrepair, because the Far Corners was a brutal and treacherous country. Rinaldi had warned him; he had now experienced the place at first hand.

Moss chipped in to say that he had been casting his mind back as well. Tranquil, starlit Camp Yarrow lent itself to introspection. The kid was now of the view that he'd missed a chance at Comfort

Hall. He ought to have used Roscoe's gun on all three Grady boys. He ought to have made them kneel down and close their eyes. Then he'd have stood behind them and taken aim, one-two-three.

Coughlin looked up. "You still got that gun with you?"

"Yeah." He patted the pocket of his overalls.

"You ought to get rid of it. You don't want it going off when we hit a pothole."

"It's out of bullets anyway."

"All the same," Coughlin said. "Riding into New York with a gun. Black vagrant with a firearm. I'm serious, Moss, that's only asking for trouble."

It was full dark in the woods, closing in towards midnight and they ought by rights to be up early the next morning. But for the time being he was happy to sit at the lake edge and listen to the kid play his music. Coughlin let his mind wander, partly led by the melodies, and he forgot about how his jaw was still aching from when Virgil Grady had socked him, or how his right knee had seized up from too long on the road. Instead, he imagined that all the forest creatures—bears, foxes, raccoons and deer—had slowly materialized from the woods at their back, drawn by the sound and wanting to hear it more clearly, and were now lined up in the darkness just a few yards away. Moss played The Kowaliga Song and The Floodgates of Heaven. He played scraps of new things which were still finding their range.

In a break in the playing, Coughlin recalled something once he'd told Rinaldi, what felt like a hundred years ago now. Rinaldi had been saying that good catchers loved music and Coughlin replied that everyone said they loved music when what they really wanted was for music to love them back. He'd been embarrassed at the time and wished he'd kept his mouth shut. But it was true, what he'd said, and he thought he should have shown more courage.

He found a round stone and tossed it at the lake. "It's the same with these songs. Your songs. The constellation songs and all the rest of them. It's like I think they love me back. That's a nice feeling. That's the best feeling, I guess." He cleared his throat and attempted a laugh. Thank God for the darkness; he might even be blushing.

Moss thought this through. "I don't know if they like you back. I don't know if music works that way."

"Yeah, maybe." Coughlin wished he had another stone to throw. "I'm only thinking aloud."

"Songs are just songs. They don't care about you. They're doing their own thing."

"Yeah, maybe." He raised a hand in surrender. "Well, I love them. I like them. Jesus Christ, kid, allow me that at least."

It could be that exhaustion had softened Coughlin's mind because his thoughts kept spinning and sparking strange ideas. It seemed that no sooner had he stopped imagining an audience of woodland animals than he began mulling the merits of putting all of Moss's music on wax. He liked the way the songs sounded different every time the kid played them. He liked thinking that each one was the best until the next one came along. But the minute he put Moss in the studio—the minute he angled the horn and turned on the machine—it would be like putting his music in amber and stopping its breath.

The right thing to do, he decided, would be to let the kid go. And so here it was: last chance, final choice. Because hadn't he heard tales of the angler who, having fought for hours to reel in a blue marlin, then leans over the side to release the hook? The reason being that the thrill of the catch is satisfying enough, and because the most beautiful fish should be allowed to go its own way. Returning his catch to the depths doesn't make the angler less heroic, less able. If anything, it's the opposite.

Do it, he thought, although he doubted that he would. Either turn Moss loose, or leave him here at Camp Yarrow, which amounts to the same thing. The kid had $30 in his pocket. He had a good guitar he could play. The police might pinch him first thing in the morning, but they might just as easily not. He was a smart and resourceful individual, Moss Evans. He might yet get wherever he wanted to go.

Coughlin closed his eyes and pictured the scene. Moss awakening the next morning to the sound of birdsong. Stepping out of the cabin to find the van gone. He'd check around the back of the cabins. He'd walk a short way up the track. He might think at first that the catcher had driven to buy food. And so he'd wait by the lake, watching the fish break the surface and the trees shake their branches. And he might sit that way for an hour or more until he realized what had happened and began the process of deciding what to do with his life. There were several small boats tied up in the shallows. The wind made them buck and dip like painted horses on a carousel. The birds and the crickets chatted back and forth. He'd slide the guitar from the case, tune it up and join in.

A black happy ending, Lucius might have called it. A black happy ending. Different from a white happy ending.

30

T HE HOMECOMING HERO. The song-catcher, John Coughlin. Sort yourself a raise, Rinaldi had advised him. Young
Animals in Love is bound to sell half-a-million. Ask for eight thousand dollars and make the bastards beat you down. Which was
crazy, he knew. There was no way in hell that Humpty was going to
pay him eight thousand. Probably Rinaldi himself didn't earn close
to that. But they might pay him six. They might pay him six-five.
And if they paid him six-five he could move out of King Street. He
fancied renting a place in the west 70s; the second or third story
walk-up in some handsome brick townhouse. Bookshelves, potted
plants and a tabletop phonograph. Stick your head out the window,
you can see Central Park.

Allentown, Nazareth, Easton and Bridgewater. They came out
of the woods and bounced across the lush farmland. Riptides of
pink blossom glued themselves to the glass. Coughlin risked a glance
over his shoulder to ask the kid whether he still had Roscoe's gun
in his pocket. Toss it, he suggested. We don't need a gun any more.

"It ain't loaded anyway," Moss said.

"You're sure about that?"

"Pretty much."

"Flip it open and check," he said, only Moss wouldn't do it. The
kid was nervous of the snub-nose and reluctant to handle it any
more than he had to. He didn't even know if he was able to work
the catch with his thumb. What if he started poking it and there
was one last round in the chamber and the thing went off in his
hand? It was Roscoe Grady's gun, after all. Who in their right mind
would trust Roscoe Grady's gun to behave itself?

"Jesus Christ, though, this isn't good," Coughlin said. "We'll have to offload it when we stop someplace."

Bound Brook and Queen City. Signs for Westfield and Newark. And here the country changed again, turning more pale and powdery, so that they ran through a dust-blown district of factories, filling stations and wood-framed tenements. To their right lay an open graveyard of rusting automobiles and engine parts. To their right, giant billboards carried advertisements for Lifebuoy Soap and The Garden of Allah.

"Hoboken ferry," Coughlin said. "That's where we're crossing over."

The day was warm and the world was bright. He couldn't look at the white road without narrowing his eyes. But closing in on the city, nearly within sight of the skyline, they caught the tail of a storm—perhaps the last squall of the spring—and were forced to pull over and wait until the clouds parted and the sun broke through again. And then afterwards, on the drenched approach to the ferry terminal, they came upon a mass of vehicles which had been so blinded by the downpour that they had run onto the verge or into one another. Coughlin peered through the glass and rotated the wheel, threading his way between the upturned cars, twisted bicycles and the incontinent goods trucks laid out on their sides.

This scene of devastation extended a quarter-mile or more. Scores of stricken motors ticked and cooled in the mid-afternoon heat. Steam hissed from radiator grills and from beneath crumpled hoods. And incredibly, so far as Coughlin could tell, it appeared that nobody was dead or even especially hurt. It was as though these collisions had somehow occurred in slow-motion, allowing the motorists the time to open their doors and step out to safety while the vehicles concertinaed and crimped and spun in lazy circles beside them. They milled in the street, the happy survivors, drunk from their revels and thrilled to have shared the same experience. They marveled at the extent of the mess they had made. They waved the van through like they were ushers at a wedding.

The tires crunched on glass. Sunlight pummeled the passenger-side window. Moss's voice was dry; he sounded shaken. He said, "Is that it there? I mean, sure, what else would it be?"

"There it is," Coughlin said.

"It doesn't look real," said the kid. "It looks like something from the future."

He'd been so intent on navigating a path through the wreckage that he only now became aware of the Hudson playing peek-a-boo behind the apartment blocks. And all it took was a turn of the wheel for the city skyline to spread itself across the windshield, so close that he could see traffic moving on the crosstown streets and hear the distant fugue of car horns. The clouds in the east had been torn like tissues. Down in the Village it looked like high summer. Midtown, it was dark. The rain was still falling.

Moss had gripped the seat-back with both hands. "I don't know," he said softly. "Do you reckon this is going to be alright?"

"Moss," Coughlin said. "It's going to be better than alright. It's going to be everything." And he wished it was so. You rolled the dice and you hoped.

He swung out onto the steep exit ramp, hitting the brake with such force that they were both propelled forwards. Coughlin braced his arms against the steering wheel. He felt his blood quicken; instinctively he knew he was home. But in those final seconds before the van made the turn and joined the line of cars to the dock, he believed he had seen the place as Moss would have seen it, blurred in the glass and smeared with flyspecks and pink leaves. A mountain range, a termite mound, buzzing and humming and crawling with life. The end of the world and the start of it, too. Gorgeous and awful, the future, New York.

ACKNOWLEDGMENTS

T HE CATCHERS IS a piece of historical fiction, which is to say that it's a flagrant fabrication of the past, not to be trusted as a journal of record. The 1927 Mississippi flood was real, as was the song-catching trade that flourished around the same time, but some of the facts have been altered and many of the details invented.

Fortunately, both these subjects (the Mississippi flood and the early years of recorded music) are covered by a number of excellent non-fiction books. These include Barry Mazor's *Ralph Peer and the Making of Popular Roots Music*, Lyle Saxon's *Father Mississippi*, Robert Palmer's *Deep Blues*, Pete Daniel's *Deep'n as it Come*, Philip R. Ratcliffe's *Mississippi John Hurt*, Ann Douglas's *Terrible Honesty: Mongrel Manhattan in the 1920s*, Fiona Ritchie and Doug Orr's *Wayfaring Strangers*, Alan Lomax's *The Land Where Blues Began*, and John M. Barry's brilliant *Rising Tide*.

This book was made possible by a project grant from Arts Council England, which funded crucial research and writing time. It was also made possible by the help of people on the ground in Mississippi and elsewhere. Huge thanks to Sandra Stillman of the 1927 Flood Museum, who showed me around Greenville and made me feel at home. Thanks to Bobby Thompson of the Mississippi Levee Board and Benjy Nelken of the Greenville History Museum. Thanks, too, to John Ruskey of the Quapaw Canoe Company up in Clarksdale, and to Paul Hartfield of the US Fish and Wildlife Service. I'm also indebted to the late Hank Burdine, unofficial "Mayor of the Delta", who schooled me in the ways of the Mississippi River.

Thanks, too, to Pamela Junior of the Mississippi Civil Rights Museum, Rachel Myers of the Museum of Mississippi History Museum and Stephenie Morrisey of the Mississippi Department of Archives and History. All three were unstintingly generous with their time and expertise.

It takes a publisher to raise a book, and I'm enormously grateful to my extended family at Salt: to Chris, Jen, Kirsty and Tabitha. That this novel exists in the world is down to the love, care and attention they've shown it.

Thanks, finally, to the amazing Sarah. First reader, best editor. This one took a while, but we got there in the end.

This book has been typeset by
SALT PUBLISHING LIMITED
using Neacademia, a font designed by Sergei Egorov
for the Rosetta Type Foundry in the Czech Republic. It is
manufactured using Holmen Book Cream 65gsm. It was printed
and bound by Clays Limited in Bungay, Suffolk, Great Britain.

CROMER
GREAT BRITAIN
MMXXIV

**Based on the novelization
by Danny Fingeroth**

**Based on the screenplay by
Simon Kinberg & Zak Penn**

LEVEL 3

■SCHOLASTIC

Editor: Helen Parker

Designer: Susen Vural

Cover layout: Emily Spencer

Picture research: Emma Bree

Photo credits: Cover image and film stills provided
courtesy of Marvel Characters, Inc.
Page 56: 20th Century Fox/Rex.
Page 57: J. Sohm/Corbis.
Page 58: Marvel.
Page 59: Marvel.
Page 60: G. Rowell/Corbis.
Page 61: JG/TS/Keystone USA, J. Banks/Rex;
Bettmann/Corbis.

Printed in Singapore